CALL OF FRANCE
A Trilogy

Book 1
BARFIELD SCHOOL

Barry A. Whittingham

Copyright © 2015 by Barry A. Whittingham
Print Edition

The moral right of Barry A. Whittingham to be identified as the author of this work has been asserted by him in accordance with sections 77 and 78 of the Copyright, Designs and Patents Act 1988.

All rights reserved. No part of this publication may be reproduced, stored in a retrievable system, or transmitted in any form or by any means, electronic, mechanical, photocopying, recording or otherwise, without the prior permission of the copyright owner. Nor can it be circulated in any form of binding or cover other than that in which it is published and without similar condition including this condition being imposed on a subsequent purchaser.

While some aspects of this book may be considered to have been inspired by personal experience, it has been conceived as nothing more than a work of fiction whose main aim is to entertain. The characters and names depicted are, therefore, either the product of the author's imagination or used fictitiously, and any resemblance or correspondence to real persons, living or dead, is purely coincidental. Apart from certain obvious exceptions, names, places, entities, events, incidents or descriptions have been invented, re-created or re-assembled for literary effect. The portrayal of Barfield School and its staff is based on the author's personal knowledge of the workings of English secondary schools in general, and is in no way a representation of any past or present teaching establishment or staff in particular.

To Ann

TABLE OF CONTENTS

One	1
Two	6
Three	9
Four	16
Five	23
Six	26
Seven	30
Eight	35
Nine	39
Ten	48
Eleven	51
Twelve	57
Thirteen	59
Fourteen	68
Fifteen	74
Sixteen	78
Seventeen	84
Eighteen	90
Nineteen	101
Twenty	109
Twenty-One	113
Twenty-Two	117
Twenty-Three	125
Twenty-Four	131
Twenty-Five	135
Twenty-Six	141
Twenty-Seven	144
Twenty-Eight	164

Twenty-Nine	172
Thirty	178
Thirty-One	183
Thirty-Two	186
Thirty-Three	189
Thirty-Four	192
Thirty-Five	201
Thirty-Six	205
Thirty-Seven	208
Thirty-Eight	210
Thirty-Nine	217
Finale	225
About the Author	227
Other Books by Barry A. Whittingham	228

1

BARFIELD SCHOOL

"Twenty years from now you will be more disappointed by the things that you didn't do than by the ones you did do. So throw off the bowlines. Sail away from the safe harbor. Catch the trade winds in your sails. Explore. Dream. Discover."

H. Jackson Brown Jr., *P.S. I Love You*

ONE

The classroom door burst open and in marched Ron Cooper. Michael hadn't heard a knock and he was sure there hadn't been one.

'Hey, you!' Cooper barked, pointing an imperious forefinger at a boy sitting in the middle of the second row.

'Wipe that stupid grin off your face, lad, and sit up straight! Where d'you think you are? At home watching telly?'

The boy spun round.

'No, I mean you, you idiot.' The finger was waggled with simulated impatience. 'What's your name, boy?'

'Me sir?'

'Yes, you sir. I'm talking to you, you half wit!'

'Higgins sir.'

'Stand up when you speak to me!'

Higgins shot up. It was as if Cooper's command had triggered some jack-in-the-box-like spring sunk into the seat of his chair.

'Mr Morgan, the headmaster would like to see you at break,' Cooper announced, hardly bothering to lower his voice, his glowering face still half turned towards the boy. Without one word more he stormed out with the same studied theatricality as he'd swept in.

'OK. You can sit down, Higgins!' Michael said gently. Though it was obvious that this intrusive display of gratuitous authority was yet one more calculated attempt by the deputy head to reinforce the reputation of fierceness he had among the pupils, Michael suspected it was also his way of expressing contempt for the more enlightened approach followed by young teachers like himself; but the indignation he felt was prompted just as much by the retrograde effect this sort of random victimization might have on the boy. Higgins was not the easiest of pupils to manage, and Michael was even tempted to think that he might be suffering from some form of emotional disturbance which could be affecting his concentration; however, he'd recently had proof he was a good, sensitive lad at heart, and had been congratulating himself on having obtained a kind of co-operation based on a still tenuous strand of respect. So, what it suited Cooper to have seen as nothing more than an imbecilic grin was simply Higgins's way of demonstrating to his young French teacher that he was doing his best to show interest in his lessons. One thing Higgins reacted against – and this with his own special brand of obdurate tenacity – was what he considered to be an injustice; and what was more unfair than this type of adult bullying which he was probably all too exposed to at home, and which Michael himself – though he did have the excuse of mitigating circumstances – had been guilty of not long ago?

It had all happened at the beginning of this new school year. Several times during their first lessons Higgins's restless determination to reject his teacher's efforts to encourage his participation in the process of learning French had reached such an uncontrollable paroxysm that, without the slightest warning, he pushed his chair gratingly back, stood resolutely up and, gazing out of the window next to him, announced to the rest of the class in his broad Yorkshire accent, 'I can see seagulls on t' football pitch.' A chorus of loud guffaws had followed. The first time Michael had ordered him to move to a vacant desk in the middle of the second row in the hope that the simple expedient of increasing the distance between pupil and window would significantly reduce the likelihood of any future repetition. It had the opposite effect. Each time he'd told him patiently but firmly to sit down and look at his text book. The boy had grudgingly obeyed. But the final straw was when it occurred three times during the same lesson. Michael had lost his self control, marched up to the boy and given him a solid clip round the ear. In a fit of rage Higgins's had seized his book, flung it across the classroom before lapsing into a deep sulk.

'Right. You'll stay behind at the end of the lesson, my lad. I want to have a word with you!' he'd simply said. Higgins had glared at him with sullen dissent.

The end of lesson came, the class filed out and the boy trudged out to the front. He was the first to speak.

'You shouldn't hit people smaller than yourself!' he declared, his eyes blazing with defiance.

'What did you say, lad?' He'd heard perfectly well the first time but his question was intended to grant the boy a chance to moderate the tone and wording of this undisguised challenge to his authority while giving himself a second or two to think.

'You shouldn't hit people smaller than yourself!'

The words were spoken with the same dogged determination. It flashed through Michael's mind that this might justify a second slap, but he was lucid enough to see it would probably be the cause of an irretrievable breakdown between them.

It wasn't the first time he'd been brought to ponder on the fact that a show of physical force by a teacher could in no way be a solution to establishing a mutually respectful relationship with his pupils. His memories of that first time were still painful. It had been during the second term of his teacher training course when student teachers had each been appointed to schools where they could observe seasoned teachers at work and gain direct teaching experience by taking classes alone. Michael had been assigned to a traditional boys' only grammar school where a 'streaming' system was in operation: pupils were placed in 'A', 'B,' 'C', or 'D' classes according to their level of ability. Usually he was given easy 'A' or 'B' forms where pupils were eager to learn and class discipline never posed any great problem. However, there had been one notable exception: trainee teachers had to present a second teaching subject as part of their course and, as Michael had chosen English, he had regularly sat in on the lessons of a 'D' form of fifteen year olds. He remembered asking himself at the time if the 'D' didn't stand for 'dustbin'; for it was a motley class of low academic achievement where some thirty pubescent youths were dumped together as so much waste. He couldn't help feeling undercurrents of resentment, hopelessness and low self esteem. However, their regular English teacher was extremely gifted in his ability to understand and communicate with his pupils. It made Michael realize that a good teaching *rapport* is a mixture of sincerity, empathy and vocation. The lessons took the form of class discussions – so many question and answer sessions where pupils could give vent to their problems and frustrations. Michael was struck by the trust they had in their teacher, the involvement they showed in his lessons, the frankness with which he answered their questions, and the resulting atmosphere of respect that reigned. One day the teacher suggested that Michael should take them alone. It was a total disaster. The minute he stepped into the classroom he knew they were determined not to give him the slightest chance. Their sole motivation was to make this student teacher suffer for the humiliation the system had forced on them by creating a riot from the start. Perhaps things have changed since then, but in those days teacher training courses did not include advice on how to establish and maintain classroom order. Teachers were simply expected to learn from hard experience. Michael's reaction to this collective aggression was to give those he considered to be the ringleaders a violent swipe across the face. It only made matters worse: such was the racket that a teacher from the classroom next door had to come and re-establish order. The class was immediately taken from him. It had served as a mortifying yet salutary lesson.

So, it must have been this humiliating experience along with one of those vaguely understood bursts of spontaneous empathetic feeling we are all at some time or other seized with that prompted him to say, 'O.K. Higgins, you're right. I'm sorry I hit you. I promise it won't happen again. And I hope this won't stop us from being friends.'

It briefly occurred to him that it might be dangerous for a teacher to expose such emanations of the heart so nakedly to a pupil; but the boy's reaction had not disappointed him. His face had lit up, they'd shaken hands, and since then the seagulls on the football pitch had gone unnoticed. Moreover, this morning as they crossed paths in the corridor he'd been considerably gratified when Higgins greeted him with a cheery, 'Hello, sir! Did you see that programme about France on telly last night?' He'd taken this as a sign that he hadn't associated Deputy Head Cooper's loutish weight-throwing with teachers in general, and that there had been no resulting deterioration in the relationship of respect he was congratulating himself on having established with his pupil.

TWO

Headmaster Fowler was almost unanimously disliked by his teaching staff. He was even detested by some. Rumours from some quarters had it that he'd been a submarine captain in the Royal Navy before abandoning the sea and embarking on an educational career. Though no definite proof of this had ever risen to the surface there were reasons for lending it some credibility: for one thing, Mr Fowler seemed incapable of imparting to his speech that subtle warmth of intonation which goes to prevent a politely-phrased request from assuming the ring of a cold, peremptory order. And his insistence on the scrupulous respect of rules had an acute sartorial list: for parents been given firm warning that their progeny must present themselves fully attired in the official school uniform, and that any deviation would result in the strong probability of them being placed on detention. The wearing of jeans, moreover, was perceived as something akin to mutiny – so much so that in those days when corporal punishment was still allowed in English schools, repeat offenders ran the considerable risk of finding themselves on the receiving end of a vigorously-applied caning. Not even the teachers escaped Headmaster Fowler's obsession with vestimentary uniformity: for reasons he himself could perhaps not clearly explain he'd decreed that boots and slacks were unbefitting coverings for female legs. On the men he'd inflicted the compulsory wearing of 'classically-cut trousers' which had in all circumstances to be accompanied by a soberly-patterned jacket and tie, worn at all times over a long-sleeved shirt; and while it was admitted that the latter might be discreetly striped or checked, its underlying colour had to be white or, in the worst of cases, the lightest possible shade of grey.

But though Mr Fowler's impositions supplied a regular subject of indignant staffroom conversation nobody dared defy him to his face: for, as an English school headmaster, the almost arbitrary power he had over his teachers' present professional comfort and future career prospects alarmed them into outward deference, if not subservience. Michael was no exception. Last December a staff Christmas lunch had been laid on in the staffroom the day school broke up for the holidays. The French *assistante* – a short, plumpish, unattractive girl of *pied noir* extraction – was sat quietly reading a magazine when Fowler came marching in. Michael thought she'd been invited to lunch with them; but on seeing her Fowler had taken him to one side and said, 'We don't want *her* cluttering up the staffroom while we're having our Christmas meal. Just tell her to disappear, will you?' He'd been both shocked and embarrassed by this display of crass rudeness but had meekly complied – with as much of an apologetic tone as he could muster. While the humiliation was certainly felt, it was not expressed: for the poor girl had walked out without a murmur. He'd hated himself for this spineless display of servility.

The only teacher to have shown downright insubordination was Dave. Dave was a recently-married English teacher, fresh from training college who, like Michael, was now in his second teaching year. One morning last summer term Fowler had strolled into the staffroom where Dave was enjoying a free period and asked him if 'he'd be a good chap and run along and pace out the gym.' Dave had pointed out with some indignation that it wasn't a teacher's job to do this kind of thing and that if he wanted to know the dimensions of the gymnasium the caretaker was the person to ask. Fowler had marched out in a huff. Dave was still outraged by the demeaning nature of the request and was adamant he'd been in the right. Michael, along with most of his colleagues, admired him for his display of defiance. He wondered what he'd have done had he been in the same position as Dave. He couldn't quite rid himself of the gnawing suspicion that he would have meekly obeyed. Some consolation was, however, drawn from the thought that his compliance was mainly due to a desire not to come into direct conflict with the headmaster: for he'd applied to *The Bureau for Foreign Exchanges* in London for a place on a teacher exchange scheme to France and had just sent off the corresponding application form. He knew Headmaster Fowler would shortly be solicited for a reference. The last thing he wanted was to jeopardize his chances.

THREE

It was the second time he'd applied. During the year Michael had spent training to become a teacher it was his luck to have had a former French schoolmaster as his educational tutor. During their first tutorial together Michael had learnt that Mr Naylor (for this was his tutor's name) was from the same northern English county as himself, and had even started his teaching career at a secondary school in Michael's home town of Bridgeford. Though he hadn't been born at the time, this geographical proximity had generated in Michael a feeling of strong personal affinity in which a mixture of both envy and admiration occupied a considerable place. It was obvious that in his younger days Mr Naylor had studied in France: not only did he speak French to perfection (Michael couldn't detect the slightest trace of an English accent), but in addition to a B.A. (Hons) he bore a *licencié ès lettres* after his name. And despite now being on the eve of retirement his enthusiasm for all things French had remained intact. Somewhere he had re-awoken in Michael a desire to seek a deeper acquaintance of a country and language for which he'd felt an attraction from an early age but which a combination of extraneous circumstance and personal choice had over the previous two years caused him to relegate to a less pre-eminent place. So, he'd confided in Mr Naylor that before getting a first teaching job he'd very much like to improve his spoken French by spending a year at a French *lycée* as an English-language *assistant;* and he'd asked his tutor to advise him on how to proceed. Mr Naylor had supplied him with the address of a bureau in London specializing in official foreign visits and exchanges. Michael had promptly written a letter of enquiry – only to be informed that language undergraduates alone could be considered for this type of post. However, as a result of a teacher exchange scheme which had recently been concluded between the two countries he would be eligible to spend a year as an English teacher in a French *lycée*. He'd resolved to go into more detail once he'd obtained his teaching diploma and was settled in a job. Last year – his first at Barfield School – he'd written to request more details along with an application form. He was informed that the aim of the scheme was to provide qualified French teachers with the opportunity to improve their language skills and gain direct experience of the workings of a French state secondary school while extending their knowledge of the culture and everyday life of the country. Since he would remain officially employed by his English education authority he would continue to receive his present salary along with an allowance to compensate for the higher cost of living in France. Apart from this he would enjoy the same working conditions as the French teacher he replaced and would be expected to return to his English teaching post at the end of the exchange year. If he decided to apply they would require two references: one from his headmaster whom they would contact directly, and another from a suitably qualified person of his own choice.

The more he read the more excited he grew, and he lost no time in writing to Mr Naylor. He'd posted his application off in the middle of October and some six months later he'd received his reply. His application had been refused: it was felt that after just one year in teaching he lacked the necessary experience to draw full advantage from the exchange. While he had to admit that the reason invoked did not come as a real surprise he suspected that a hesitant reference from Headmaster Fowler had also had a part to play. Though he did gain some comfort from being informed that any future application might be viewed in a more constructive light he was immensely disappointed.

And so, it was partly by way of compensation, partly from the wish to see for himself some of the country's natural and historical splendours which gave him the idea of spending the following summer vacation on a tour of discovery. It was true he'd been to France twice on summer trips with his school. The first time had been at the age of eleven in the mid nineteen fifties when he and a group of some 60 pupils accompanied by half a dozen teachers had made the long train journey to Nice where they'd stayed for two glorious, sun-filled weeks. Up to then it had never struck him that life could be lived other than in grimy, gas-lit streets under cloud-filled skies, and that summer holidays didn't necessarily involve the threat of windy, rain-swept beaches and a chilly green sea. But after all how could it? For this was all he had seen in his short life. The trip had been a revelation: he'd had the privilege of spending two short weeks in a sort of terrestrial paradise he'd never for once imagined could have existed beyond his book-nourished fantasies. The second occasion had been three years later – by the more flexible form of transport afforded by coach. This time it had been for three whole weeks. They'd spent two days in Paris viewing the usual tourist attractions – *la Tour Eiffel, la Cathédrale de Notre Dame, les Champs-Elysées, l'Arc de Triomphe* – before travelling on to the picturesque, lake-side town of Annecy where they'd stayed for almost a week. Then it was on to Nice where they spent the rest of the holidays with day excursions to Cannes and the Italian border town of San Marino; and this exotic cocktail of sounds, sights and smells had produced in him an even headier elation than that procured by his previous sojourn.

But his longest stay had been while at university: in order to enable students to gain some insight into French culture and, above all, to improve their everyday spoken language it had been part of his course to spend a whole academic year in Grenoble. It was not the success he'd hoped for; moreover, his limited financial means had meant that, apart from one occasion when they'd taken the train to visit friends in Besançon, all other travels had extended no further than a day trip to the liqueur-making monastery of the *Chartreuse* and the occasional hitch-hiked winter visit to the ski-ing resort of Chamrousse. But now, while waiting to re-apply next year wouldn't this miniature *Grand Tour* provide him with an exciting opportunity to meet French people, speak the language and to explore for himself some of those things he'd heard, read and so often dreamed about? Not only would it be the very first time he'd be venturing into this foreign country alone, but wouldn't it serve as a prelude to that promise of a more unique and testing adventure which a year-long stay would involve?

Though Michael was aware he would be stepping along well-trodden tourist ground this didn't detract from the thrill which his plans aroused; for the shelves of Bridgeford's Central Library contained a rich enough selection of travel books on France to offer him an abundant indication of the sights to see as well as a vicarious foretaste of the delights they would inspire. And his accumulated readings had a sort of mental kaleidoscopic effect where the original, frequently trite descriptions were reflected by the mirror of his fancy into a fascinating, constantly-changing association of varying movements, colours and forms: a rocky island abbey fortress dominating a sweeping bay where the tide came racing in with the speed of a galloping horse; the tapestry film of a brutal, history-changing battle fought more than nine hundred years ago; a westerly rock looking out onto a vast tumultuous ocean with the Americas far beyond; glistening, fairy-land *châteaux* rising like monumen-tal white incrustations along a broad river's banks; a heaven-sent peasant girl seeking out her king in a crowded castle hall; the remnants of Roman viaducts, arenas and theatres languishing beneath an immaculate Mediterranean sky; legendary vineyards basking in the promise of precious, first-growth wines; a vast wetland delta of roaming bulls, wild horses and pink flamingos.

Little by little he began to trace a route out. It was in no way fixed: if along the way he came across anything presenting unforeseen interest, he would have no hesitation in modifying his plans. When it came to accommodation the choice was simple: wasn't France a camper's paradise where even the smallest town had its own well-equipped site? Wouldn't this arrangement have the advantage of providing an ideal place for easy contact with others? And even though he'd have to purchase a small tent, a sleeping bag, an inflatable mattress and a camping stove wouldn't it all work out at a reasonable price? What's more, in larger towns he could always spend the occasional night in a youth hostel where the shared sleeping and cooking areas would provide him with an even better opportunity to meet French people of his age.

It is, alas, a constantly verifiable fact that what we preview in the cheery glow of our imagination can sometimes be cast by reality in a chillier, more shadowy light. I am happy to say this was not the case with Michael. The only downside – and it was one of importance – was that the frequent opportunity he was given of speaking French with young native people made him even more painfully aware of his linguistic limitations, especially when it came to understanding and expressing himself in the language of every day.

I will not go into our young man's tour in any detail. Suffice it to say that it did not include Paris. As he'd already stayed in the capital and seen its main attractions during the course of his second school trip he considered his time would be better spent discovering other regions. In addition, that romanticized image which prompts so many foreigners to dream of visiting, or even living in this *ville lumière* had been somewhat tarnished by him hearing on French radio that the dream of a not inconsiderable number of Parisians was simply to get out. So, I will simply limit myself to the narration of two events which, though not without being a source of apprehension at the time, now stand out fondly and amusingly enough in his memory for him to take delight in relating to others.

The first had occurred at the very start. As he'd planned to begin his tour in Normandy he decided to take the ferry from Newhaven to Dieppe. There were two sailings per day – one at midday and the other in the early evening. In view of the long drive down from his home in the North to Newhaven, he'd reserved a place on the second. It was scheduled to arrive at around 11 p.m. The problem was that at this late hour it would be impossible to book into a camping site or youth hostel; so the only solution was to camp in the wild. After driving off the ferry he would head out of Dieppe and then take the first country lane he came to. It would certainly lead to a field where he could pitch his tent – even though he would have preferred this first experience of sleeping under canvass to have taken place in a more secure area: for he couldn't help feeling some apprehension at the idea of spending his first night in France with only a thin stretch of fabric between him and the great unknown. He did, however, find comfort in the self-persuaded view that the risks involved in spending a few nocturnal hours in such an exposed configuration lay mainly within the confines of his alarmist imagination.

So, after disembarkation, he'd driven out of Dieppe and proceeded for a few kilometers in the direction of Rouen before taking a narrow, hedge-bordered lane off the *Route Nationale*. He soon came to a gate opening on to a field. The night was dark and he could only catch an occasional glimpse of the moon and stars as they peeped through breaks in the clouds. He pitched his tent by torchlight a few yards beyond the gate, blew up the mattress, slipped into his sleeping bag, and fell into an uneasy sleep. The sun was just rising when he was woken by strange trampling sounds. He could see great looming shadows through the east-facing side of the tent. Suddenly, the whole structure began to sway. It was with some trepidation that he'd scrambled out – only to find himself surrounded by a herd of grazing Normandy cows!

The second incident came right at the end. So much did he enjoy his tour that he'd prolonged it to a point where he was becoming preoccupied by the rate at which his cash was running out. When he drove off the evening ferry at Newhaven he had only enough money left (these were the days when credit cards had yet to make their appearance) to buy a tankful of petrol for the 300 mile or so journey back home. As he drove up the motorway he noted with increasing alarm that if the fuel gauge indicator continued descending at that same rate he would be reduced to helpless immobility at a distance considerably more than that remaining between him and the safety of home. The only solution was to reduce consumption by lowering his speed to a snail-like 40 mph. It must have been around 2 o'clock in the morning when a police car pulled alongside. Its driver beckoned him to pull over onto the hard shoulder. After being invited to step out of his car there then followed questions as to where he was going and why he seemed to be in so little hurry to get there. After hearing his explanation they let him continue. He inwardly smiled at the thought that it was probably the first time they'd stopped someone for not driving fast enough on a motorway. He was only a hundred yards or so from the parental home when the engine started gurgling and finally spluttered to such an irremediable stop that he was obliged to complete the remainder of his journey on foot.

Fortunately, it was a Sunday and his father ran him to a petrol station where he filled a jerry can, poured its contents into the tank and brought his Mini back to its point of departure some five weeks before. But what he had seen and done over these five glorious weeks had exceeded the most optimistic of his expectations. It strengthened even more his resolution to escape to France.

FOUR

Though he couldn't say he was especially fond of Headmaster Fowler the person he came nearest to detesting was Cooper – not only because of the loud-mouthed authoritarianism the deputy head systematically resorted to as a means of instilling fear in the kids, but for the overbearing manner – even open contempt – he was all too inclined to display towards those young teachers whose pedagogical convictions caused them to seek classroom order on the more liberal basis of reciprocal respect. But what had rankled most was when he'd called Michael 'a failed businessman' to his face and in the presence of others. It had stung so much because of the element of truth it contained.

After graduating from university he'd got a job working in Birmingham as an area supervisor for a large brewery which operated a 'tied-house system'. In this type of organization the public houses and off-licences (a liquor store where the alcoholic drinks sold can only be consumed 'off' the premises – mainly at home) are owned lock, stock and barrel by the brewery, and serve as an outlet for its beers, ales and wines (usually imported by an affiliate company) on a more or less exclusive basis. The brewery appoints a pub or off-licence manager who is responsible for all aspects of their running and who receives a fixed salary (along with a bonus if justified) for his pains. It is, therefore, the brewery which takes the profits (unlike a tenancy where, as a general rule, the landlord is simply under the contractual obligation to buy the brewery's products, to pay it a rent, but keeps all net profits for himself). As a tied-house supervisor Michael had acted as a controlling intermediary between the brewery and its outlets. His job had been varied and included interviewing and appointing managers, draught beer cellar management, stock control, order vetting, renovation and refurbishing these licensed premises as well as promotional work with the general aim of increasing customer frequentation and optimizing the profitability of the 50 or so on and off-licences he'd been placed in charge of.

But Michael soon became painfully aware that this first employment fell far short of his initial, admittedly naive expectations; for his moral sensibility was considerably shaken on discovering that, as well as being a sobering introduction to the humdrum realities of the world of work, it provided him with almost daily exposure to some of those less enviable, sometimes sordid manifestations of human nature. For one thing it was generally recognized in the trade that most managers were 'on the fiddle' – that is to say considerable ruse and ingenuity were used to skim off into their own pockets what should normally have gone to increase their employer's profits. It was all part of a dangerous game played out between the Brewery Cat and the Pub and Off-Licence Mice; if the Mice stepped over a clearly-indicated line the Cat would pounce. This line was defined by a system of financial control which took the simple, yet viable form of regular, usually monthly stock taking.

To this effect, the brewery employed a dozen or more stocktakers who, as their job designation so clearly indicated, had been entrusted with the task of going round the company's tied-house pubs and off-licences taking stock. This consisted in simply (though, as Michael was later to find, it was not as easy as he'd first imagined) counting and recording on a dedicated stock sheet the exact quantities in stock at that particular moment of everything the tied-house sold (beer, both bottled and draught, spirits, cigarettes, crisps, etc.), while taking into account the results of the previous inventory as well as the invoiced goods delivered in the interval between. In this way a stocktaker was able to calculate what had actually been sold during that period. If, for example, six bottles of brown ale had been counted in stock at the previous inventory, an invoice proved that four dozen bottles had been delivered since and now there were only ten bottles remaining, this meant that $6 + 48 - 10 = 44$ bottles had been sold in the period between. Then, each evening they would post their completed stock sheets back to the brewery stock office where a dozen or more clerks spent their days costing out the quantities of all the items delivered and sold in order to work out their profit margins: for instance, 44 bottles of brown ale bought at a unit price of £1 gives a total cost price of £44 and, when sold at £1,50 a total sales amount of £66. A gross profit of £22 or 50% has, therefore, been made on the sale of brown ale in the period between the two inventories. The same calculations were applied to all items sold, and the corresponding amounts worked out in each case. These were then added up, and a total gross profit figure and percentage (i.e. profits before overheads such as wages, heating, etc. are deducted) established for that particular outlet. Any discrepancy between the total amounts really sold, as calculated by the inventory, and the actual takings meant that something was amiss: if the inventory showed that the total sales of a specific tied-house over a given stock period amounted to £5,000 whereas the takings were only £4,000, there was an unexplained deficit of £1,000. How could this be accounted for? There were only two possibilities: either the stocktaker or the stock clerk had somewhere made a big mistake, or the manager or even his own bar staff (and sometimes both) were 'on the fiddle'.

As Michael soon came to discover it was usually the second case: for he soon came to admire the speed and accuracy with which the stock clerks and especially the stocktakers could count and add up. It was a source of amazement to him that, in spite of the repetitive nature of their work and the permanent concentration it required, the stocktakers seemed to enjoy their job. He'd put this down to the fact that they'd all been stock clerks previously and for them it was a step-up. But, above all, it was due to the relative independence the job gave. Stocktakers were supplied with a small company car, and since they posted the result of each day's work back to the brewery every evening, they only had to go into the office on Monday mornings when they were given the ten or more stock sheets for the pubs and off-licences they would be required to take stock of during that week. As part of his training to become a tied-house supervisor Michael did a four-week stint working as a stock clerk, after which he went round with an experienced stocktaker before being allowed to take stock alone. He had previously viewed with some scorn this grindingly monotonous work which he'd described to himself as 'counting your life away'. The experience had proved to be a lesson in modesty: for he was hopeless at both jobs – much to general incomprehension at the brewery where nobody could understand why a supposedly intelligent university graduate couldn't even count and add up! And he himself never really understood why; he was something of a perfectionist and always made an effort to do the job well. As he was later to analyze, the difficulty lay in establishing some form of compatibility between two seemingly irreconcilable things: permanently applying the whole of your concentration to an activity of a basically mindless nature.

Whenever a stock take revealed that the manager's performance fell short of pre-calculated expectations, it was part of Michael's job to give him a stern warning. And sometimes, in order to limit the accumulated proportions which these losses could assume, to recommend that stock should be taken at shorter intervals – every week, or in some extreme cases every day. If, thereafter, the tied house's profit margin didn't return to normal Michael simply informed the manager of his dismissal. What made matters worse, however, was that announcements of this kind frequently gave rise to dramatic scenes where reactions could range from a deluge of tears to explosions of fury: for the manager lived on the premises with his family, and depriving him of his job also meant placing him in the unfortunate and sometimes desperate position of having to seek a new abode. And here lay another problem: since the brewery was legally obliged to give the offending manager a month's notice of his dismissal, nothing stopped him from continuing to 'fiddle' or to steal stock during this period. To prevent this, what was termed a 'lock-out' was implemented: a locksmith was called in to change the locks on all the doors leading from the living quarters to the pub or off-licence premises so that the manager was physically prevented from acceding to his previous place of work. A temporary manager was then called in to replace him and, on expiration of the dismissed manager's four weeks' notice, this substitute manager, or a newly-appointed one moved in. Michael had found himself temperamentally unequipped to resist finding these situations at best highly unpleasant, at worst acutely distressing. What's more, he was still liable, more than two years later, to mull over in some detail what he'd considered as the straw that finally broke the camel's back. The event dated back to the beginning of his second working year, and had acted as the irrefutable confirmation that it was as inconceivable for him to adapt to this type of job as it is to deny that geometrical law which states that a square peg can never be made to fit into a round hole.

He'd interviewed a young woman who had applied to become manageress of a small off-licence in a working-class part of the city. She had a young baby which created some doubts in his mind as to her suitability. But though he'd expressed his doubts regarding her ability to manage the shop while at the same time having to look after a six-month old infant, she'd assured him there'd be no problem: she had relatives in the neighbourhood who would take care of it during the day, and her husband would be there to give her a hand in the evenings. She'd also informed him she was the sister of a well-known pop-singer of that time. It had all served to reassure him. Her spouse, she added, was 'Jewish'. He remembered thinking this strange as her baby had frizzy black hair and a dark complexion; but he'd thought no more about it; and, since she seemed eager to take on the job, he decided to give her a chance. It was a horrible mistake. The takings immediately began to drop and, though he'd called every day, this quickly assumed dramatic proportions. Now each off-licence was equipped with a small safe in which takings were placed at the end of each day; and for obvious reasons of security managers were instructed to bank the accrued amount once it had reached a pre-determined figure. To this effect the brewery provided dedicated paying-in slips on which the manager indicated the amount and the date on which it had been paid in. The bank itself, of course, stamped the slip and gave the depositor the duplicate as proof that the money had actually been deposited with them on this specific date. So Michael decided to count the cash in the safe. It amounted to only the previous evening's takings. She assured him that she'd paid all prior amounts into the bank the afternoon before; but on asking her for the duplicate she told him she'd lost it. He'd immediately gone to the bank – only to be informed there was no record of the deposit. It was becoming horrifyingly clear that she was both a brazen thief and a pathological liar.

As a result, he'd had no choice but to go back to the brewery to organize a lock-out and consult a list of temporary replacement managers. He returned to the off-licence in the early-evening with the intention of giving her notice of dismissal. Not only was she looking extremely sorry for herself but he was mortified to see that she had bruises on her arms and face along with the beginnings of a spectacular black eye. It was obvious she'd been on the receiving end of a thorough beating. He could only surmise that the culprit was the man standing beside her: for her 'Jewish' husband was, in fact, a beefy, furious-looking West Indian (the city had a large Jamaican population). For a moment he feared he was going to suffer a similar fate but the husband's wrath seemed directed solely at his wife. It crossed his mind that, even if the man's reaction was brutally expeditious, it at least suggested that he was far more honest than his spouse. After doing his best to calm him down, Michael decided that discretion was the better part of valour, and beat a hasty retreat. He'd come back just before evening opening time with a substitute manageress, and had taken advantage of the young lady's husband's absence to quietly inform her that she'd been dismissed. Perhaps she had some remorse as tears began rolling down her cheeks. From this moment onwards he became obsessed by the desire to get out.

But now, with hindsight, he couldn't really say he regretted those two years spent with the brewery. He was even convinced that he was a more mature person for the experience. For this raw confrontation with down-to-earth, often unsavoury reality had shaken him out of the ingenuous ideality which had been so much a part of his ivory-towered student life. It had also taught him things unknown or which he'd only been vaguely aware of in himself. So, he now knew what he didn't want and what he was not suited for. For while the financial rewards were not negligible and he'd been granted the luxury of a small company car, he felt ensnared in a system which inflicted more pain than pleasure. Some of his unease was caused by the guilty thought that the material rewards he was enjoying were being obtained fraudulently, and that the time he was devoting to pleasant, homely chats with his managers and manageresses over morning coffee or afternoon tea should have been spent confronting them with the deficiencies of their management, and their lack of satisfactory results; some of it was prompted by the depressing realization that he would never be able to come to terms with the fact that the next few years – perhaps the whole of his working life – would be spent in much the same narrow, dingy urban environment where conflict with others was a daily reality, and where his objectives were limited to the banal and frequently ignoble pursuit of financial gain; some discomfort was also occasioned by the growing consciousness that his temperament was more in keeping with a job which would allow him to play a part in the personal development of others. But most of the pain came from the nagging thought that he was wasting precious time: for he throbbed with excitement at dreams of making a fresh start to life in a land of sunny beaches, warm blue seas, dazzling white buildings, wide shaded avenues, and orange trees gently caressed by a deliciously-scented evening breeze.

FIVE

It now seemed quite natural that what in his final student year he'd contemptuously dismissed as little more than an extension of the cloistered life he'd been leading should now present itself in a far more redemptory light. Wasn't teaching the type of vocational job he now realized would provide him with that opportunity of finding the personal fulfilment he was seeking? And wouldn't the possession of a teaching diploma give him the means of earning a stable living in those far-away countries he was so much tempted by? So, why didn't he apply for a place on a teacher training course? Why not at the university where he'd studied for his first degree? The thought of freeing himself from the stifling confinement of his present job and returning to the refreshing *insouciance* of student life filled him with all the anticipatory joy of a prisoner contemplating his impending release.

It must not be imagined, however, that Michael belonged to that category of devil-may-care young men who took radical decisions concerning their future life orientations without giving careful consideration to the detrimental effects these might have on present circumstances. So, before handing in his official resignation he decided to cover himself by first obtaining a place on a teacher training course at his former university. Soon after applying he'd received an invitation to present himself at the university's school of education where its head, a Professor Ibbotson, would be happy to interview him. His reactions had been mixed: he'd been delighted at having been granted an interview but apprehensive as to the form it might take and, above all, the outcome it could have.

He now felt some shame (though it hadn't caused any real compunctions at the time) at having taken advantage of the independence his job had given by granting himself a day off work, and using his company car and petrol to drive there; and was it some strange immanent justice which, in punishment for this blatant abuse of company time and money, caused things to get off to the worst possible of starts? Being a scrupulously punctual person, he set off from his lodgings at a time he'd estimated as being early enough for him to arrive well before the appointed hour of two o'clock. But as he neared the end of the journey he became more and more despairingly aware that he hadn't taken into account the delaying effects of heavy lunchtime traffic. The result was that he arrived at Professor Ibbotson's study door more than a quarter of an hour late. He was convinced his chances of being accepted were seriously compromised. Perhaps it was because this academic wasn't the most punctual of persons himself that he accepted Michael's explanation and profuse apologies with a casual wave of the hand and a benign smile before inviting him take a seat and proceeding to question him on his motives for wanting to embark on a teaching career. Michael had tried to anticipate the questions, and had mentally prepared their answers. When he actually gave them they appeared trite in his mind and seemed to have little effect. It was only when he spoke about his brewery experience that he saw he'd hit the mark. He didn't at all regret it. It had enabled him to see what he was not suited for and where his path really lay. It had made him a more mature person. And it was also perhaps the obvious sincerity with which he'd spoken that prompted Professor Ibbotson to gratify him with an understanding smile and an acquiescent nod of the head before informing him there and then that he was prepared to offer him a place on the course. He'd even added that, as far as his future student accommodation was concerned, he would recommend him to the warden of a newly-built hall of residence. The relief was immense and Michael had driven back to Birmingham on a cloud. A few weeks later he'd received a letter from his local education authority informing him that he'd been allocated a corresponding grant. He could now contemplate handing in his resignation in all tranquillity.

An opportunity was not long in coming. One morning his boss called him into his office to tell him that the managing director wanted to speak to him. 'It could be to inform you of your dismissal. If I were you I'd get in there first,' he'd advised. Though Michael was privately aware of his own professional inadequacies this confirmation emanating from his direct boss came as something of a shock as it placed them in a more far-reaching, publicly-known light. It was with some trepidation that he'd gone along. Much to his surprise he was greeted with a broad smile, a firm handshake and a warm invitation to take a seat. After a few enquiries about how the job was going he was even more astonished to be informed that it had been decided to give him a rise. While there was no question of him going back on his decision to leave, this unanticipated display of undeserved confidence had made him feel ungrateful; and when he explained that he felt unsuited for the job and wished to announce his resignation, the bubbly relief which often results from a lengthily-ruminated decision being finally made irrevocable was deflated by a prick of remorse.

So, he'd countered Deputy Headmaster Cooper's humiliating public staffroom declaration that he was a failed businessman with a remonstrative, 'You know, you couldn't be more wrong! When I handed in my resignation I was offered a salary rise to stay!' It was a rather loose interpretation of the truth but he was determined to bring a check to bear on Cooper's infuriating readiness to pronounce loud-mouthed, ready-made judgements.

SIX

Another no less painful effect of Deputy Head Cooper's public aspersion was to remind Michael that over the last three years the outcome of other important challenges had fallen well short of his own standards, let alone those that others expected of him. One of these barely-met challenges had such a direct bearing on his sense of personal satisfaction, his professional conscience, and future career prospects that it reinforced his resolution to draw up the anchor of his present life and set a course for more redemptory shores. This challenge had been provided by the nature of his third student year.

With a view to giving students the best possible chance to improve their spoken language skills and gain a first-hand insight into French life and culture, Michael's university had required them to spend the whole of the third academic year of their four year degree course studying at a French university (most English university language courses of that time were of a three-year duration with students spending just two terms in the country whose language they were learning). They were four fellow students to have chosen the same university town, and it had been the task of their French department back home to find suitable lodgings. It being generally admitted that in matters of foreign-language learning the most effective way to speedy progress lies in speaking the target language to a maximum –necessarily to the proportional exclusion of one's own – it might have been thought that the most satisfactory arrangement would have been to accommodate them as distantly from one other as the four farthest corners of the town would have allowed. The opposite couldn't have been more the case. Perhaps it was the result of a significant lack of student accommodation in the town that they found themselves lodged in pairs in two adjoining study bedrooms of the same three-bedroom flat – the third being occupied by a French student whom they hardly ever saw. The flat was located some 30 minutes' walk from the main university buildings which also contained the student self-service restaurant whose interminable queues the four of them would join twice a day for lunch and dinner. And so it was perfectly natural that on those prolonged occasions they found themselves together our four English friends communicated in their mother tongue.

Their predicament was further exacerbated by the fact that contact with French students was almost non-existent: for the university had created a separate section dispensing daily lectures on French language, literature and history for the exclusive enlightenment of the town's large foreign student population. These were diffused through the medium of *le cours magistral* – a formal, one hour, microphone-assisted monologue which took place in a huge and often crowded *amphithéatre* where the lecturer remained an anonymous and, for those seated right at the back, microscopic figure. It was a far cry from the lectures back home where the number of students rarely exceeded 30. In addition, these were supplemented by regular tutorials during which just three or four students met their academic tutor for informal discussions on previously-penned essays.

This is not to say that the French university hadn't made perfunctory attempts to organize social events conducive to personal encounter with native speakers. These took the form of occasional gatherings – theme parties and dances – held after the evening meal in a corner of the student restaurant. While being better than nothing, they bore no comparison with the numerous parties and animated Saturday evening 'hops' Michael had known at his university back home where they often danced to the accompaniment of well-known groups, and where unattached students stood a remarkably good chance of striking up an acquaintance with similarly unengaged members of the opposite sex. Moreover, these French get-togethers seemed to be snubbed by most native students, and were mainly attended by Anglophones like himself who naturally conversed among themselves in English. One occasion he remembered in particular. They'd attended a cheese and wine party and, after a couple of glasses of doubtful red wine, he'd lost enough of his inhibitions to invite one of the rare French girls present to dance. But after they'd been jerking around for a couple of minutes, she suddenly remembered something mysteriously urgent, obliging her to take instant leave. Before departing she did, however, extend a vague invitation for him to come and see her; and she even scribbled down her name and the address of the *cité universitaire,* the hall of residence where she lived.

To make matters worse, though at home he'd got on well with his room mate, their friendship didn't withstand the constant assaults made on it by the stifling intimacy which their living conditions imposed, and they began to find each other's company insufferable. One evening, shortly after his brief encounter with the French student, Michael made up his mind to go and seek her out. The *cité universitaire* was quite a long walk away and, on arriving, he was both astonished and dismayed by its size. Despite making several enquiries nobody seemed to know exactly where she could be found; so he finally gave up and, bitterly disappointed, trudged back home. His room mate, who must have guessed where he'd been, could barely conceal his delight at this miserable failure, and even turned it into a subject of sarcastic derision, repeatedly alluded to over the following days. Fortunately, they did have a fair amount of personal study to accomplish. Apart from a weekly *thème,* a translation from English to French which they were given to do by the university, their French department back home had set them a project: that of writing a mini thesis on a subject of their choice which they had the daunting task of submitting in French. He chose to write about Diderot's *Le Neveu de Rameau.* As a result, enough of his time was occupied in research at the university library for him to escape some of the increasingly oppressive atmosphere which had now turned what should have been an agreeable, fruitful stay into something akin to a nine-month prison sentence. He couldn't help heaving an immense sigh of relief when it all came to an end in June. While he did make some progress in spoken French, he was left with the frustrating feeling of a mission only half accomplished and of having let a golden opportunity slip irremediably by.

What's more, the French conversations he'd forced himself to have last year with the school's French *assistante,* Mademoiselle Berthet (she had even sat in on some of his lessons), had only served to confirm the suspicion that his level in the spoken language left much to be desired: though she seemed to make a point of assuring him that he spoke the language well, something in the way she said it made him suspect it was a wary kind of politeness speaking. This deficiency on the part of a French teacher was something so much approaching the shameful that he couldn't rest until it had been rectified. So, when he'd learnt that an official teacher exchange scheme between French and English schools now existed, he was determined to seize on it as that second chance he'd always dreamed of. This time he'd leave no stone unturned to make it succeed.

SEVEN

The convocation which had given rise to Cooper's ill-mannered classroom intrusion reminded Michael that, while he had from time to time exchanged a few words with Headmaster Fowler in the staffroom or corridor, the meeting it summoned him to would be only the second occasion he'd had to converse with him in the privacy of his study. The first time had been more than a year ago now when he'd presented himself for the job interview in July, just before school broke up for the summer holidays. He'd emerged from his training course as a qualified teacher the month before, and as the end of the final term drew near had become increasingly aware that what had been previously consigned to some distant recess of his mind was now occupying his thoughts with disquieting insistence: that this refreshing re-immersion in student life was now nearing its end and that the time was fast approaching when he'd have to give some serious thought to laying the foundations of a future career. He had to admit that the prospect of finding a job filled him with only moderate enthusiasm. It was not so much that he was beginning to regret his decision to go into teaching as the thought that he would soon have to buckle down to what he had difficulty in perceiving as anything more than a daily grind. He consoled himself with the thought that it was a necessary evil in so much as it would give him that precious teaching experience he already suspected would be a *sine qua non* condition for him to be accepted on the exchange. For the more he viewed his plan of spending a year in France the more it presented itself as a way of opening up a new, more adventurous and stimulating chapter to his life.

It was with the same muted enthusiasm that he came to the conclusion it would be preferable to look for a teaching post in the familiar surroundings of his home town. After all, he hadn't the slightest intention of remaining in this first post for very long. And what would be the point in getting a job where he'd be alone among strangers? What's more, as far as his future accommodation was concerned, it would have the advantage of enabling him to look no further than the parental abode. While not perhaps being the ideal solution for an unattached young man of his age, living at home would allow him to enjoy an appreciable number of comforts; and even though his father would certainly insist on him paying for his keep it would be far easier on his pocket than renting a flat. Wouldn't he need some savings behind him for the French exchange?

As a result of these reflections he'd written to Bridgeford Education Authority to enquire whether they had any vacancies for a newly-qualified French teacher in one of their secondary schools. He'd received what seemed a promising reply: a position was available at Barfield Comprehensive School, a recently-opened establishment catering for pupils aged 11 to 18 of all ability ranges; its headmaster, a Mr Edward Fowler, would be happy to interview him with a view to assessing his suitability for the post. Michael was seized by the dispiriting thought that, by a strange twist of fate, his life's wheel had come full circle within a span of only ten years: for Barfield School was located little more than a stone's throw from the primary school he'd attended, the streets where he'd played, and the small semi-detached house he'd lived in up to the age of 16.

The interview with Mr Fowler proved to be not much more than a formality. Even as he walked into his study Michael discerned the hint of an approving smile which followed the all-embracing glance the headmaster had given to his person. Somewhere he couldn't avoid thinking he'd already been weighed in the balance and found not to be lacking in what his interviewer considered to be the job's sartorial requirements. And the benign superficiality of the questions that were posed on his previous work experience and personal interests gave him the impression that what was being sought, above all, was the certainty of having a French teacher available for the coming September term and that, as long as the candidate conformed to certain conventional criteria, more or less anybody would suit the bill. Michael had expected to be told he would be informed by post of the result of the interview; it was with surprise, almost disbelief, that after a mere ten minutes Mr Fowler announced his decision to appoint him on the spot. It reminded him very much of his interview with Professor Ibbotson. Barfield School, the headmaster confirmed, was a new establishment named after Geoffrey Barfield, a local man who had been posthumously awarded the Victoria Cross for an act of heroism during the First World War. Michael had vaguely heard of him. The school had opened only five years earlier with pupils mainly of working class parents. Some 5% were of immigrant, mainly Indian and Pakistani origin. From an academic point of view the school was, as the headmaster put it, 'still seeking its way.' Michael had taken this to be a roundabout way of saying that general academic standards were low.

As he knocked on Mr Fowler's study door this second time he was conscious of an uneasiness he hadn't felt that first time. Was it a sign that he attached more importance to the result of this meeting than that of the job interview? For though he was in no doubt as to the reason for the convocation he wasn't at all sure what his headmaster's attitude would be. He did, however, draw some reassurance from the reflection that Fowler not calling him to his study for a similar meeting last year could be taken to mean he had opposed his first application. So, couldn't this present summons be interpreted as a sign that he was now more favourably inclined?

'Ah, come in, Mr Morgan.' The headmaster gave a vague nod in the general direction of the chair on the other side of his desk. This time there was not the slightest trace of a smile on his face.

'I just wanted to have a few words with you.' he began. 'I don't want to deprive you of your morning coffee, so I'll get straight to the point. I had a letter this morning from the *Bureau for Educational Exchanges* asking me for a reference for that French teacher exchange business you appear to have applied for again.'

It was true that Michael hadn't informed him of this second application – not because he hadn't meant to, but simply because his headmaster had been contacted much earlier than he'd anticipated.

'Yes, well I had every intention of informing you, but they seem to have beaten me to it. I didn't expect them to write to you so soon.'

'Well, that's by the way. I just wanted to tell you that, frankly, what bothers me is what *I* will get in exchange.' The emphasis he placed on the 'I' was especially heavy.

'I know you don't seem to have any great discipline problems now but, assuming, of course, your application is successful, I ask myself whether your future exchange partner will be up to the task of keeping on top of some of the bright sparks we've got with us here. What with this, the language and the reputation the Frogs have with pupils, I can't help feeling he could find himself struggling.'

'Well … errr….' Michael's hesitation was caused not so much by an absence of any reassuring arguments to counter Fowler's fears as a feeling of surprised irritation that someone in his position should allow himself this type of popular batrachian comparison. In addition, he found himself torn between addressing his headmaster by a deferential 'Sir' or a less formal 'Mr Fowler'. He decided on neither.

'Well, my French exchange partner will certainly be a qualified and experienced secondary school teacher, and he'll have spent a year as an *assistant* in an English school as part of his studies – just as Mademoiselle Berthet did last year here. So his English should be pretty much up to par. In any case, I don't think the risk will be any greater than if he were English. I think the experience will do both of us good. It'll certainly make us better teachers. And being taught by a real Frenchman might even prove to the kids that the Frogs are only human after all. In any case, it's only for a year.'

He had contemplated detaching the word 'Frogs' to give it a slightly ironical ring, but thought better of it. And he'd done his best to make it all sound convincing, especially the end. Didn't he want Fowler to think he'd be coming back next year as a matter of course?

'Mmm. Well, all I can say is that I hope you're right. In any case, Mr Morgan, I'd like you to know that I won't stand in your way.'

Michael was seized by an immense feeling of relief which he tried his hardest not to show. At the same time it crossed his mind that simply adding 'this time' to Fowler's last sentence would have meant he'd been right in thinking his headmaster had, in fact, opposed his application of the previous year.

'Thank you, Mr Fowler. I very much appreciate your support.'

There had been some warmth in his voice and this time he had no hesitation in using his surname. But, as he was getting up to leave, he couldn't avoid wondering whether 'I won't stand in your way' meant that this year his project would be given Fowler's full and active endorsement, or that he merely intended to remove his previous resistance to it. Nevertheless, he was more than tempted to think that, all things considered, Headmaster Fowler wasn't quite the bad chap he was made out to be.

EIGHT

'Hey Mike, you know what? She's sitting in the staffroom all on her tod!' Ian said in a tone of bantering amusement. An ear-to-ear grin split his face. Michael had just finished an after-school game of badminton with the gym teacher, and was wiping himself down when Ian had sauntered into the changing room.

'Have your shower and head over there quick, man. She might just get fed up of waiting for you and piss off home!'

'Who's 'she'?' he asked. He had a vague idea of who Ian was referring to, but his colleague's observation had caused him enough uneasy incredulity to justify a display of half-feigned ignorance. After all, he didn't want to give the impression he was vain enough to believe that one of the women teachers could have set her sights on him to this extent.

'Come off it, don't tell us you don't know!'

'No, honestly, I don't!'

'It's your secret admirer, Sylvia Schofield. She just can't wait to get to know you better! She's got you marked as a future hubby.'

'She's probably just stayed behind to do some marking!'

'You must be joking. She's sat in a corner reading *Time Magazine!* She's waiting for you, you twerp! If you listened to the voice of experience you might learn something about the way female minds work – especially when they're 23 years old and it's beginning to dawn on 'em they could be left on the shelf!'

It was true that Ian was quite a bit older than himself – he'd estimated him to be in his late thirties – and was married with two children; but he still couldn't totally subscribe to what he was being asked to believe. Sylvia and he had started at Barfield at the same time, and during the

35

year they'd now been teaching there they'd never exchanged more than a few casual words. What's more, he couldn't really say he was attracted enough to want to go beyond. And she'd never given him cause to think it wasn't the same with her. Nevertheless, he couldn't quite rid himself of the uncomfortable feeling that Ian might not be completely wrong and that, even if she hadn't yet gone to the extreme of considering him as a potential husband, this could be a planned attempt to create circumstances leading to them getting better acquainted. After all, she was the only young, unmarried female teacher among them and she might not have a boyfriend. And even more unease was caused by the fact that him not noticing what Ian, and perhaps others, seemed to consider obvious could be taken as a sign of his own naivety. He was still in two minds whether or not to dismiss it all as nonsense and drive straight home when he remembered he'd left a pile of exercise books in his staffroom locker for marking at home that evening.

As he strolled in she was sitting there alone in a corner. The magazine was resting open on her lap. She looked up with what seemed genuine surprise and gave him an apparently spontaneous smile. He did his best to give her one back. Opening his locker he took out the books.

'It looks as if you won't be watching much telly this evening,' she commented. As she spoke she closed the magazine in a gesture of finality. He had the impression she wanted to bring it to his notice that between him and the magazine it was the former she considered to be a more interesting subject.

'Oh, not really. This little lot won't take me all that long – an hour at the most. Have you done all your marking?' He'd noticed her earlier that day sitting at one of the staffroom tables with a pile of books in front of her.

'Yes, I only finished ten minutes ago. I got so engrossed I missed my bus. I've got an hour to wait for the next. I was hoping that *Time Magazine* would live up to its name and help me pass the time away!' He responded with a weak smile.

'I thought you had a car?'

'Yes, but I took it in for servicing this morning. I'm collecting it this evening. That's why I'm having to catch the bus.'

Even though her explanation seemed plausible he couldn't help thinking of Ian's words. Was this story of missing her bus really a scheme she'd carefully contrived to put herself conveniently in his way? Was her show of innocence all an act? Or was it just typically Ian? For, when in the sole company of men, he'd noticed that Ian frequently displayed a facetiously deprecatory, sometimes cynical attitude towards the women teachers – especially the younger ones. And their physical attributes were rarely spared. Only the other day he'd quipped, 'We never seem to get perfect beauties here at Barfield. I mean, there's always something wrong with 'em ... boxer's shoulders, horsey teeth, hairs on their chest ... a gammy leg.' Michael didn't know whether this last remark was a direct reference, but he had noticed that Sylvia walked with what could possibly be viewed as the trace of a limp. Being a tall girl with long legs it was as if she had difficulty in controlling her feet at the ends – especially the left one which turned slightly inwards as she walked. It seemed to impart just a hint of imbalance to the whole. But no, he couldn't for the life of him imagine all this was part of a carefully hatched *mise en scène*. How could she possibly have known he'd be staying behind after school to play badminton?

'Can I run you to your garage?' His proposal was prompted by little more than the pleasure it gave him in showing a modicum of gallantry towards a female colleague.

'Oh, it's very nice of you to offer, but I don't want to put you to any trouble.' He had the vague feeling that her resistance was little more than a show of token politeness.

'It's no trouble at all. Where is it?' She mentioned a place a couple of miles away.

'That's no problem. It's on my way home.' His words of reassurance came less from a wish to tell the strict truth than from an awareness that he had now gone too far for his play of gentlemanly consideration not to be acted out to a convincing end.

'Well, if you're sure I'm not putting you out of your way.'

'Not in the slightest.'

In the car she did most of the talking. The conversation began on the subject of Deputy Head Cooper. Like Michael, she didn't appreciate him at all. He was too much of a loud mouth for her liking, and he treated the kids as if they were all delinquents. And as for Headmaster Fowler, she was outraged by his ruling on women not being allowed to wear boots and slacks. But hadn't he heard? Next year would be his last. He was retiring. She didn't know who they'd be getting in his place but it could hardly be anyone worse. Even though Michael made no mention to her of his future French plans he found himself wondering how they might be affected by this news. As far as he could judge there was nothing that could be considered as presenting the slightest threat. On the contrary, his fast approaching retirement could explain why Fowler now seemed relatively favourable. After all, even if his exchange partner did have discipline issues the headmaster would be able to console himself with the thought that he didn't have long to go before this sort of problem would no longer be part of his responsibilities. Michael mostly listened and agreed with what she said. He also learned she was Bert Schofield's daughter. In his youth Bert Schofield's *Majestic Ballroom* had been a popular dance hall in one of the town's suburbs. In his later school days he'd been there two or three times with his mates in the hope of 'picking up a bird'. Being shy and not much of a dancer he'd contemplated these evenings with enough trepidation to welcome the fortifying effects of the beer they would ingurgitate at the bar prior to summoning up enough courage to ask a girl to dance. But he'd had no success. The final time they'd been the horrified witnesses to a savage fight of trembling hands, broken bottles and gashed faces. He'd never set foot there again.

She eased herself out of the car, thanked him profusely and wished him goodbye. Had our young man looked her more closely in the face he might have detected something very much like a glow in her eye.

NINE

He pulled into the drive of his parents' house. His father had been a commercial traveller for a wholesale grocery firm until they'd bought a grocery shop some twelve years before when Michael was barely sixteen. It had meant leaving the familiar places of his childhood and early youth and going to live some distance away in another part of the town. 'We're going to make some real money now,' his dad had boasted. But the move was ill-considered and under normal circumstances would have had disastrous consequences. For this was at the beginning of the nineteen sixties; and not far from the centre of Bridgeford a shop-keeping pioneer, intent on fulfilling an entrepreneurial dream, had only two years previously converted an old cinema into a large retail store with an extensive car park where customers could serve themselves to groceries, low-priced meat, fruit, vegetables and dairy products all in one go, and which was to herald the gradual demise of the small corner shop. After six months they had to face up to the inescapable evidence that takings were showing an uneven, but inexorable decline. While it was never mentioned openly, the growing realization that buying the business had been a ghastly mistake stifled all in a blanket of palpable gloom which frequently exploded into bitter, mutually incriminatory quarrels. But Michael's grandmother's prophetic declaration to her daughter just before her marriage that, 'You'll never go far wrong with Albert. He was born under a lucky star,' was about to prove itself true: for in the space of not much more than ten minutes everything had come good.

The shop was situated on a busy main road opposite a large textile mill, and one morning its personnel manager called in to see them. Having been built at a time when the well-being of workers had not been an object of much consideration, if any consideration at all, the factory was now unable to provide eating facilities for its staff. Though the management had recently installed a number of hot and cold drink machines, workers were complaining more and more that, unless they brought their own food, it was impossible to get a bite to eat at lunchtime or during their morning and afternoon break. Since the firm was reluctant to invest in cafeteria facilities, it had been suggested at a recent staff welfare committee meeting that outsourcing might be the solution. And who better to ask than the grocery shop across the road? He thought that a good variety of plain, reasonably-priced sandwiches, buns and cakes, proposed in the mornings and afternoons, was all that would be required. Would they be interested in catering to this demand?

It was a golden opportunity, and his dad had been quick to seize it. He immediately commissioned a joiner to make a large trolley equipped with rollers and wide removable drawers which he could wheel around the factory twice a day. And he soon got things moving. Though this meant them rising early and working hard to make the sandwiches and bake the confectionary, profit margins were generous, and their business soon began to prosper. However, his mum had never liked living on these old premises next to a busy main road and opposite a grimy Victorian mill. So, four years later they decided to invest in a four-bedroom detached house on a newly-built estate in a residential suburb a few miles away, and commute from it to the shop early each morning. The only problem was Grandpa.

Shorty after they'd moved into the shop, Michael's grandma, a longstanding chest angina sufferer, had committed the irreparable act of departing this life while hanging out the Monday morning washing in the back garden of the house she and Grandpa had retired to five years earlier. While her demise was regretted by all – especially since it had had the indecency to occur at the relatively early age of 63 – the person who suffered its most unwelcome consequences was Grandpa, who now had to face the disheartening prospect of living out his remaining years companionless.

Now Grandpa was the youngest of a brood of twelve children (his parents had even adopted a thirteenth) living in a cramped, back-to-back terrace house in the main street of a small Yorkshire mining village. Like his six brothers he'd left school at the age of thirteen (this was at the beginning of the last century) to start his working life as an apprentice coal hewer down the village pit. However, a combination of personal ambition and rejection of the hard labour and abominable working conditions that were the miner's lot of that time had prompted him to enroll at what then went under the name of 'night school' in the neighbouring town where, twice weekly, after a day's hard toil, he studied for, and was eventually rewarded with a mining engineer's diploma which enabled him to rise from his lowly beginnings to spend most of his working life on top as undermanager in charge of the early morning shift. But despite Grandpa calling the morning tune at the pit, he had to play second fiddle at home: for when it came to conducting domestic affairs his wife had the leading part; and her conception of female marital duty even extended to sitting her husband down, and pulling his boots off when he came home from work, or running his bath and scrubbing the coal dust from his back whenever his managerial responsibilities obliged him to descend into the depths of the mine.

It is a widely-observable tendency of human nature that the more people are looked after by others, the less effort they are inclined to make to look after themselves. Grandpa was no exception. It wasn't that he couldn't manage on his own in a rough and ready kind of way – especially when it came to rooting up his meals; but, having been required during the whole of his married life to lift considerably less than what his little finger was capable of, he was blind to, or chose to disregard, both at home and in his own person, what his wife would have immediately spotted and rectified. The result was that both house and Grandpa were slowly but relentlessly falling into a state of grubby neglect – a situation which his daughter had neither the time nor the energy to remedy in any appreciable way. Even though he was frequent-ly invited to come and stay with them at the shop – an event which was enjoyed and looked forward to by all – when he left to go back to his life of solitary rumination his daughter was deeply saddened by her father's forlorn looks. So, when they moved into their new abode it was suggested he should sell up and come to live with them. Grandpa didn't even need to be told that he agreed. It was a grave mistake: for what four years of periodic, week-long visits had accommodated with cheerful benignity, four weeks of permanent co-habitation began severely to condemn.

It soon became irritatingly clear that, despite his managerial career at the mine, so accustomed had Grandpa become to being waited on hand and foot that he had to be told to do everything at home: to pull out a few weeds in the garden, to clean the oven, or set the table in readiness for the evening meal when his daughter and her husband came home after a tiring day at the shop. Otherwise he could show a remarkable ability to sit for long periods in his armchair, occasionally reading, but often simply puffing on his pipe: 'just staring into space,' as his son-in-law would ruefully remark. And growing up as part of a numerous, closely-knit family had acted on Grandad's already gregarious nature to produce a person of lively, irresistible sociability: for Grandpa was a good conversationalist, not only capable of maintaining a lively discussion on matters of topical concern, but keeping his audience entertained by a well-rehearsed repertoire of stories, anecdotes and jokes. As a result, there was nothing this mild-mannered, generous and intelligent man loved better than being in the company of others; so whenever his daughter and son-in-law's friends came to visit, he took an active, often predominant part in the conversation for as long as they stayed. 'He sticks it out right to the bitter end!' his daughter would comment to her husband who would slowly shake his head. Grandpa just didn't seem to realize that, after an appropriate moment, he should have been thoughtful enough to have said goodnight to everybody and despatched himself off to bed.

And was it this innate affability combined with the cramped family circumstances of his formative years, with all the lack of personal privacy this entailed, which had gone to develop in Grandpa a strong inclination to think he had a right to share in what is normally restricted to those who are directly concerned? Or was it simply curiosity? After only a couple of weeks of co-habitation Grandpa had to be told to drop the infuriating habit he seemed to have adopted of opening both the household bills and his daughter and son-in-law's personal mail. While the former was considered to be an annoying impingement on their private living space, the latter was its shameful annexation. But things really came to a head that Saturday evening when they had come back home at midnight after dining with some friends. There sat Grandpa calmly awaiting their safe return, enthroned in his armchair and drawing meditatively on his pipe. It was with some indignation that his daughter had told him she was no longer a child, and that whenever she and her husband came home at this late hour in future he would be expected to have long since retired to bed.

What caused displeasure in the daughter drove the son-in-law to fury. Michael's father was a reserved sort of man, more at ease among the flowers and vegetables in his garden and greenhouse than in the company of others, and who could meet his father-in-law neither in depth of intelligence nor breadth of conversation. Perhaps it was also the place this old man occupied in his wife's heart which brought out other, more deeply-felt inadequacies: did he also sense that his son had sometimes to struggle against the thought that he might have preferred the gentle, easy-going man his Grandpa was to his less benevolently-disposed father whose temper could quickly turn him white with rage? Whatever the cause, his cup of jealousy soon brimmed so full of his father-in-law's faults that it left no room for his merits: for Michael's father – like all of us, I suppose, at some time or other – sought facile justification for his resentment rather than subjecting himself to the more painful process of self-evaluation. The result was that the home atmosphere soon became poisoned by an accumulative pressure of simmering tensions which the slightest spark could ignite. One evening he'd come home from school later than usual to find Grandpa lying prostrate on the sofa, his daughter perched worriedly by his side, pressing a glass of brandy to his trembling lips. Through the window he could see his father furiously digging over the back garden. Fortunately, they had a married daughter living on the other side of town who would regularly invite Grandpa to stay for a week or so. His absence brought a temporary breath of oxygen to the vitiated home air.

When at the beginning of his first year at Barfield Michael had taken the decision to live with his parents he'd been away for so many years, with only the occasional short visit home, that he hadn't been able to assess the extent to which relations between his father and Grandpa had now deteriorated. After a week or two his discomfort was enough to induce him to take a surreptitious look at the flats-to-let column in the local evening newspaper. He realized, however, that it was now too late, and that the slightest inkling of his desire to move would be considered by his parents as a form of rejection, even betrayal. He was reluctant to cause them this additional pain. In any case, they were well aware of his dreams of going to France and knew that these present accommodation arrangements were limited in time. All he could do was to wait patiently for events to unfold. If he couldn't get what he liked, he could only make an effort to like what he could get.

He had, nevertheless, quickly resolved to reduce his exposure to these domestic tensions by the simple expedient of organizing his non-working hours in such a way as to spend the least possible time at home. Once he'd settled into his new job he'd extended his involvement well beyond his normal teaching time table by accepting the gym teacher's invitation to take full charge of the junior soccer and cricket teams. As a schoolmaster in England it was expected of him; and he was not without thinking it would act in his favour when it came to obtaining a reference from his headmaster. This meant organizing and supervising weekly after-school practice sessions and refereeing or umpiring Saturday morning matches against other schools. He'd also started a table-tennis club with similar training sessions and matches; and being something of a sportsman himself he'd joined a squash and badminton club with regular weekly meetings throughout the year. All in all, he was relatively satisfied with the variety and degree to which he'd mobilized his after-school hours. The problem was the weekends – especially in winter: for though Bridgeford had a first division soccer team, the Saturday afternoon matches he went to watch ended before five o'clock, and all too often he found himself spending the evenings gazing at uninspiring television programmes in the company of his parents and Grandpa. When he first started at Barfield he'd even taken the desperate measure of going to the city-centre dance hall in the hope of meeting a girl. But this wasn't a student dance, and it had been a great let-down. He'd danced with three or four girls whom he'd found plain, stupid, or simply vulgar. With one it was all three. He couldn't help reflecting that, since he didn't speak with much of the local accent and was capable of aligning words of more than two syllables in length, they probably thought he was something of a snob. To make matters worse, when he'd walked back to his Mini, alone and dejected, he found the side window had been smashed and the radio stolen. He'd cursed himself for being stupid enough to leave it in such an unlit spot. In the light of the next morning he discovered that his fog and spotlight had disappeared, too. Even though he spent his summer Saturday afternoons playing cricket for a local team his initial hopes of finding pals in whose company he could prolong the evenings were short-lived. Matches usually ended not much later than seven o'clock, and at the end of the first he'd invited some similarly-aged team mates to have a drink with him in the pavilion bar. He had hoped they might be willing to carry on their drinking in a town-centre pub. But his suggestions to this effect came to nothing: he was pointedly informed they'd now 'settled down'; they were married men with families, and they either politely rejected his advances, or allowed themselves just a quickly-expedited 'half'. As a result, after a quarter of an hour or so he found himself abandoned to his solitary fate. It was a far cry from those student days when a party was always going on somewhere or other and, if the worst came to the worst, there was always the Saturday night hop. But then he'd hit on the idea of retiring to his bedroom on Saturday evenings and Sunday afternoons with a view to improving his French. On these occasions he would tune into French radio, or re-read some of those literary works which had formed part of his degree course.

This is not to say that our young man hadn't had the opportunity of attending one or two parties over the last year. But he was of a reserved and serious nature. 'You're like your father,' his mother would frequently say. 'You can't let your hair down!' He himself had to admit that he needed the liberating effects of alcohol in order to relax. And even then his conversation would all too often take on a serious, philosophical tone. He didn't seem to realize that most girls were seeking light-hearted, transient fun; and his attempts to make himself sound interesting by a detailed explanation of the difference between 'existence' and 'essence', and his existentialist conviction that the first preceded the second tended to bore rather than entertain. What's more, he couldn't avoid reflecting that a profession which everybody has had at least a decade of almost daily contact with and which can bring back memories of the more disagreeable kind may, in the eyes of many, have difficulty in raising itself above the painfully banal. It all went to confirm that any quest for female companionship should be limited to that provided by young women operating in his own occupational sphere.

One result of these reflections was to persuade our young man that he wouldn't be against the idea of getting better acquainted with Sylvia Schofield. Wouldn't this be a good way of getting him out on a Saturday evening? And if there was enough affinity they could go out for Sunday runs in the car, too. So, when the opportunity presented itself why not invite her out for a drink? She was certainly an intelligent girl, they had similar professional preoccupations, and perhaps a closer acquaintance might reveal they had other things in common. Since their recent chat he'd been watching her more closely. Ian was definitely being unfair. She was more attractive than he'd first thought; and the limp he'd accused her of – if you could even call it by that name – was barely perceptible. However, on no account would he let things get too serious. It would only be a temporary arrangement. He wouldn't allow anything to get in the way of his dreams of starting life afresh in France. For unlike many young men of his age and position who might have thought the time had now come to turn their thoughts to marriage and the founding of a family, Michael had now come to view the state of matrimony as not much more than a self-inflicted prison sentence; or, at best a kind of consented probation. 'I understand why it's called wed*lock*!' he frequently joked to his married male colleagues while heavily emphasizing the final syllable. It was not always said in jest. When they moaned about the scrimping and saving involved in keeping on top of their mortgage payments, or how underpaid they were, he couldn't help feeling scorn for the suffocating confinement of it all. It was the same when they spoke of their hopes of a rise at the end of the year, their petty ambitions to become departmental head, how difficult it was getting to control the kids, and how much they detested Headmaster Fowler. In moments like this he saw himself as a bird enclosed in a sunless cage. A shimmering horizon beckoned to him beyond; he longed to take flight on the wings of adventure.

TEN

I hope to be forgiven for not yet revealing whether those conditions conducive to Michael Morgan and Sylvia Schofield becoming better acquainted soon presented themselves, or whether they presented themselves at all, and that I will once more be permitted to delve into our young man's past – this time in order to dwell at some length on an amatory episode which had impressed itself enough on him for it still to be a frequent subject of reflection. While these retrospective ponderings did not so much entail the reopening of deeply painful wounds as bring an immensely-felt relief that favourable circumstances (or was it simply his destiny?) had rescued him from an official union whose consequences, he was now sure, would have quickly revealed themselves to have been disastrous, what is more understandable that they should have had some bearing on his present aversion to the marital state in general?

Not long after the beginning of the first term of his final university year Michael had been introduced to the heady elation, the sensual delights, not to mention those unsuspected perversities which may frequently lie concealed beneath that innocent-sounding wrap called 'first love'. It had all begun at the weekly Saturday night 'hop' or 'meat market', as it was cynically referred to by many students – not without some justification: for it was generally considered as providing an ideal place to acquire for future consumption varying cuts and qualities of human flesh. The group had just struck up in the main hall, and a covey of girls were perched in uneasy anticipation on the score or more chairs encircling the dance floor. He'd immediately noticed her sitting apart in a barely-lit corner. She didn't seem all that bad-looking, though he couldn't make out any confirmatory details. Knowing she'd soon be solicited by others, this shy, bespectacled, unprepossessing youth, previously fortified by a couple of beers, had plucked up enough courage to go up and present her with a tentative, 'Would you like to dance?' along with the bravest of smiles. He was almost surprised when she'd accepted without the slightest sign of hesitation. The music was loud, and while they were dancing he'd done his best to engage her in, and keep up a semblance of conversation. He was encouraged by her beaming face and readiness to talk. Even though the lights were low his discreetly directed glances were enough to discern a pair of nicely-shaped legs below a slightly-above-the-knees skirt as well as the contours of a generous bosom; and it wasn't possible for a 'bag' to move with such light, feminine grace. While they gyrated she seemed only too happy to answer those banal questions he ventured to ask her. She was studying English and, like him, in her last year. Having spent most of the day swotting for finals it wasn't going in any more: so she'd decided to grant herself an evening's respite; the change would do her good. She lived at Saint-Catherine's, a nearby women's hall of residence. As the first dance ended he half expected her to thank him and go back to her seat. When she didn't he just stood there awkwardly, hardly knowing what to say. But she stayed up for a second and then a third dance and his confidence began to grow. It was only when she accepted his shy invitation to go and have a drink with an enthusiastic-sounding, 'Oh yes, that'd be really nice!' that he was sure he'd scored. In the less subdued light of the Students' Union bar he was presented with a more substantial confirmation of her physical charms. Though there was a reassuring homeliness about her manner, her wide-set eyes and high cheek bones lent to her face an exciting, yet at the same time vaguely disturbing exotic look. It was as if he'd netted what he'd thought was an attractive, yet indigenous butterfly which, on closer examination, had revealed itself to be of an unknown species. She quickly provided an explanation. Her name was Vicky Nielsen. Her father was of Danish extraction and her mother was a French-speaking Belgian. And this mixed parentage of contrasting genes had engendered a girl who was neither pretty nor beautiful in the strictest sense of the words, but whose features and gaze – helped by the slightest of casts in one eye – lent to her person just that *soupçon* of wanton sensuality which the French call *du chien*, and which the warm simplicity of her demeanour could do little to efface. They'd spent the rest of the evening chatting together cheerfully in the bar. And they'd held hands while he'd walked her back to her room. Though she seemed as pleased with him as he was with her, he didn't want to run the risk of compromising such a promising beginning by too hasty a display of fondness, and a simple 'goodbye' had been their only form of parting. He'd walked back home on a cloud. She'd invited him over to her room for coffee the following evening.

ELEVEN

Is it all that surprising that in those more and more emancipated university days of the mid 1960's a beaker of watery instant coffee imbibed by a healthy young man and woman within the narrow confines of a student study bedroom should be the hastily despatched prelude to encounter of a more intimate kind? Up until then his physical relations with the opposite sex had amounted to not much more than holding hands along with the occasional cautious peck – though, admittedly, he had been presented once or twice with the opportunity of indulging in exploratory versions of what is commonly termed a French kiss. With Vicky he soon discovered that this fusion of disparate foreign genes had engendered a girl whose appetite surpassed his wildest imaginings: for her unabashed enjoyment of their sexual engagements frequently induced her to take the lead to a point where he quickly became aware of how innocent he was. Her reputation had even gone before her. His room neighbour, who happened to be the boyfriend of one of Vicky's friends, had one day joked with a roguish wink, 'You'll be all right there, Mike! She's like an Ever-Ready battery! Once you've turned her on she'll never let you down!' Though not appreciating the comparison he had forced a weak smile and said nothing. And it didn't take long for him to have his first confirmation of her indefatigable readiness to participate in the joys of sensual gratification. One evening he'd got fed up of studying and had gone to see her. She wasn't feeling well and after their cup of coffee she lay down on her bed. He sat down beside her. The sight of her reposing there excited him so much that after a while he began their usual foreplay by slipping his hand up her skirt and down into her panties. He was surprised by the degree of receptivity his digital penetrations encountered. 'I thought you were a dying duck!' he joked. 'I hope you think more of me than that,' she replied. He'd immediately regretted saying it.

During their preliminary chats, however, she would often take time to talk about herself and her family. She was of modest origins. From what he could gather, her father was some sort of office clerk for an insurance company. Her mother didn't work at all. They lived in a small, semi-detached bungalow in the suburbs of a West of England cathedral town. Judging from what was hinted she'd had several boyfriends. Somewhere he was left with the feeling that her previous relations with men had frequently been a source of dissatisfaction and had never lasted long. She soon disclosed that she tended to attract 'the wrong sort of man' – the 'smoothie' womanizer who saw her as little more than a decorative extension to himself. She was looking for someone who would love her for what she was, and not for her looks and the desire which they aroused. She was an only child, and it was perhaps for this reason she seemed especially close to her mother. Just before the beginning of the present term they'd had a heart-to-heart talk. 'Why don't you find yourself a nice boy, Vicky?' Mrs Nielson had asked.

This seemed to be what her mother had done. She'd met her husband in Brussels at the end of World War Two. Apparently, he was a gawky, shy and unprepossessing young private in the British Army who'd fallen head over heels in love with this Belgian beauty some five years older than himself. Though they spoke no more than a few words of each other's tongue it was the depth of love she saw through those windows to the soul that were his eyes which made her consent to marry and accompany him back to an unknown country whose language it remained for her to learn. Michael couldn't help asking himself – not without some unease – whether he himself had been chosen because of what Vicky imagined to be his own conformity to her mother's representation of this male marital ideal. Her last boyfriend had graduated and left the same university the previous year. She'd even invited him home to meet her parents; but she hadn't appreciated his tendency to want to take control. 'He was always bossing us around,' she told him. 'We were preparing a meal together one evening when he started telling my mum what to do in her own kitchen!' He'd been more experienced than her. On one occasion their sexual play had got out of control, and it had all ended in what she deeply regretted. She'd spent three weeks or so in an agony of worry.

'But why did you let him do it?' he asked.

'I didn't realize what was happening!' she replied.

He began to feel more and more out of his depth. One evening as they lay together she'd said, 'Michael, be rough with me!' Not only did he have difficulty understanding what exactly was expected of him, but he couldn't help being disturbed by the thought that drawing excitement from being manhandled rather than caressed was one of the more perverse manifestations of female sexuality. Feelings of inadequacy and jealousy began to smoulder in him. Up to then they'd simply indulged in manual stimulation. He wanted the experience of making real love.

'You let him do it so why not me?' he asked her.

'I promised God I wouldn't do it again until I was married. I hope He'll forgive me for what I did,' she replied.

Her evocation of a censorial God had been a further subject of unease. His existentialist readings were causing him to be more and more tempted by the idea that God had no presence beyond the superstitious imaginings of Man. 'But don't you prefer *me* to your God?' he'd answered in a wild surge of jealousy. He immediately felt deeply ashamed for having said it.

The holidays came and they went back home to spend Christmas with their respective parents. Before leaving he'd promised to write to her immediately on arrival and she'd assured him she would do the same. But after four or five mornings the postman had brought nothing. He was in agonies of anguish. Was she ill? Had she had an accident? A small parcel finally arrived on the morning before Christmas. It contained a narrow, green corduroy tie. 'Some mod youth told me they're in fashion,' she'd commented in the short letter attached. He was cruelly disappointed by both its brevity and detached tone; and without really knowing why he was tormented by the growing certainty that there had been a radical change. When he got back to university the first thing he did was to go and see her. As he knocked on the door of her room a strained 'Come in' brought the heart-rending confirmation that she had a grave announcement to make. She was sitting stiffly upright at her desk in preparation for his arrival. Without her even asking him if he'd like a cup of coffee it all came straight out. During the holidays she'd had a heart-to-heart talk with her mother. She'd asked her daughter to think carefully about whether she wanted a jealous man. What's more, she'd met someone back home. He was the brother of an old school girlfriend of hers, and was studying at Oxford. In fact, she'd known him on and off for quite some time; up to then she'd never viewed him in more than a sisterly light. He'd asked her to dance at her friend's Christmas party; they'd chatted and, even though he wasn't much to look at, she'd been struck by what a nice boy he was. Couldn't they now just be friends? Though he'd heard the ominous hum of the approaching plane he was no less devastated when the bomb actually fell.

In view of this first experience of strong amorous attachment with all the blind finality this may bring, what is more understandable that Michael should have been incapable of entertaining the thought that what he now considered to be a life-shattering disaster could be viewed in a more relative light in less time than he might have been prepared to believe? At that moment he was unable to conceive of a future without her, and could only resolve to concentrate all his efforts on winning her back. And not only did he find comfort in that adage which states that the course of true love never runs smooth, but his trembling hopes clutched at the straw which her apparent wish to remain on amicable terms had provided. But, for the moment at least, he had no alternative but to accept her conditions; and the only possible strategy he could adopt was to maintain their channels of communication as widely open as the downgraded nature of his present status would allow. He would just have to resign himself to the inescapable fact that any attempts to reconquer his beloved's heart would be confined to the verbal, and be considerably limited in space and time. In addition, he would also have to find the mental strength to combat that additional source of anguish caused by the more and more worrying thought that his final exams were looming up, and that he should now be focusing his efforts on subjects of a more academic purport.

Despite his resolve he was unable to get her out of his mind during most of the day; and her corporeal form frequently encroached upon territory usually reserved for thoughts of a more cognitive kind. The faculty of arts building was a modern, red brick, two-winged construction standing among cedar and elm trees in an extensive parkland setting. The theatre where Michael's lectures took place was located on the ground floor of one of the wings adjacent to which ran the final 30 yards or so of the wide, straight drive leading from the main road outside to the faculty entrance. And so it took only a slight turn of head from the lecturer on the stage towards the large, east-facing window on the left which, during morning lectures bathed listeners in light, to be able to follow the thin but steady trickle of student comings and goings outside. Shortly after meeting Vicky he'd happened to look casually out, and had caught a glimpse of her strolling past. He came to know to the minute when she would appear. She was easily recognizable in the short, glossy white raincoat she wore in anticipation of the autumn rain. It brought out all the richness of her tumbling auburn hair. She'd drawn the contrasting black belt tight enough to bring out all the slimness of her waist, and reveal the outline of those full, firm breasts he was getting to know so well. He was seized by desire at the sight of those shapely legs. And was it her foreign origins which imparted that lightness to her step? Could such an enchanting girl really be his? But what had previously set him in a flutter of excitement now produced throbs of anguished pain. Was it because she was now unattainable that he yearned for the fragrance and feel of her even more?

He had been struck by the fact that she invariably walked alone, and he couldn't help thinking it was her striking looks and the rivalry this might cause which had set her apart from English girls. Though she never mentioned it, he suspected that somewhere she felt lonely: for on those occasions when they met inside the student common room café she would often ask him over for coffee that same evening or the following one. These invitations were always extended with what appeared to be a casual air – as if acceptance was a matter of indifference to her; but he could detect just enough of a strain in her voice to suggest she would have been disappointed had he declined. Not that he ever contemplated refusal. These occasions made him feel there was still room for hope: that somewhere she needed him – even if it was only his presence as a conversational partner. He sometimes took the liberty of inviting her to his room. Usually she accepted. These moments were not without causing pain as what had previously been just a short verbal preamble to a prolonged close exchange now consisted in them remaining firmly seated apart, and him having to endure glowing reports on the subject of her newly found *amour*. Even so, one of these evenings had been exceptional enough to stand out in his mind. They were sitting opposite each other in his room, sipping their coffee and chatting about something and nothing, when the rays of the setting sun suddenly pierced the dark clouds outside, bathing her head and shoulders in an iconic light. And this normally reserved, inexpressive young man was seized by a passion which caused the words of a fervent eulogy to come tumbling out. 'You know, I've never known a girl as divinely beautiful as you look now! It's as if your hair was intertwined with threads of burnished gold!' he'd said. As she was studying English literature he couldn't quite rid himself of the thought that such hyperbolic praise might sound overworked and could be mocked. It was perhaps the obvious sincerity with which the words were spoken that caused his Goddess to respond with beams of pleasure. Can we blame him for taking this as an indication that all was not quite lost?

TWELVE

As Michael had feared, one of the effects of this break-up was to cause the results of his final exams to fall short of his hopes: for though he obtained his degree its classification was lower than what he'd set his sights on. Even if this didn't represent a total failure he couldn't in any way conceive of it as being a success. He did, however, draw some consolation from the fact that, as one of his similarly-positioned friends declared, 'a degree is a degree', and that once they were out in the great wide world this would be all that mattered.

Their student days ended, and after the summer holidays he started his job with the brewery. She was still all too present in his thoughts. During the daytime it wasn't too bad – his work gave him plenty to think about and he could sometimes push her to the back of his mind. It was not the same when he found himself alone. He had rented a bedsit on the top floor of a large suburban Victorian house; and in the solitude of those autumn evenings when daylight was conceding more and more territory to an invasive night he would gaze through the window into the growing darkness outside. He was haunted by shimmering visions of her face floating incandescent-like in the gloom.

I am certainly not the first person to have observed that a young and ardent lover, estranged from the object of his desire, may clutch at the flimsiest of straws in an attempt to glean the hope that Destiny may have planned their reconciliation. Was it this wild expectation which caused our young man to interpret these twilight apparitions as the flickering embodiment of her distressed spirit beckoning him to fly back to her rescue? Moreover, he was beginning to realize it was only when he had been given irrefutable proof that this chapter of his life was irreversibly closed that he could turn to another page. It was as if someone dear had disappeared beneath the ruins of some earthquake-ravaged town. As long as he hadn't been presented with the body he could never come to terms with the death. So, wasn't writing to ask if she would agree or not to see him the only way of bringing conclusive proof that for him she was truly dead? After all, what did he have to lose? That evening he penned the following note:

Dear Vicky,

I'll be in Melchester next Saturday. Would it be possible for us to meet at 2 o'clock in front of the Cathedral? I shall consider silence on your part as a sign that all is irremediably finished.
Michael.

There was a postbox at the end of the street. Fearing that the night might bring second thoughts he went straight out to post it.

He'd mailed it on Friday evening and had reckoned he'd receive any reply by the following Friday at the very latest. When Saturday arrived he'd lost all hope. It was only after breakfast that he'd trudged downstairs to see if there was any mail. As he reached the first floor landing he looked down over the bannister onto the front door entrance hall. A single letter was lying on the doormat. Even before he could see the writing on the envelope he knew it was from her. He rushed down and tore it open with trembling fingers and wildly thumping heart. It read as follows:

Michael,

I'll meet you at the time and place you suggest.
Vicky.

He was engulfed by a wave of triumphant exultation in which mingled a sense of the unreal. It was as if this brief sentence had released some mental anesthetizing substance which produced a benumbed feeling this was not happening to him. But the wondrous stupor he felt on stepping back up to his room couldn't quite allay the anguished thought that it might now be too late for a train to get him to their appointed meeting place on time.

THIRTEEN

His fears of arriving late proved to be unfounded. Melchester was on the main line to Wales and a train halted there every hour. But the nearer it came to the station the more those brief words of hers which had been the cause of so much stupefied elation became the source of nagging doubt. Had he really been reinstated as sole pretender to her heart? What if her acceptance was simply to renew their previous 'friendly' relationship? Or could it merely be a way of assuring some kind of substitute if things didn't work out with John? He arrived early in front of the cathedral. A chilly wind made him step inside. He'd just walked through the vestibule into the nave when she was walking down the aisle towards him. She was wearing that same, glossy white raincoat. A tense half-smile froze her face. She was paler than he'd ever seen her before.

You will, I hope, forgive me for repeating that platitude which states that the stronger our emotions are the more we become aware of how difficult it is to find those words necessary to give adequate expression to them. This was the case with Michael: for despite those passionate hopes that this moment would finally come he couldn't find it in him to declare, 'I'm so wonderfully happy to see you again!' All he could murmur was, 'Hello Vicky. How are you?' But it was spoken with tenderness.

'Oh I'm fine. What about you?' she said softly.

'Shall we go for a drink?' he replied, unaware that he'd not answered her question. Before entering the cathedral he'd noted the presence of a pub on the other side of the square.

'Yes, all right.'

The cold autumn wind had now given way to a light drizzle and

59

apart from trite remarks about the weather they hurried there in silence. Neither had brought an umbrella; and neither knew what the situation required them to say. When he brought the drinks to their table she'd unbuttoned her raincoat, and her rounded, high-boned cheeks were taking on a pinkish glow. Though her features were still slightly drawn she was as desirable as ever. Perhaps it was the warmth of the pub lounge and the chattering conviviality around them which prompted her to talk. She was living at home with her parents and working as a child safety officer with the local authority. As with him this first encounter with down-to-earth, sometimes squalid reality had been something her studies had in no way prepared her for and had come as a considerable shock. Life now was a far cry from those sheltered student days when the decisions they took had little impact on the lives of others. She was now faced with choices which caused her gnawing worry and painful, self-questioning doubt. At the moment she was in charge of a case involving a young, abused girl; she would soon have to decide whether to withdraw her from her parents' custody and place her in out-of-home care.

Though he listened with patience and sympathy he was longing for her to open a way leading to confirmation that he still held a place in her heart. He was beginning to doubt it would ever come when, all at once, she declared, 'You know I've broken with John!' Then, like a dyke suddenly collapsing beneath the constant poundings of a raging inner sea, it all came gushing out. That 'nice boy' had revealed some failings she couldn't excuse. The final straw was when he'd sent her a cartoon-style birthday card (it had been her birthday a few weeks before) showing a young man hanging out of a bedroom window jubilantly swinging a pair of bras aloft. She had not found it amusing. It was even offensive. She had never thought he could be so disrespectfully immature. Despite his inner exultation Michael couldn't help comparing this act of puerile naivety with that moment when his jealousy had overflowed to the point of him asking why she didn't prefer him to God. But perhaps his jubilation was a little premature. Could her words be taken as full confirmation that he'd been reinstated in her heart? It was only when she said, 'I'd like you to come and meet my parents.

They've invited you to tea,' that his triumph was complete.

It is a frequently confirmable fact that even the flames of passionate young love will sooner or later be smothered, if not completely doused by the pernicious tendency life has of slotting our daily and weekly activities into those same temporal cubby-holes we agree to call 'routine'. Michael and Vicky's romance was no exception. Their lives soon settled down into a regular course which consisted in him taking the train on Friday evenings (he hadn't yet been entrusted with a company car) to spend the weekend with his beloved and her parents in their tiny bungalow; while the following Saturday morning she took the opposite direction to join him at his cramped bedsit in Birmingham. However, on coming home one evening, a few weeks after their blissful reconcilement, he was surprised – even puzzled – to find a letter from her not only informing him that she was delighted to accept his proposal of marriage but suggesting that their engagement be made official by his purchase of an appropriate ring. Could they have a look round some jewellery shops when she came on Saturday? She'd also like to offer him a ring in return. Michael's perplexity was caused by him being unable to recollect anything that might have been construed as a direct offer. They'd certainly talked about marriage the previous weekend at her parents', but he'd been left with the impression that their conversation had been on the subject of matrimony in general rather than its particular application to them. Moreover, if indeed he had proposed, why hadn't Vicky accepted on the spot? Why had she waited before informing him by post? And why this haste to make it all official? While, at bottom, he would have preferred their romance to have been free of any formal commitment for the moment, it did, all things considered, constitute an agreeable surprise. After all, what did it matter? Wasn't she the love of his life? Nevertheless, he couldn't quite rid himself of the thought that somewhere his hand was being forced. He'd phoned immediately to tell her how much he loved her, and how blissfully happy he was that she'd agreed to become his wife. He then got in touch with his parents to inform them of the good news. But with the cold hindsight provided by the last three years, a remark which he'd paid little attention to at the time now made him more than suspect that Mrs

Nielson had, once again, had had a not negligible part to play in her daughter's decision. The remark was prompted by the contact lenses he'd bought only a couple of weeks before.

Now it is another no less frequently observable trait of human nature that most young people – and even those more advanced in years – are not without a certain vanity regarding their person. Michael was no exception. So, on receiving his first month's salary the first thing he'd done was to treat himself to a pair of contact lenses. He'd been wearing spectacles since the age of 14 and mentally had never felt comfortable with them: they neither reflected the image he wished to have of himself nor the one he would have liked to project to others. At that time contact lenses were made of hard plastic, and normally required a relatively lengthy period of gradual adaptation. But so impatient was he to rid himself in the shortest possible time of those ocular hindrances to him being viewed – especially by the girls – in a more advantageous physical light, and to have that confidence boost this would certainly bring that he'd made a determined effort to wear them all day right from the start. While the immediate result was a pair of red-looking eyes he'd been rather flattered to have rapid confirmation of their hoped-for effects when, during the weekend prior to him receiving his beloved's letter of matrimonial acceptance, Mrs Nielson had announced in her approximate English, 'Vicky, now you lucky to 'ave got a boy nice and good-looking!' Had she advised her daughter to net this eligible fish right away just in case it might be tempted to swim away?

Whatever the explanation, the following Saturday afternoon they went to choose an engagement ring and she bought one for him. As he slipped hers onto her finger she'd announced, 'Well now, I'm all yours!' That evening they became lovers. It was as if this publicly-recognizable betrothal had removed that last impediment to them enjoying true marital relations. The thought vaguely crossed his mind there might also be some correlation between her decision to make their union official and her desire to make love. It was his first time, and there had been some hesitancy; but she'd been understanding and helped him find his way. He'd finally made it. This was as much to her relief as his. For her the physical side of marriage was very important, she confessed, as they lay talking together afterwards.

Their appetite grew with the eating. They began to make love everywhere, any time and almost all the time. He would meet her at the station on Saturday mornings and they would take the bus straight back to his bedsit. Immediately after lunch they would eagerly strip before making straight for the double bed which occupied most of his room. There they would lie until early evening. He had exciting memories of that deliciously cool, naked body which would quickly turn hot with desire. It was the same on Sundays. Their love-making was all that seemed to matter. She was always willing, and he was eager to give her satisfaction. Sometimes they would jump out of bed and come together lustfully on the floor. However, during those alternate weekends he spent in Melchester Vicky's parents' almost permanent presence along with the cramped nature of their abode was not without posing limitations on their ardours. For one thing the bungalow had only one bedroom. This was occupied by her parents while Vicky herself slept in a narrow bed which spent its daytime hours discreetly folded away into the dining room wall. Michael spent the night on a sofa bed in the sitting room. On Saturday mornings, however, Mr and Mrs Neilson were in the habit of doing the week's errands; and during their absence our two lovers would slip into their bedroom and come together on the still unmade parental bed. The risk of them coming back earlier than expected made it even more exciting. But most of these intimate moments took place beyond the family roof. Only a short time after their engagement Vicky had acquired a small, second hand car, and on Saturday evenings after a rapidly-despatched drink in a pub, she was often the first to suggest they drive off to the local lovers' lane where they would devote the rest of the evening to eager preliminaries on the front seats before making contortionist love at the back. It was with some amusement they noted how the heat generated provided enough contrast with the outside temperature to cause the inside of the car windows to run in rivulets of condensation. While they were recovering from their gymnastic couplings he was not always able to resist the sobering thought that the inebriating effects of this wine-filled loving cup they were so lustily sharing was preventing them from savouring the delicate fragrance of its *bouquet*.

One evening she'd suddenly said, 'I want to be loved by someone I'm in awe of.' This caused him some discomfort: not only did her declaration strike him as being the result of a certain romanticized idealization of the male, but the thought crossed his mind that the comparison she was making was to his detriment. It also occurred to him that what she seemed to be seeking was a sort of incestuous father relationship, but found rather distasteful the terms in which this was conceived. Or perhaps in her book-nourished mind she was thinking of a mature John Knightly type of guide who would cast his wise, benevolent gaze over the blind error of her ways but still adore her for what she was. After all she was a graduate in English literature and had certainly read Jane Austen's *Emma*. But what contributed most to his unease was not so much his impression that this type of masterly male figure existed only in the Romanesque recesses of her mind than the awareness that she was coming to suspect he himself was still groping his way along too many dimly-lit, circumvolutory paths.

Little by little, he became the object of more direct reproval. When he stayed at her parents' he was in the habit of spending a good part of the morning in close perusal of the Sunday newspaper. She'd pointed out that some of this time could be spent washing her father's car or digging over the garden. But the problems really started when he went on holiday to Belgium with her and her parents. They spent the week with her mother's brother and family who lived in a modest flat in Zeebrugge. She found he ate too much, or didn't play as leading a part in conversations as she would have liked. At the end of the holidays she'd had to tell him to give her uncle some money to pay for his board. But what counted the most against him was that he'd lost the ring she'd given him. It must have slipped off his finger while they were bathing. She'd taken it as an ill omen; and when they got back home she'd told him that, 'She didn't know why, but she no longer wanted to make love.' Though these signals were not without causing him some alarm, he clung to what he would have liked to think: that this was all a normal part of a couple adjusting to each other, and that everything would come right in the end.

That drop which causes the nectar-filled cup to overflow is not necessarily composed of the same liquid as that which the cup holds. A similar effect can be observed when that small globule consists of nothing more remarkable than water. It was an occurrence of the utmost banality which hastened on the end. They'd bought tickets for a concert. It was being held on a Saturday evening in Melchester Cathedral and she'd told him to have his suit dry-cleaned for the occasion. He'd only remembered on the Friday evening; but it was too late. He'd hastily borrowed his landlady's iron and board, dampened a cloth, smoothed out the jacket, and imparted a sharp crease to the trousers (during his student years spent far from home he had mastered most of the intricacies of ironing). When Vicky asked him whether he'd had his suit cleaned he'd replied with a casual, almost jocular, 'Yes, of course!'

It must not be imagined by this that Michael was an inveterate liar. Up to then he'd been inclined to consider untruths as falling into two distinct categories: there were those he dismissed as innocuous enough to affect nobody in any detrimental sort of way – like inventing an excuse when his parents invited him to go with them to their friends'. Moreover, his work at the brewery had brought him to accept the fact that in business falsehoods or half-truths were inevitable and, therefore excusable in their necessity; and then there were those fabrications he considered to be of a more reprehensible nature. If, for example, he'd been involved in a car accident which was entirely due to his own carelessness or negligence he'd have no hesitation in admitting this. But he'd made the mistake of placing his untruth in the first category, and experience had not yet taught him that it was the flimsiest of barriers that separated the two. She'd inspected his jacket and trousers in detail and, on detecting some traces of dirt, had curtly announced that she didn't believe him. She'd then asked him again. He could still have told the truth by replying, 'No, I must admit I forgot, but I did iron all the creases out and press the trousers!' It was perhaps the hurt to his pride that such an admission would have involved which caused him to repeat the same denial. The more vigorous his denials the more conscious he was that they failed to ring true. She knew he was not telling the truth and she told him so in a voice which was now assuming a chillingly serious tone. What he had considered to be a minor omission was now being made to assume the proportions of a heinous crime. Suddenly, almost before he knew it, he'd reached a point from where there was no escape. He'd become the prisoner of his lie. As he left to go back home that Sunday evening there was a stinging coldness in her attitude and she declined his offer to kiss goodbye. When he asked her if she'd be coming the following weekend she'd replied with an evasive, 'I must see! I need time to think!' He couldn't help being seized by the thought that the wine of love which had been coursing through their veins was now turning irremediably sour.

The following Saturday morning he received a small package containing her ring along with a short letter informing him that she considered their engagement to be at an end. Though the finality of her decision had disturbed him he couldn't say it had really come as a bolt from the blue. And the initial shock it had prompted soon gave way to a feeling of relief: how would it have been possible to live happily with someone who could be influenced to this point by such a triviality? Wasn't she simply taking advantage of the slightest pretext to end it all? Wasn't he better off without her? He was not without suspecting, moreover, that, once again, her mother had had a hand in it all. What's more, with someone who was just as quick to fall out of love as she was to fall in it, he suspected that her decision had been hastened by her meeting someone else. After taking up all these reasons, and turning them round in his head, he'd presented himself with the comforting conclusion that the fault was more on her side than his and that, all in all, it was a blessing in disguise. He'd written a brief reply to the effect that events had proved they were not meant for each other, and had ended by politely wishing her every happiness for the future. It was the standard epitaph to their now deceased love.

That afternoon he went back to the shop where he'd bought the ring. They couldn't refund its cost but would be only too happy to exchange it for an article of equal value. He chose a lady's gold watch which he presented to his mother on his next visit home. He didn't know whether her delight was prompted by this unexpected gift or the fact that his engagement had been broken. Perhaps it was a little of both.

But that sense of desperate, unbearable loss he'd felt at the first break-up with Vicky existed no more. He'd tidied her away forever. What mattered was that he was now free to plan his future way. A year later he learned through a mutual friend that she'd married. He felt not the slightest regret.

FOURTEEN

'Yep, you're another beauty!' Adrian exclaimed as he examined the dark red armadillo printed on the white T-shirt he was holding at the end of outstretched arms. His words were preceded by the kind of boyish wolf whistle he might have bestowed a few years earlier on a shapely young factory lass strolling down their street. He handed the T-shirt to Michael who, after likewise holding it at arms' length, gingerly stepped out of the kitchen into the tiny back garden where he pegged it onto a clothes line by the side of the dozen or so others flapping in the breeze. Before starting two hours ago they'd pushed the kitchen table right up to the sink, and when Michael walked back in Adrian had already washed the residual ink from the wood-framed silk screen and squeegee spreader.

'I dunno about you, Mike, but I'm beginning to have hallucinations. I keep seeing a shiny red Dino Ferrari sitting out there in front of the house! An' I swear I haven't been smoking any pot!'

'An' just think of all those birds we're gonna pull!' Michael added with a laugh. It was said for his friend's sake. He himself liked to think he could never be tempted by the type of girl whose attraction for a man was clearly prompted by the outward show of wealth or position he presented rather than the person who resided within.

Plucking another T-shirt from the pile on the table Adrian inserted a sheet of cardboard inside and smoothed it out over the table oil cloth. The cardboard was to stop the ink from seeping through the front and staining the back during printing. Then, while Michael pressed the edges of the wood frame tightly down against the T-shirt, his friend poured an even blanket of red ink across the end of the screen nearest to him and, with a smooth, gentle away stroke of the squeegee blade, spread it over the stencil before pulling it firmly back towards him and forcing the ink through the porous silk fabric leaving the armadillo design imprinted on the shirt beneath.

It was Adrian's first year at Barfield; Michael and he were only just getting to know each other. Adrian had qualified as an arts and crafts teacher in June and, as is quite natural with two young single men of a not too dissimilar age, their interests and preoccupations contained enough common denominators for them to have decided to extend their relations beyond the confines of Barfield School. One evening while they were having a drink together, Adrian had talked with enthusiasm about a business venture he'd been contemplating. As part of his studies he'd opted for a course in silkscreen printing; it had given him the idea of using the technique to print motifs and inscriptions on T-shirt supports. This, it must be remembered, was at the beginning of the seventies when T-shirt art in Britain was still in its infancy. After seeing a sample of what he'd produced, Michael could only agree that printed T-shirts had a promising future.

So, when Adrian invited Michael to join him in the project he'd accepted without hesitation. It appealed to the *entrepreneur* in him. Wouldn't it be a novel way of passing his leisure moments while waiting for the French exchange to come about? And wouldn't it make a refreshing change from teaching? If the truth were to be known, however, it faintly crossed his mind that if the French exchange ever came to nothing he might be tempted to abandon teaching and engage himself full-time in their project. This wasn't to say he didn't like teaching in itself: he drew considerable satisfaction from the chance it gave him to contribute to the development of young minds. But though it also gave him job security along with generous holidays and a reasonable level of pay, enough of the adventurer lay within for him to feel dispirited at the prospect of finding himself irremediably entrenched in this same narrow, humdrum school environment where his life would be more or less mapped out ahead. Somewhere he wanted to take advantage of those opportunities which might enable him to impart a more personalized stamp to his existence outside the conventional mould.

From then on their conversations were focused on the project. Adrian had come across the design on the record sleeve of a pop group of that time – a stylized armadillo, called Xarkus, moving on World War One tank tracks and endowed with a side canon. As the artwork was subject to copyright law Adrian had written to the record company asking for permission to use the name and design. Even though he was still waiting for a reply he'd taken the liberty of producing a dozen or so samples. He'd also explained the basic silkscreen printing process to Michael: a screen is made from a piece of porous silk stretched out and fixed over a wooden frame; a stencil of the *motif* is then created by using a photo-reactive technique to copy the design onto the silk as a negative image of the pattern or inscription to be printed; a chemical emulsion is applied to block off those parts of the silkscreen design not to be printed on the T-shirt substrate – thereby leaving only the corresponding pores through which a special ink can be forced by a stroke from the squeegee blade. The actual procedure wasn't all that complicated; it simply needed a bit of practice. Since he didn't have the necessary equipment the present Xarkus stencil had been produced by a pal using the facilities of the local art college where he was a day student.

The more they talked about the project the more seriously Michael began to view it. The two years he'd spent working for the brewery had gone a considerable way towards ridding him of his head-in-the-clouds student impracticality to reveal beneath a temperament of a more down-to-earth inclination; and he'd begun sketching out a mental synthesis of the problems they would have to face if ever they decided to commit themselves fully. For a start, it was obvious they wouldn't get far working in Adrian's mother's tiny kitchen in this present hit or miss, pre-artisanal sort of way. It was a long and painstaking process with too much waste. Though Adrian had now had enough practice to know the amount of pressure he needed to exert on the squeegee to produce a clean imprint, he'd sacrificed half a dozen T-shirts or more in the process; and an acceptable *motif* was still not guaranteed every time. What's more, even after the print had dried they weren't at the end of their pains: in order to prevent the design from fading dramatically when the T-shirt was being washed, they had to set his mother's rickety iron at the highest heat that wouldn't scorch the cotton fabric; and then, after putting a cloth between it and the T-shirt print, they had to iron on each side for at least three minutes. And to cap it all, Adrian's mother was beginning to complain. Apparently, she'd asked her son several times when she'd be getting her kitchen back. So, if they wanted to turn the idea into something resembling a feasible project a first step would be to find suitable printing premises to rent. But, above all, if ever they decided to develop their plans at an industrial level they'd have no alternative but to invest in a mass-production, multi-colour screen printing machine. The screen-printing technique had been developed in the U.S.A. as far back as the thirties, so he was pretty sure automatic machines of this kind now existed. But what would be the price? Since the investment would be far beyond their present means they'd have to ask for a bank loan. Would a banker consider the success of their venture credible enough to grant them one? Even if he did, what sort of security would be required? In addition, as far as the present moment was concerned, wouldn't they be foolish to lose sight of the fact that they were using somebody else's design for commercial purposes without the owner's written consent? While they could probably get away with it at this embryonic stage where sales wouldn't exceed more than a few score, any decision to use the design on a larger scale would expose them to the risk of legal action for breach of copyright. Then, even if permission was forthcoming, they'd certainly be required to pay royalties on sales; so, they'd quickly have to provide themselves with the resources necessary to creating their own designs and producing their own silkscreen stencils.

Another problem they'd have to face was where to obtain wholesale quantities of blank T-shirts at the lowest possible price. Adrian had bought the original three dozen at a local open air market, but it was obvious they couldn't continue in this way. Apparently, they were imported in bales of several thousand, mainly from India. And if they wanted to pursue their undertaking seriously they'd first have to register as an official company. Michael was also realistic enough to see that if they decided to go ahead together in any significant way he would have to enter into some kind of official co-operation with Adrian. This meant they'd need to be able to trust and rely on each other as responsible and firmly committed partners. Though at the moment they got on well as pals, the prospect of a more serious business relationship had prompted him to begin viewing his friend from a more objective angle. What he saw was not without imparting a vaguely-felt unease.

I'm inclined to think it is a fact of human nature that, while some people are less indulgent with themselves than they are with others, most of us are more demanding with others than we are with ourselves. Adrian, on the other hand, seemed to belong to that category of easy-going young men whose pursuit of life's more immediate gratifications makes them as equally indulgent towards themselves as they are with others: so much so that Michael couldn't help wondering whether his pal was really conscious that the favourable time and place they now seemed to be enjoying could only be transformed into success by strong commitment and hard work, and that this required the stubborn application of a certain steadfastness of purpose in both themselves and others. While he was aware that he might be doing Adrian an injustice he couldn't quite dismiss the thought that their venture drew much of its attraction from his pal's hope that it would provide him with the means to extend the diversity, intensity and duration of his enjoyment of life's pleasures in the shortest possible time and with the least possible effort. He could only conclude that, in his present configuration at least, this potential business partner could perhaps not be counted on to be the most effective manager of men, machines or money.

It must, nevertheless, not be thought that Michael was one of those people so conscious of the dangers of devoting one's time to an excess of amusement that he actively seeks to discourage all but its most limited form of expression in others. On the contrary, he was well aware of both the necessity and the benefits of partaking in the more pleasurable aspects of life. But it was an indulgence which had to remain moderate. For though he wasn't much into philosophy there was much of the philosopher in him; and he tended towards the balanced view that the pleasurable and the serious should, in an ideal world (if here we can talk of ideals), be considered as constituting two opposite, yet equal parts of a single, indivisible whole, and that any attempt to cleave the two apart and pursue just one as a goal in itself can only lead to disaster. In short, he preferred not to let the extent and frequency of enjoyment to encroach upon those bounds which he considered reasonable. As a result, he was tempted to believe that when it came to their respective attitudes towards the taking of pleasure the difference between his pal and himself could be resumed by the comparative thought that Adrian, on waking up with a head-ache after a night on the tiles, would in all probability declare, 'What a great night out that was!' whereas he himself would say, 'What an idiot I was for drinking so much!'

Our young man was, nevertheless, honest enough to admit that when it came to social pleasures he felt a tinge of envy with regard to his pal: for not only was Adrian quick-witted by nature but he could captivate an audience by what seemed to be an inexhaustible repertoire of amusing stories and jokes. He also had an eye for the girls; and they were attracted by his repartee, his engaging looks and, above all, his frizzy Afro-style hair. He'd grown it during his first year at college, and since then he'd never looked back. They'd been to one or two parties together where Michael had quickly become aware that his pal's white-negro looks and jocular sociability made him a far greater source of attraction than he was. He was vaguely contemptuous that young women could prefer these frivolities to a quieter, more seriously-minded person like himself.

One consequence of these reflections was to prompt in Michael the thought that it might be a good idea to ask Roland for advice. Or even, if things showed real promise, whether he'd be interested in joining them. Roland was a maths teacher and fifteen years or so older than himself. The wool company he'd worked for as financial manager had gone bust, and the redundancy which followed had made him seek the security of teaching. Roland's previous experience would be useful to them; and Michael had been struck by his solid common sense. Yes, he'd put it to Adrian that perhaps they needed some guidance from a more experienced hand. He was pretty sure he'd agree. But as far as the immediate future of their venture was concerned the next step was to seek proof that a demand really existed for their T-shirts. They decided to spend the following Saturday morning hawking the products of their printing session in Bridgeford's covered market.

FIFTEEN

That opportunity enabling Michael Morgan and Sylvia Schofield to get to know each other, or at least begin to get to know each other soon presented itself. At this embryonic stage in their relationship I would point out that my use of the words 'presented itself' is in no way caused by a wish to infer that the origins of this occasion were entirely circumstantial, and not at all the result of any initiative on the part of either of our two protagonists. My words are simply intended as a verbal reflection of a certain authorial neutrality, prompted by a desire not to over-influence you in deciding whether, in confirmation of Ian's premonitory declaration, what I am about to relate was the first phase of a pre-meditated female action plan designed to assess both Michael's readiness and suitability for matrimonial union.

At Barfield School, as in most English state-funded secondary schools of the time, school assembly marked a statutory beginning to the day. Each morning before the start of lessons pupils and staff met in the main hall in an act of communal worship of a basically Christian nature, conducted by the headmaster, and consisting of a prayer and a hymn. There then followed various announcements – sporting or otherwise – concerning the life of the school. In an attempt to inject a little more diversity and, hopefully, interest into a gathering which, in his estimation, was showing signs of lapsing into a tedious routine, Headmaster Fowler had recently come up with the idea of inviting his staff to extend their participation beyond that of mere sedentary (and often sleepy) presence on a platform by giving a short talk on a subject of their choice, considered to be educational or generally enlightening. Though not obligatory, he had let it be known that those who consented would be helping him out, and that he would leave it to them to decide whether, in consequence, this would allow him to view any future hopes of promotion in a more positive light. Many teachers had protested, one or two had refused, but most had accepted. Michael and Sylvia were among the latter.

During the morning coffee break two days later Sylvia Schofield came up to him. By some process whose logic, if logic there were, belonged solely to her, the deputy headmistress (a Miss Dobson by name), who had been entrusted with scheduling the talks, had decided that Miss Schofield would have the privilege of being among the first to address the school. The topic Sylvia had decided upon was the abolition of slavery. On doing some preliminary research she'd come across a Frenchman called Toussaint Louverture, himself born into bondage, who had risen to be an important figure in the history of emancipation in the Americas by leading slaves to victory over their French and British colonial oppressors. But he'd been taken prisoner, shipped to France, and held in solitary confinement in freezing conditions in a fort in the eastern part where he died of pneumonia less than a year later. Had Michael heard of him? Did he know exactly where the fort was? Could he supply her with more information, or even recommend a book in English on the person? There was nothing in the school library. She'd be most grateful for any help he could give her.

I will not allow it to be thought that Michael's understanding of the workings of the female mind, though far from being comprehensive, did not cause him to suspect that Sylvia's desire to involve him in her talk had something of a pretext about it, and that her real motives sprang more from a wish to develop their relations enough for her to be able to examine him in closer detail. After all, why should she be so interested in an obscure foreigner like Toussaint Louverture when such a famous English abolitionist as Wilberforce existed? What's more, there was a well-endowed library in the town centre where he was sure she could find all these details for herself. I can only surmise that our young man was no exception to that common form of human fallibility which consists in ignoring reality – in part at least – merely because a particular web of circumstance makes it seemingly advantageous for us to do so. For his male ego was not without being flattered by this feminine appeal for assistance and by the interest in the man he was tempted to consider it implied. The result was that he was more than happy to play along. During the days which had elapsed since their brief conversation in his car he'd been eying her discreetly and he now took notice when she walked into the staffroom. It was as if some strange magnetic force was pulling him in her direction. Or was it simply because she'd been paying more attention to her make-up, hair and clothes? Whatever the explanation, she was far more appealing than he'd previously been inclined to think. And now he barely noticed what Ian had so unfairly described as a limp.

Michael's studies had, in fact, included a brief outline of French history; but, though he was vaguely aware of the personage of Toussaint Louverture, he didn't remember enough about the man and his claims to historical recognition to supply Sylvia with all the information he would have liked. For, by way of impressing it upon her that he had taken her request to heart, he had resolved to provide her with considerably more than he knew she would need. As a result, by a curious inversion of what might be considered the normal order of things, it was he who spent the following Saturday morning in the reference section of Bridgeford Central Library researching the topic and writing a *résumé* of his findings. The following Monday morning he presented her with the results. She couldn't thank him enough. Since it was she who had made this first step he was now determined that any further attempts to produce a closer acquaintanceship would be initiated by him. I will again leave it to you to decide whether it was circumstances alone which caused this not quite to be the case.

One damp morning of that same week when day was making only the feeblest of efforts to extract itself from the previous night, Michael turned into the school car park. The drizzle he'd noted on leaving home had now turned into a steady rain. She must have arrived just a minute or two before him as her car was already there. Its door was open and he caught sight of her two long legs swinging themselves out. Pulling into a space opposite and half turning his head he reached behind him for his briefcase. He'd expected her to hurry on towards the school entrance, but as he glanced through the rear window he saw she was standing there beneath her open umbrella.

'Hello. After all the help you've been, the least I can do is offer you a half share in my umbrella. It's a bit on the small side and I hope you don't mind pink,' she said with a laugh.

It might have been the scarcely growing daylight which made it seem too dark to be pink; and it occurred to him that her verbal lightening was simply a way of presenting the invitation in the least serious manner. But he'd gone along with her, and had even tried to produce a similar jocular reply in return. All he could manage was a, 'Not at all, I just love being in the pink!' He was sure Adrian would have done far better.

As they strode towards the teachers' entrance his shoulder gently nudged against hers, and he caught a smell of her light perfume as it hung in the damp air. This unexpected intimacy both troubled and embarrassed him. He found himself vaguely wondering whether he'd ever be on close enough terms to be able to slip his arm round her waist. She seemed unperturbed by his presence.

'By the way, are you doing anything on Saturday evening?' she asked. He was caught unawares and paused for a moment to reflect.

'No, I don't think so.' He couldn't for the life of him guess what was coming next.

'I was just wondering if we could have a chat about my talk and all that information you gave me on Toussaint Louverture. I've been looking it over and there are one or two questions I'd like to ask you. I'm giving my talk next Monday morning of all days. So I'll be working on it this weekend. Just the thought of it makes me quiver! I've never spoken in public before. I'd like you to tell me what you think. And I might even be able to find a drop of French wine.'

'Well that's an offer I just can't refuse.'

'You know where we live. The Majestic Dance Hall in Bankfield. It's closed down now but we still live in the flat above. The entrance is round the back. There's plenty of space for you to park there. Will half seven be OK?'

'That's fine. See you on Saturday evening then. And try not to work too hard!'

As they strolled into the staff room she left him with what he took to be intended as a lingering smile.

Sixteen

Despite Michael's doubts as to Adrian's ability to maintain that tenacity of purpose and effort necessary to the achievement of any worthwhile goal, it was with a feeling bordering on exhilaration that the following Saturday morning he took the road to his friend's parents' house situated in a modest council estate on the other side of town. His excitement was caused by an awareness that he was about to embark on a totally new adventure, and that the events of the next few hours would probably be decisive in providing him with a measure of the likelihood of its success. But what is more normal that a young man of his age should be too absorbed by the present novelty of it all to give much thought to where this future success could lead? However, one thing he was now receiving daily confirmation of was that, whatever his future might have in store, it didn't lie within the classrooms of Barfield School. For he'd recently been observing the more senior members of the staff: their eyes were dull, their steps were leaden and they never spoke with hope or joy. Wasn't this a preview of what he himself would eventually become?

As he came nearer to Adrian's parents' house his elation was tempered by the sobering thought that it was he who would be mainly responsible for ensuring the success of the morning's events. They'd previously agreed that in view of his previous commercial experience he would play the salesman's part while Adrian's would be limited to answering any queries of a technical nature. The screen-printing process was a relatively unheard-of technique in England at that time and potential customers might require some explanations or even reassurance as to its viability. It was true that his previous job had given him a certain self-assurance and glibness of speech. What added to his unease, however, was that when he'd walked into a tied pub or off-licence it had been as a superior in a hierarchical system. As a result – though he'd always hesitated to do so – he could always use his position to impose his wishes on those he'd been appointed to supervise. But here they were in a free market situation of supply and demand where the only way to achieve a sales objective lay in his ability to convince others of the desirability of the product he was selling; and since they'd be cold calling, he couldn't quite exclude the fact that they might be received at best with indifference, at worst with hostility.

He had, therefore, mentally rehearsed his act by preparing a number of arguments in advance: an original fashion product with an exceptional sales potential, a high-profit margin and a significant discount if six were taken. Furthermore, as a final resort, he'd even be prepared to offer the T-shirts on a sale or return basis. So, what did the customer have to lose? But the biggest argument he'd be relying on would be a pleasant, patient manner and a friendly smile. His experience at the brewery had also taught him that in the world of business appearances play an important part. As a result, the evening before he'd resurrected that same suit which had set the seal on his rupture with Vicky. The jacket was crumpled, the trousers were in need of a crease, and both exuded a strong smell of mothballs; and he'd spent a good half hour at his mum's ironing board bringing it back to something like its pristine state before leaving it out overnight to air. As he was setting off the following morning she'd assured him that he really looked the part. He'd allowed himself to be moderately convinced. He'd also found himself hoping that Adrian wouldn't be wearing that 'ice-cream man's' jacket he was in the habit of sporting at those parties they'd attended together. It wasn't at all in keeping with the situation. Michael didn't really know why they'd agreed to give his sports jacket this name as neither of them had ever seen an itinerant ice-cream vendor attired in this way. Perhaps it was because its bright, motley jumble of red, blue, green and yellow brought back pleasant memories of those warm, bright summer afternoons during which he plied his wares.

He'd barely finished rapping on the back door when Adrian's smiling face appeared. It was with some dismay that he noted he was wearing the jacket in question – though the yellow shirt which usually accompanied it on social occasions had been replaced by one of a more sober green. And he wasn't wearing jeans. It was more as a joke than from any wish to bring to his pal's direct attention the inappropriateness of his dress that he said, 'God, if Fowler could see you now, he'd have a fit!'

'I'd prefer a fatal heart attack of the more painful kind.' Adrian replied. 'You know, Mike, if ever we make a go of this and I hand in my resignation, I'll put this jacket on with an open-necked pink shirt and a pair of dirty jeans with holes in the knees, knock on his study door and then just stand there praying it'll have that effect! And I hope I'll be able to tell him to get stuffed before he kicks the bucket!'

'You look as if you're going on holiday,' Michael said in gentle allusion to his pal's attire; but, above all, because his pal was clutching a small, cheap-looking suitcase. He presumed he'd borrowed it from his parents.

'Yeah, I'm off to that olde worlde market town of Bridgeford. And we might just be able to flog a few T-shirts while we're there!'

By 'olde worlde' Michael presumed his pal was referring to the town's majestic, Late Victorian covered market whose spacious interior accommodated a hundred or so stalls offering enough diversity of food and wares to provide most of those things necessary to the comfort of its citizens' daily lives. Alas, what should have remained an inviolable part of the city's architectural and historical heritage was, only a few years later, the victim of the stubborn dementia of its worthies who, despite general and frequently outraged opposition, decided that this stately monument (among others of a similar style and age) to a proud past should be pitilessly demolished and replaced by a characterless, American-style shopping mall. Not only did the wrecker's ball tear out the heart of the city but it destroyed its soul. Michael had been there many times before: in his childhood on shopping trips dangling at the end of his mother's arm; and in youth as an alternative to insipid school dinners when he and his pals would taste the delights of the pies and peas or fish and chips provided by numerous stalls.

The moment they walked in what they would never have noticed before immediately met their eye: a stall selling teenage casual wear — jeans, sports shoes, pullovers, cardigans, and shirts. The dozen or so T-shirts dangling on a line strung above the counter seemed to indicate that a vague specialization was being made of what they had come to sell. Michael was slightly dismayed on noting that, while they bore no artwork, they came in several different colours. Even though the Xarkus *motifs* offered a choice between red, white or blue theirs all had the same white background.

'What do you reckon?' Michael whispered.

'Well,' his friend replied, lowering the suitcase gently to the ground and pausing for an instant, 'As the bishop said to the actress, I think we'd better get stuck in right away.' His face creased into a broad grin. Michael could only respond with a nervous half laugh.

A small, plumpish man with his back to them was busy transferring some cellophane-wrapped shirts from a box on the floor to one of the shelves at the rear of the stall. As they approached, Adrian bent down to open the suitcase, extracted three crumpled T-shirts, positioned himself discreetly behind Michael, and holding them in front of him began shaking the creases out. The introductory patter which Michael had rehearsed went something like, 'Hello there. We're just launching our new range of U.S. style, screen-printed T-shirts. They're all the rage over there, and it won't be long coming here. So if you'd like to get in on the act before everybody climbs on the bandwagon here's your chance now. Just have a look at these. It'll only take a minute.'

It all felt a bit false and pretentious but he hadn't been able to find anything better. He'd come to the conclusion that much depended on his attitude and the way he said things more than what he had to say.

'Excuse me,' he pronounced in what was intended to be a clear, confident voice. 'Could I have a word, please?'

The man finished arranging the shirt he had in his hand before slowly turning round and focusing a pair of small, closely-set eyes on him. They betrayed a glint of suspicion. It flashed through Michael's mind that his approach might have sounded too official, and that he'd been taken for some kind of inspector – perhaps of the fiscal kind. Or was it simply because he hadn't spoken with enough of the local accent?

Though he'd spent the years since leaving school polishing up his speech and had congratulated himself on having smoothed out most of its more salient northern protuberances, he realized that the occasion now required him to polish it down. And perhaps he hadn't imparted enough modesty to his words. After all, he didn't want to sound like a patronizing southern snob.

'Sorry to bother you but can I just show you our new range of printed T-shirts? It won't ...'

He'd lowered his voice to as much of a murmur as the requirements of productive verbal communication would allow. The stallholder's look of suspicion relaxed into one of relief, and before Michael could finish he nodded his consent and strolled up to them. Plucking the three T-shirts from Adrian's outstretched hand Michael laid them out on the counter before him. The man picked them up one by one and examined them at arms' length. While he was doing so Michael gave him details of the sizes and prices. He'd expected some kind of resistance – perhaps some reservations regarding the artwork, or the lack of choice as to their underlying colour and, above all, an attempt to haggle the price. There was only silence. Then, without any further solicitation, he reached into his back trouser pocket, extracted a wad of folded one pound notes, peeled off three which he slapped down onto the counter before announcing, 'OK mate, I'll take one of each size in red and blue'. Michael couldn't believe it had been so easy.

Would I be stretching your credibility to tearing point when I say that their visit to similar stalls in Bridgeford's covered market produced much the same reactions with very much the same results? For in little more than an hour they'd sold the lot. And though Michael had anticipated some enquiries as to the origins of the Xarkus design he was relieved to find that no questions were asked. One stallholder did, however, request a receipt. It was an eventuality Michael had neglected, and he'd felt foolishly amateurish at having to ask him for a sheet of paper on which to write one out by hand.

It was in a state approaching euphoria that they'd deposited the empty suitcase into the boot of Michael's car before stepping into a nearby pub to celebrate their success and discuss their next move.

Adrian suggested they should try their luck at an even larger covered market located in the centre of the neighbouring town of Middlebourne. After all, there was no reason to think that what had worked in Bridgeford wouldn't produce the same, even better results there. He'd also had a look in the Yellow Pages where he'd found the name and address of some importers of both white and coloured cotton T-shirts. As he had thought they came in bales from India. He didn't know exactly how many a bale contained but thought it must run into thousands. Perhaps they could make enquiries about minimum quantities and prices. Meanwhile, they'd have to go on buying blank white T-shirts from the local markets and print them in the same manual way. This could be a problem, however, as his mum was making it increasingly felt that she was fed up with him 'messing up' her kitchen. He'd done his best to explain that what they were doing could have important repercussions on her son's professional future but she'd remained unconvinced. All in all, he didn't know how long the present arrangement could last.

As they were strolling back to the car Adrian suggested they made a detour via the showroom of an exclusive, sporting *marque* of Italian car. For at that time Bridgeford was the seat of a heavy woollen industry in all its exuberant affluence which, alas, was soon after to commence a vertiginous decline. They stopped in front of the showroom window, transfixed by the sight of the glossy, low-slung red models reposing within. And I'm not able categorically to deny that at this moment one of them at least couldn't prevent himself from dreaming of the day when the success of their venture would enable him to stride confidently in.

'Well,' quipped Adrian ruefully as they made their way back to the car, 'I suppose we're now 24 quid nearer to buying one!'

Just before dropping Adrian off back home Michael told him of Sylvia's invitation for that evening.

'See you at school on Monday, then. And don't do anything I wouldn't do tonight!' his pal said as he closed the car door.

'Well that doesn't give me much latitude, does it?' he'd replied with a collusive wink and the broadest of grins.

SEVENTEEN

It might easily be imagined that the result of that first amorous experience so full of twists and turns was to produce in Michael a feeling of disenchantment as to the real content of that package we persist in labelling 'true love', and that his disillusionment might even have caused deep feelings of rancour towards those more nubile members of the fair sex. I am happy to state this was not really the case. And though its main consequence was a stubborn determination not to include marital union in his foreseeable plans, it was not without producing a more positive result: for unlike many of his sex who, when contemplating marriage, limit themselves to the question, 'Will *she* make *me* happy?' this failed romance had made him self-critical enough to ponder on whether *he* would make *her* happy, too. He derived much consolation from the fact that the reply to both questions was a firm negative. Without bringing a resolute 'yes', the romance which followed (if it can be called such) might have encouraged him to consider the tentative possibility which the word 'maybe' implies.

Not many months after his break-up with Vicky he'd met another girl. On the eve of the first term of that teacher training course it had been his great pleasure to have been admitted to, the school of education had laid on an informal buffet supper with a view to presenting staff and students with those conditions enabling them to get to know one another a little before lectures and tutorials actually began. If the truth were to be known, however, he'd gone there more in the hope of making the acquaintance of a girl whose future companionable presence was what he'd persuaded himself he needed to make the year a total success. Having no precise notion of what such a person could be recognized by, he comforted himself with the thought that he would know her when he saw her.

Though his inner reasoning had not expressed itself in quite the same proverbial terms past experience had taught him that on student social occasions of this nature it was the early bird that caught the worm. With this in mind he'd arrived some ten minutes before the officially-indicated start, and had positioned himself strategically enough to be able to vet all arrivals with as much discretion as the barely occupied state of the room would permit. She'd walked in only a few minutes later, and had given a timid, exploratory look around before strolling past him and seating herself in a corner. Her weathered jeans and thick patchwork shirt over which a white fleecy waistcoat brought out the bushy, slightly frizzy blackness of her hair made her appearance original enough for him to be aware of his own more conventional presentation. It was certainly his reflection that the purpose of the evening was to bring participants together which decided him to take the bull by the horns (though once again his reasoning was not expressed in these same epigrammatic terms). He strode up to her and said, 'They've got some scrumptious-looking cream buns over there. Would you like me to get you one?' He was conscious of being briefly but thoroughly looked up and down before being gratified with a, 'That's very kind of you, but I think I'd prefer just a *nice* cup of tea.' It had been spoken in a voice decisive enough for him to be seized by the ego-boosting thought that, physically, he'd not been found wanting. Had she also been attracted by his reassuring air of confidence and bold resourcefulness of manner? He'd been intrigued by the way she detached the word 'nice'. It was as if she wished to impart a tone of irony to alleviate the triteness of the word. What's more, he'd been pleased, even flattered to note she spoke with an accent which, though without the slightest trace of affectation, said much about the social class she was issued from and the exclusivity of the school she'd certainly attended.

He brought their teas and sat down beside her. Her name was Susan and she'd just completed a degree course at a well-known college of fine art. Without wishing to imply it was love at first sight, in the space of a few minutes he'd felt the stirrings of that pull – the elements of which I won't attempt to analyze – drawing two people as invisibly together as north and south-facing magnetic poles. They quickly introduced themselves. Her name was Susan. But it was her surname which he found intriguing. It was that of a famous Jewish banking dynasty. Strangely, he thought, she gave it to him along with her first name. He had the impression this was more to lighten herself of a weight than to bring to his immediate notice the fact that she might be issued from a world-renowned family. He decided not to seek any further details: after all, he didn't want her to think his interest in her was prompted by the name rather than the person. What's more, wasn't it all irrelevant to student life? The more they talked the more he recognized the facial type. It worried him vaguely: it was not so much her Jewishness as the fact that he'd heard Jews always went with their own kind, and he feared it might act as a scotch to their relationship. His fears, however, seemed to be without foundation. During his two years at the brewery he'd saved up enough to purchase a small second-hand car, and after driving her back to her lodgings he'd said on parting, 'See you at our first lecture tomorrow.'

'Yes, of course,' she'd replied with a smile.

A bond had been established and they always sat together during lectures. It seemed the natural thing to do, and he felt a glow of pride in the knowledge that she was present by his side. But that check he had feared was soon brought to his notice. Though it didn't come from the quarter he'd anticipated it wasn't entirely unexpected. One evening, not long after their first encounter, she informed him she was committed to another man. He lived in her home town on the south coast and was some kind of scientologist. He'd certainly been an influence in her conviction that the movement was a precious aid to self fulfilment. It was one of the rare subjects on which they agreed to differ: for Michael tended to share the commonly-held view that it was a potentially dangerous sect, capable of exploiting those in a state of mental vulnerability. Like Michael her fiancé was not a Jew. It was a strange partnership, she declared – not without some humour – for a Jewess to be with a Gentile – especially when he was a scientologist!

Otherwise, she rarely mentioned her fiancé during their first term together. And he never really wanted to know. She did, nevertheless, inform him that he occasionally came to see her at weekends. Once, on the eve of one of these visits, she'd extended a mischievous invitation for Michael to come and meet him. He didn't really understand why. Was it yet one more example of female perversity? Or was she simply looking for some endorsement of her choice by using a face to face comparison – probably to his detriment – to remove any doubt? Whatever the reason, it had made him uneasy and he'd hastily declined. She was in private lodgings and on another occasion she confided that her boyfriend had stayed over in her room one Saturday night. After he'd gone back home the following evening she'd been upset by her landlady taking her to one side and sternly informing her that it mustn't happen again.

Curiously, during the first term, the relations she entertained towards a man with whom she was to all intents and purposes engaged didn't prevent their own friendship from developing at a more intimate level. This was facilitated by the nature of Michael's own accommodation: for the hall of residence where he lived was occupied by older post graduates preparing a master's degree, a doctorate or a teaching diploma like himself. As a result, unlike the hall where he'd resided as an undergraduate, students were allowed much greater freedom: it was both self-catering and, above all, no limits were imposed on the hours during which they could receive female guests. So, he frequently invited her to his study bedroom for a late-evening 'coffee'. He remembered that first time in particular. They'd gone to a party and had danced closely together. She'd filled him with desire and he had every reason to believe he'd had the same effect on her. After only a few minutes he suggested they drove back to his room. She'd accepted without hesitation. They'd thrown off their clothes, laid down on his bed and begun much the same preliminaries as those he and Vicky had indulged in together. His caresses and penetrations soon had her sobbing with pleasure. And she'd drawn her finger nails down from the top of his shoulders to the bottom of his back. The sting he'd felt was exquisite. He had the impression it wasn't the first time she'd enjoyed such play when suddenly she said, 'Ah you're so experienced. I never thought sex could be such a powerful thing!' He couldn't help feeling satisfaction at the thought that this time he was in command. It was as if he'd delivered her of some barely-known creature she was now contemplating with wondrous delight. The comparison occurred to him that, while Vicky had wallowed in the effects the beast had on her, part of Sue's interest lay in the nature of the beast itself. He felt much closer to her for this. One evening he'd gone so far as to try to make love; he was concentrating his efforts to this end when she began a distressed weeping. It all came out: she wanted to save herself for her fiancé; she'd supplied him with a detailed confession of what they were doing together and he'd told her it all had to stop. Michael even suspected he'd presented her with an ultimatum. She was adamant that her boyfriend was right in maintaining that her transgressions were unacceptable – even more so since she'd been the one who'd insisted on them keeping themselves for each other. And stop it did. For though they continued seeing each other almost as frequently as before, now she wouldn't even allow him to hold her hand. She seemed to feel lonely in her lodgings, however, and at weekends would often telephone to suggest they go for a walk or to the cinema, or to ask if she could come to his room for a chat. He'd found the situation frustrating and once, in an attempt to break her resolve, he had told her he loved her. It was not without truth. He'd even felt the temptation to exert some kind of pressure by leaving her to marinate in her own solitary juice. Perhaps it was out of respect for her fortitude and a desire not to hurt that he could never bring himself to do it. He would always have fond memories of this refreshing, intelligent, artistically-inclined, and finally strong-minded girl who introduced him to the plaintive songs of Leonard Cohen and the high-decibel rock of Ginger Baker, Eric Clapton and The Cream, and who sometimes took it upon herself to mockingly correct the mispronunciations of his northern accent. If he'd been absolutely honest with himself he would have had to admit that, given more propitious conditions, she was the kind of girl whose company he could have been tempted to embark upon a longer journey in; but somewhere they had always understood that the terms of the contract they had tacitly made excluded any extension beyond that brief student year. He did, nonetheless, receive a short letter from her just after the end of the final term. He'd arrived back home only a few days before and was wistfully trying to reconcile himself to the fact that he now had no choice but to bend to the implacable realities of working life. It gave him pleasure to learn that she'd been offered a post as art mistress in a rather exclusive girls' school on the English south coast. But what delighted him the most was when she'd declared there were 'some people you should be able to hang up in your wardrobe (with mothballs) just in case you needed to take them out later'. It was typically Sue. He'd taken it as a vast personal compliment but had seen no point in replying: for somewhere he knew the wardrobe would remain forever closed. Now, more than a year later, he couldn't help wondering what she had become. His memory of her was like a vaguely-remembered dream, a haunting echo of which he sometimes heard ringing in his ears in a line from one of Cohen's songs:

I'm just a station on your line I know I'm not your lover

EIGHTEEN

Though the seeds of suspicion had been planted in Michael's mind and he had to struggle against the thought that the next few hours might see them grow into certitude, he found himself reacting favourably to the idea that he would not be against this impending encounter giving his relations with Sylvia just enough of a nudge in a more amicable direction to provide him with regular female company over the next few months, without in any way compromising his hopes of spending the following year in France. However, he wasn't without remembering that he'd viewed the beginnings of his relationship with Sue in very much the same restrictive light. But with Sylvia wasn't there too much incompatibility for there to be any great danger of him becoming romantically involved? It was true that her apparent desire to produce a competent talk suggested a conscientious mind; and the down-to-earth jocularity with which she enlivened her speech indicated a sensible, feet-on-the-ground type of girl with a cheerful, sociable attitude to life. But hadn't she been formed in too standard a mould? Didn't she lack that touch of the artist, that original way of looking at things which had made him feel so much in tune with Sue? Though he couldn't deny there was a physical attraction, wasn't it one which any normally-constituted young man would feel for an agreeable-looking girl? As he drove along the thought came repeatedly back to mind that it was this same levelheadedness which might have decided the time had now come for her to give some serious thought to settling down in life, and that this seemingly innocent invitation smacked very much of a scheme enabling her to examine his marital eligibility in the comfort of her home. The idea that he might be being manipulated irritated his male pride, and he resolved to be particularly attentive to the slightest indication that this was the case.

The former dance hall was a wide, solid-looking, two storey, stone and brick building which had originally been purpose-built as a picture theatre a year or two before the onset of the First World War. It had been purchased by Sylvia's father in the late 1930's, and converted into a ballroom lavish enough to have endowed it with the reputation of being among the most splendid in the North. Now, what had been for decades a garishly illuminated scene of almost nightly animation reposed in a sullen darkness which the glow of the nearby streetlamps had only the feeblest of effects upon; and the large-lettered sign *A. Jackson & Co. (Household Furnishings)* prominently displayed above what had once been the grand entrance for many a youthful dream provided the sobering indication that it now led into the prosaic mundaneness of a furniture and carpet showroom.

As Sylvia had suggested he parked his car round at the rear. A damp evening mist was imparting a nimbus-like circle to the light of the carriage lamp above the doorway. It had certainly been turned on in view of his impending arrival. As he rang the doorbell he noted the names *Mr and Mrs Herbert Schofield and Sylvia* displayed on a small bronze plaque above. Almost immediately a light came on and through the door's frosted glass panels he could make out a blurred presence stepping down the stairs behind.

'Hello, come on in,' she said. The smile on her face was more re-laxed and confident than the slightly forced one he'd noticed she frequently bestowed upon colleagues at school. Her grey blue eyes seemed to have more emphasis and depth, and the straight blondish hair which at school fell freely over her shoulders had been combed tightly back and gathered into a pony tail. It lent a sleek, slightly hollow-cheeked appearance to her face. Her sleeveless, V-necked black dress fitted close enough to give just a hint of the contours beneath while having the decency to stop just an inch or two above the knees. A discreet gold pendant hung round her neck. He had to admire the sober elegance of it all. It crossed his mind that a woman dressed for a man and that her dress was often a reflection of the image she had of that man. As he followed her up the stairs he couldn't avoid taking a discreet look at her legs. He could almost hear Ian declaring with a mischievous smile, 'Yep, they could be worse. I'll give 'em six out of ten!' When they reached the top of the staircase she led him through the open door of a room on the right.

'This is my *boudoir*,' she announced with a laugh. 'Don't come down too hard on my accent. At school I was worse than hopeless at French.'

'You know, I'm sure the French would find it charming. It'd have the same effect on a Frenchman as Sacha Distel's accent has on his English lady fans!' he replied.

'Really? Then I'm delighted to know I'd have no problem making a Frenchman swoon. But don't get the idea I'm given to sulking all the time. I just like my own little private living quarters where I can do my own entertaining or just be quiet on my own. It's out of bounds for parents – though they're allowed to visit by appointment. Make yourself at home. Go and sit down while I take your coat.'

She gave a slight nod in the direction of a sofa and two opposite-facing armchairs arranged in a semi-circle around a rectangular, glass-topped coffee table on which reposed two glasses, a corkscrew and a bottle of red wine. He chose the chair nearest to the bottle, picked it up and began scrutinizing the label. She disappeared with his coat into what he presumed was an adjoining bedroom and when she came back he was still holding the bottle.

'I'm afraid I'm not much of a wine connoisseur,' she said. 'I just drink it. I know it's French but that's about all. You'll know much more about it than me. I won't even attempt to pronounce the name. As a domestic science teacher I suppose I should know more. My dad says 1970 was quite a good vintage.' Her voice had a controlled, modulated tone which carried a flat northern inflection. Though not unpleasant, he couldn't help comparing it to Sue's faultless accent.

'Well, I'm not really a specialist but you can see where a French wine comes from by the shape of the bottle. This one's a Claret. You can tell by the high shoulder.' His demonstration was accompanied by a light caress of its curves.

'Saint-Emilion is a wine-producing area in the Bordeaux region. When the wine's from Burgundy the bottle's got no shoulder at all.'

He had to confess there was an element of false modesty in what he'd said. When he'd been with the brewery he'd attended wine courses and knew much more. He didn't want to appear a know-all. It occurred to him that his wish to create this kind of favourable impression might be due to the seductive effect she was having on him. It was as if he was speaking to some mysterious person totally unlike the one he'd known at school. She gave her dress a self-conscious tug down before perching on the edge of the armchair opposite, her legs joined together in elegantly oblique union.

'Has it got to be drunk at room temperature? If that's the case then I've made my first boob. I only brought it up from the cellar an hour ago. And shouldn't it have been uncorked?'

'Oh, a few degrees won't make all that much difference. And it's probably warmed up since then. I suppose the real wine *connoisseur* would want his wine to breathe for an hour or two before, but personally I think there's a lot of snobbery in all this. I'm like you. I prefer just to drink it. Is wine your favourite tipple?'

'Well yes, I think it is, but I don't swill. I only have a glass or two when friends come round.' He briefly thought about informing her that in France wine was always associated with eating, and that the concept of 'sofa wine' was an Anglo-Saxon invention. He was diplomatic enough to think better of it. After all he didn't want her to feel it might be an indirect criticism of her own ignorance of what the done thing was.

'I think some English women do tend to drink far too much. And it's not always wine. It can be anything alcoholic. A girl who works in the same office as my sister told her that a good Saturday night out for her is when she can't remember anything about it when she wakes up the next morning!'

'Really?' It's the first time I've heard that. I thought it was more the boys. When I was a little girl and my dad had the dance hall they usually had to throw quite a few drunks out on Saturday evenings – especially during the *Teddy Boy* years. I never heard of girls drinking themselves stupid.'

'Did you enjoy living over a dance hall? It must have been a bit noisy.' He thought it better not to mention he'd been there once or twice in his youth, let alone the savage brawl he'd been witness to.

'Well yes, I suppose it was. But you get used to it. There were ballroom dancing classes two evenings per week. I used to love joining in. One advantage is that I'm not too bad a dancer.'

'Do you go dancing very often?'

'Well, I did in my younger days,' she said with a laugh, 'but now I don't get all that much opportunity. The main problem is you need someone to dance with – preferably a man. Do you like dancing?'

He couldn't help wondering whether this apparently casual question could, in fact, be considered as marking the start of the deeper examination he suspected she had reserved for him. Or had he already passed the first part? Was it an indirect way of soliciting some sort of invitation to go out together? He was on the point of replying with an honest, 'No, I can't really say I do,' but thought better of it. Though he could never abandon himself so completely to the pleasures of dancing as to efface the feeling that he was making a rather ridiculous display of himself, he didn't want to give her the impression he was rebuffing what could simply be an initial probe into his willingness to embark upon nothing more than companionable relations.

'Oh, I can hop about a bit, you know.' He was aware of not really answering her question and immediately changed the subject.

'Is your Dad retired now?'

'Well, more or less, but he's still a director at the Odeon cinema in the town centre.'

The doorbell rang distantly below. A door opened and he could hear muffled footsteps descending the stairs. A murmur of excited voices rose up.

'Oh, that'll be my Aunt Hilda and Uncle Joe. They've come to have a look at the photos Dad took during their Mediterranean cruise this summer. Can you manage without me for a minute while I go and say hello? I shan't be a tick. Perhaps you can do the honours while I'm away?' She pointed to the corkscrew.

After uncorking the wine he placed the bottle back on the table and had a look around him. The room was elegantly furnished but at the same time cosy. He'd previously put her father in the brash, vulgar, self-made-man class; but if his daughter's *boudoir* was anything to go by there was enough taste to suggest he'd been mistaken. As soon as she came back he began filling her glass. The bottle trembled slightly and he had to use his other hand to steady it. He hoped she hadn't noticed.

'Well, cheers. Here's to your talk,' he said, raising his glass. Did you manage to finish it?'

'Yes, more or less, I think. I was at it most of this afternoon. Honestly, the things I do for our dear headmaster. I'm reasonably satisfied ... but I'd like to go through it with you all the same. By the way, I haven't talked as much about Toussaint Louverture as I'd have liked. The whole thing would have been too long. I don't want to bore the pants off everybody for more than five minutes. As a grand finale I'm going to play *Amazing Grace,* sung by Judy Collins. You probably know it was written by an Englishman called John Newton. He was the captain of a slave ship who suddenly saw the light and went on to be a minister.'

'Well now you're telling me something *I* didn't know.' He wasn't at all surprised she'd not included much about Toussaint Louverture. After all, he'd never really considered her request for his assistance as much more than a pretext. What's more, it would have been impossible to use all the information he'd given her. Hadn't he done the research out of politeness and, above all, as a means of letting her know that he returned the interest she seemed to have in him? Moreover, wasn't she too intelligent to think he was naïve enough to have seen things otherwise? The problem was in knowing how far she might want to go. Was marriage now her aim, or would she be willing to have a relationship based on his terms? And what about himself? Was he sure he could resist becoming so closely involved that he might allow himself to be led into a relationship which at bottom he didn't really want and which he would soon regret?

'Shall we get down to business then?' she suddenly asked. 'We can take our glasses to the table.' She turned her head in the direction of the round, extending dining table reposing in a corner of the room. During her momentary absence he'd noted that two places had already been prepared to receive them. A vase of roses had been pushed to the far side and two of the four chairs around it had been pulled well out and positioned side by side. A loose-leaf ring binder was lying open on the table between the two. As they sat down he was seized by a feeling of self-conscious proximity which he'd not experienced to the same degree before. It was true they'd spent that brief moment together the other morning beneath her umbrella; but then they'd been on the move, and he'd been aware that this moment of relative intimacy was of a fleeting nature and had in all likelihood been occasioned by a combination of fortuitous circumstances. What's more, the slight shoulder contact between them had been involuntary. Here the situation required them to remain seated together in conditions of pre-arranged physical closeness which they would be required to maintain for at least an hour. Though any initial form of contact could be accidental, or made to appear so, any further ones could not be viewed in the same way. What had been just a hint of perfume floating in the air had now become a heavily pervasive, jasmine scent which, together with the fragrance of the roses, seemed to add to the sensation of pleasant intoxication the wine was now beginning to induce. He was determined that any initiative would not be taken by him; but how would he react if the first touch, even if not recognizably intentional, should come from her? He couldn't really say. She opened the two binder rings, took out the sheets and laid the first one on the table between them.

'I don't feel confident enough to talk just from notes so I've written it all out in full,' she said. 'Shall I read it out while you follow? I've tried to keep it short and simple with not too many dates. I don't want to talk too much above their heads. The main problem was what not to include than what to include. Stop me if you see something you think's not quite right – especially when it's my French pronunciation!'

'O.K. I'll do my best!'

She took an audibly deep breath and then began as follows:

This morning I'm going to speak to you about what is one of the most shameful episodes in the history of mankind. I hope you'll give it your full attention. I'm talking about the slave trade. This cruel exploitation of fellow human beings, on which immense fortunes were built, can only be described as a crime against humanity which all the main European nations, including our own, were guilty of for over 300 years. From the 16th to the 19th century an estimated 12.5 million African natives were captured and shipped to North America, the West Indies and South America. The dreadful, 12-week-long sea crossing on special slave ships, where the slaves were packed and chained together in a stinking hold as if they were sardines in a can, was so terrible that it's estimated at least a million never survived to reach their destination.

'I'll just stop you there,' he interposed as she came to the end of her sentence. 'Instead of saying, "... where the slaves were packed and chained together in a stinking hold as if they were sardines in a can ...", I think it'd be better simply to say, "... where the slaves were chained together in a stinking hold as if they were sardines in a can ..." I mean, "... as if they were sardines in a can ..." conveys the idea they were packed together, so don't you think you tend to be saying the same thing twice? Do you see what I mean?'

'Yes, you're right. So I'll cross out "... packed and ...".'

'And in the same sentence you say, "The dreadful 12 week long sea crossing ... was so terrible that ...". Once again you're saying the same thing twice. "Dreadful" and "terrible" mean the same thing. You could get rid of one by saying, "The 12-week-long sea crossing was so terrible that ..."'

'You're brilliant. I'd never have spotted that.'

They were just small points but he couldn't help feeling proud of himself at having brought them to her attention; he was sure that somewhere this had raised him in her eyes. She went on:

Those who did finally make it were auctioned as if they were animals or just objects, and then put to work in sugar plantations and cotton fields for up to eighteen hours a day under the supervision of an often sadistic overseer who wouldn't hesitate to beat or whip them if he thought they weren't working hard enough. And sometimes this even led to their death. It's not surprising then that some slaves revolted. One of the most famous of these was a man called Toussaint Louverture. He was himself a slave and worked at a plantation on an island in the French West Indies where he led an uprising. In 1794, five years after the Revolution, the French abolished slavery, and Toussaint-Louverture was made the first black general in the French Army. Later, however, Napoleon Bonaparte re-established slavery, and Toussaint Louverture was captured and transferred to France where he was imprisoned in a cold, damp castle and died less than a year later. But even though Britain took an active part in the slave trade it also produced a man called William Wilberforce. William Wilberforce was a Yorkshire-man, born in Hull in 1759, who spent the last 26 years of his life fighting against slavery. He finally succeeded in 1833 when the Slavery Abolition Act abolished slavery throughout most of the British Empire. Wilberforce died only three days after the law was voted.

I think we must all take William Wilberforce as an example. Even though slavery has been abolished we can still see in our everyday lives examples of people being exploited because they are unable to defend themselves, or treated differently because of the colour of their skin. We must do all we can to fight against this. All men are equal. We are all brothers and sisters. We all have the same right to be treated with dignity and not as if we were animals or just things. I'm now going to play the record 'Amazing Grace' which I'm sure most of you have heard before. It was composed in 1779 by an Englishman called John Newton. He was the captain of a slave ship who saw the light and went on to become a minister. I want you to listen carefully to the words.'

'Well, I can find nothing wrong with the rest. It reads nicely.'

At one moment their feet touched accidentally. Though slight, the contact was appreciable enough for her to utter a word of apology. It gave him a vague feeling of displeasure. He would have preferred her to have said nothing. It was as if she wanted to make it perfectly clear that their present relationship was governed by nothing more than the rules of politeness.

'What do you think? You don't think it's too ... well, sanctimonious? Especially the end bit. I don't want to sound as if I'm preaching.'

'No, honestly, I think it's very good. You've included some interesting historical facts with a universal message at the end. And it's not too long. I don't think the kids'll find it in the least bit boring.' He'd almost said 'any more boring than the other talks' but had checked himself in time.

'As far as the sermon bit goes, I think it depends very much on the tone you adopt when you're reading it. Just try to be as natural as possible.'

'What about my pronunciation of 'Louverture?' I don't seem to be able to get that "u" at the end to sound right. It's more like "ou".'

'We can practice it a bit if you like, but frankly I don't think you should worry about that. Nobody will notice.'

There was a brief rap on the door and an erect, grey-haired, distinguished-looking man with a clipped moustache strode in.

'Oh Dad, this is one of my teaching colleagues,' Sylvia said. The man threw him a distantly neutral, 'How do you do.' It gave Michael the rather disconcerting feeling that it wasn't the first time he'd walked into his daughter's *boudoir* while she was entertaining a male friend.

'Sylvia, I'm looking for the photo album of that Baltic cruise we went on two years ago. Any idea where it is?'

'Oh yes. It's on my bedside table. I was having a look at it yesterday evening. I thought you'd only be showing Auntie Hilda and Uncle Joe the photos you took of this summer's Med Cruise.'

'And, as usual, you put it back where it belongs,' he retorted, ignoring his daughter's excuse.

'Hang on. I'll go and get it.' She disappeared into her bedroom.

As she was going he turned towards Michael, his eyes raised in mock heavenly supplication. She came back and handed it to him with a brief apology. He took it and marched out without a word.

'Don't mind my dad,' she said. 'He's really a friendly creature at heart. But he can be a bit of a fusspot and soon gets annoyed about things not always being in their right place. Now we've finished shall we treat ourselves to some more wine? It should be at the right temperature now.' She beckoned towards the coffee table they'd left an hour or so before.

'I'll leave you to pour us some more. I'll be back in a minute.'

There was still half of the bottle left, and he made a vague mental note to be careful about how much he drank. After all, he might be breathalyzed on his way back home. When she came back she was holding a tray with some sandwiches and a cake on it.

'This is the standard sponge cake I teach my girls to make. It's quite plain and simple; but in view of the occasion I've sliced it in two and put a dollop of cream and jam in the middle.'

'It looks really delicious.' It was the only thing he could find to say.

As they ate and drank their conversation took on a more personal tone. She was a bit of a home bird. She'd been to France several times on camping holidays with her parents when she was a girl. They had a caravan at the time. She enjoyed setting off on holiday but was always glad to get back home. She was born and bred in Bridgeford and had never thought of living anywhere else.

'Ah, you're just the opposite to me.' he replied. I've applied to go on a year's teacher exchange to France beginning next September. I've always wanted to go and live there. If I'm accepted I don't know whether I'll ever come back.' His words were reinforced by the energy with which he uttered them; and, as he spoke, he was conscious of a faraway look blurring his eyes. Somewhere he couldn't stop himself from thinking it was the wine which was now talking, and that it had made him say something he should have kept to himself. But, after all, wasn't it the truth? Her face betrayed nothing more than what seemed to be polite interest.

As they came out the light mist he'd noted on arriving had now turned into a thick, low-hanging fog, and the halos surrounding the door lamps had now assumed a sickly, yellowish hue. He'd vaguely thought of asking her out next weekend for a drink, or even a meal but decided against it. Where was the hurry? An opportunity would certainly present itself during the course of the following week at school.

'Hey, it looks like a real pea-souper. Be careful how you go, now,' she said. 'If you're had up for drinking just give us a ring when you get home. Dad's on friendly terms with the local constabulary! Enjoy your Sunday, and once again many thanks for your help.'

'Oh, don't mention it. It was a real pleasure. The best of luck for Monday!' She made a slight grimace. His words were accompanied by a brief wave of the hand.

NINETEEN

On looking at his bedside alarm Michael was pleased to see he'd woken up later than usual. It made the day shorter. He disliked these sluggish English Sundays which made him feel he'd been cast into a sort of limbo; that the course of his life had been momentarily suspended by uncontrollable circumstances which prevented him from doing anything of value. It reminded him of a lengthy transit stop in some foreign airport where the only way to find temporary escape from that oppressive inertia of killing time was to retire into the perusal of a newspaper, or seek the oblivion of sleep. But last year, while consulting the French travel section of Bridgeford Central Library in preparation for his summer tour of France he'd come across a shelf displaying books in their original French. Among these figured the novels of Hervé Bazin. While he'd vaguely heard of the author he'd never read any of his books; and after leafing through two or three, he'd been faced with the disturbing conclusion that they contained a plethora of richly detailed descriptions couched in a vocabulary he'd barely encountered or, in too many cases, hadn't encountered at all. He'd been so much intrigued by the psychological dissection of the conflictual childhood relations the author had entertained with his cold-hearted, authoritarian mother as described in *Vipère au Poing* that he'd taken the book out. He now spent two or three hours of these autumn Sunday afternoons diligently ploughing through it. He worked with the *Petit Larousse Illustré* of his university days at his side: it had the advantage of supplying definitions and synonyms in French which he'd meticulously copy down against the previously unknown word or expression. The work was laborious, and progress rarely extended much beyond one single page per hour; but for a conscientious, studious mind like his it brought the satisfaction of knowing he was learning. Then, when he got tired of this scrupulous labour, he'd tune into a French radio station, lean back in his chair and settle down to listen. He frequently repeated the same exercise when alone in his car; but in the silence of his room he could concentrate better; and he was charmed even more by the refined musicality of the language.

Usually, after waking up he'd slip down for the newspaper and take it back to bed. Normally, he was early enough to do this before anybody had got up and it was still lying on the hall doormat. It was of the tabloid kind. He'd tried to talk his parents into changing it for one he considered to be part of the 'quality press', but they'd adamantly refused. He'd then alternate reading and dozing for an hour or so. At around ten his mum would shout up the stairs, 'Are you ready for your breakfast, now?' He'd reply, 'Oh, yes please!' with a slightly exaggerated note of enthusiasm in his voice. Some twenty minutes later his bacon, eggs and sausage would be brought up on a tray. Occasionally, his dad would mildly grumble about him not getting up to give him a hand to do this or that, but his irritation never went much beyond: though his begetter was one of those active men who, once awake, felt the irresistible urge to rise and was unable to understand why others didn't do the same, his rectitude in money matters obliged him to admit that the monthly board his son was paying covered the right to spend Sunday mornings lazing in bed. So, Michael would only think of rising around eleven o'clock and sometimes even later.

As he walked into the living room Grandpa was peering at the newspaper, his spectacles pushed well up over his forehead. Without being asked, he relinquished it with a benevolent, 'Here you are, lad. I've read all I want to.'

'Is that you?' his mother called out from the kitchen. 'Can I get cracking with your breakfast now? I'll bring it up for you as per usual.'

'Yes please. Where's Dad?'

'Oh, he's pottering about in his greenhouse.'

He didn't really know why he'd asked the question as he already knew the answer. Perhaps he wanted to influence his mum into thinking that more consideration should be given to both the person and what he was doing. Her answer betrayed a trace of resigned irritation which he could hardly understand. His dad was never happier than when in the sole company of his vegetables and flowers, and Michael was sure she was aware that what she apparently considered to be just idle tinkering was, in fact, one of his father's ways of maintaining a semblance of family peace by creating as much of a distance between himself and Grandpa as the boundaries of house and garden could reasonably provide.

When his mum brought his breakfast up and placed the tray in front of him he could see she had something on her mind. Usually she'd say something like, 'You wouldn't get better service than this in a five star hotel!' before adding with a gentle laugh, 'And don't slurp your coffee all over your pyjama top!' followed by a, 'Right, I'll leave you to it, then!' This time she remained standing stiffly by his bedside. There was a strained look on her face and her head gave a nervous twitch. It was usually a sign she was preparing herself to say something important. He waited for her to speak.

'Michael,' she began, 'before you start your breakfast I'd just like to have a quiet little word.' It flashed through his mind it was something to do with Grandpa. Had they decided to put him into a home?

'Your dad and I have decided to sell up.' It was said without the slightest preamble. Both this and the tone of resolute finality with which the words were uttered seemed to emphasize the irrevocability of the decision.

'We've been in the shop for 12 years now and it's beginning to get us down. We've decided to move down to Rivermouth. As you know, we've always said we'd retire back down there. Well, we've decided now's the time to do it before it's too late. I want to be a lady of leisure for the rest of my days. I think I've earned it. But keep it under your hat for the moment. We'll tell your sister, of course, but we haven't said anything to Grandpa yet.'

Michael was surprised by both the unexpectedness and the precocity of their resolution. For even though the war years they'd spent in Rivermouth was a recurring subject of fond, often anecdotal conversation with relatives and friends, and retiring down there had always been presented as a dream they were determined to fulfil, he'd thought they would have waited a few more years until his dad had reached retirement age. He'd been stationed there during the whole of the Second World War as an RAF police corporal in charge of airfield security. Apparently, when he'd received his calling up papers in 1939 they'd only faintly heard of Rivermouth. For the Northerners they were it was situated somewhere in that vaguely alien region termed 'down South', and they'd had to look its precise location up on the map. However, on arrival their apprehensions had been allayed. Not only were the people friendly but it was a picturesque little seaside town they had previously imagined could never have existed. Despite the airfield being an active base for both fighters and heavy bombers, they themselves had been spared any significant exposure to the direct effects of war. The only exception – and it was a story they never tired of telling – occurred one day when they came back home to find that an American fighter plane had overrun the nearby runway, crashed through the wall of the bungalow they were renting, and ended with its nose resting on the dining-room table. Though Michael never doubted the truth of the occurrence he could never exclude the suspicion that his parents' description of this dramatic event had received some anecdotal adornment from their conjoined imaginations. But he understood why they talked about those years with so much nostalgia. They were young; they were in their first years of marriage; and both he and his sister had first seen light of day down there.

'Isn't all this a bit sudden?' was all he could find to say.

'Not really. We've been thinking about it on and off for quite a while now.'

'And what about Dad? Isn't he too young to qualify for a pension?'

'Your Dad can get a little job down there until he retires in four years' time. It's a holiday area so that shouldn't be much of a problem. Then there's Grandpa's pension.' The thought crossed his mind that, though they might have dispensed with the presence of Grandpa himself, they weren't able to do without his money.

'And if the worst comes to the worst we can always do Bed and Breakfasts in summer. Anyway, we're going to put the shop and house up for sale straight after Christmas. Finding a buyer for the shop could take some time but we're going to sell it as a going concern. I don't think selling the house will be much of a problem. It's not even ten years old and we're in a sought-after area.'

'What about finding a place down there?'

'Well, we're going to ask your Auntie Marguerite and Uncle John if they'll be kind enough to get local estate agents to send us details of properties for sale. I'm sure they'll be thrilled at the idea of us going to live there. When we close the shop at Easter we might well go down and have a look for something on the spot. If everything goes to plan we'll be moving in August.'

His mum had first met Auntie Marguerite shortly after they'd settled down there. She'd been engaged in the door-to-door selling of something or other to help the war effort, and being somewhat older had befriended the family in a motherly sort of way. Her husband, John, had been Petty Officer aboard a destroyer and had survived both Dunkirk and several North Atlantic crossings. Their friendship had developed to the point where they'd been invited to become Michael's godparents. They had accepted with great pleasure.

'Anyway we just thought we'd put you in the picture. Now I'll let you get on with your breakfast before it goes cold.'

While eating he pondered over the news. When he came to think about it was it all that much of a surprise? Lately his mum had been complaining more than usual about having to get up at five o'clock in the morning and being on her feet all day. And it was true they weren't getting any younger. So, wasn't it quite natural that they should want to reap the benefit of their labours before they were too old? Though she had presented the decision as springing from mutual agreement Michael suspected it was she who had been the instigator. On the whole he welcomed their decision with pleasure. Much of the pleasure was drawn from the common denominator it had created between his parents and himself. Wasn't their dream of escaping to a better life in many ways comparable to his? Nevertheless, he couldn't avoid thinking that it drew much of its inspiration from the hope that the simple act of moving back to a seaside town holding so many memories of long past joys would miraculously wash away their present cares. Wasn't this an illusion? Perhaps it was that common human failing which consists in us bringing our judgements to bear on others rather than first directing them at ourselves which made Michael only faintly aware that as far as his own dreams were concerned this same consideration might be applied to him.

It is perhaps in the natural order of things for a young man of his age that what principally occupied Michael's thoughts, however, was how a successful outcome to his parents' plans might affect his own future. Of course, if his French exchange application was accepted there would be no significant change: he'd simply give them a hand with the removal, help them settle in and then set off for France. On the other hand, he'd have to make some important choices if he was again confronted with a refusal. Should he resign himself to staying at Barfield and apply once more the following year? While he'd have to find a place of his own and would certainly miss the home comforts he was now enjoying, this wouldn't present any great problem. Hadn't his student days and the two years he'd spent living in his Birmingham bedsit proved he was quite capable of looking after himself? Or should he resign his post and accompany his parents down South? After all, getting a job there shouldn't be all that difficult. He was sure Headmaster Fowler would give him a good reference and he'd have two years of experience under his belt. And living in a holiday region on the English south coast would certainly bring a better quality of life. The problem was that his new headmaster might not take kindly to him re-applying for the exchange after only one year at his school. So, wouldn't this mean he'd have to wait two more years – or even longer? What's more, he was sure there'd still be the problem of Grandpa and his dad. It would certainly be better if he found his own little flat. But who knows what could happen while he was living down there? Could he trust the firmness of his own resolutions enough not to allow himself to become amorously involved to the point of doing something so stupid as to get married? If he did, wouldn't this be the end of it all? Wouldn't this mean him having to accept that soul-destroying marital and professional routine he had resolved to do all in his power to avoid? And wouldn't his life become a source of such deep self-reproach that it could plague him for the rest of his days?

Then there was their T-shirt project. Even while he and Adrian were driving back home together after their visit to Bridgeford Market, that successful outcome which had been the cause of so much exhilaration had begun prompting in Michael deliberations of a more self-questioning nature. For, beyond all reservations as to his pal's ability to maintain a strong steadfastness of purpose, some of his doubts were now focusing on himself. Did he know his own mind well enough to be sure of his reaction if over the next few weeks results exceeded their wildest expectations? If this were the case and his application was again refused might he not be in danger of viewing their project as a serious alternative to him going to live in France? And, even if he was accepted, might not this initial business success lead him to turn the offer down and concentrate all his efforts on developing their venture? Since the *Bureau for Foreign Exchanges* would certainly decline to consider any future applications on his part wouldn't this mean an even more likely end to his French dream?

In addition, his self-questionings were not without assuming a more scrupulous form. Though he'd already mentioned to Adrian that he could be spending the next year in France, he'd spoken of it in enough of a casual way to give the impression it was more a remote, inconsequential possibility than an actively sought-after goal. As a result, Adrian probably thought that in his friend's mind it was their project which had priority. But if he was offered a place and decided to accept, wouldn't he be abandoning his pal at a time and in circumstances when he needed him the most? Didn't he owe it to his friend to tell him where he really stood? Wasn't he being dishonest in not laying all his cards on the table? Couldn't it even be said that he was playing a double game?

Would it be surprising to learn that, after some reflection, our young man's qualms finally gave way to considerations of a more realistic nature? Given the fact that his future depended on circumstances beyond his present control wasn't the most astute policy one which consisted in him keeping his options open for as long as necessary? And couldn't this only be achieved by waiting to see how events would unfold? For only then would he be in possession of enough certainties to take decisions reposing on solid foundations. Wasn't it, therefore, not in his present interests to be totally frank with Adrian? So, in order to avoid any irretrievable commitment, financial or otherwise over the next few weeks he resolved to say nothing to his pal, while at the same time applying a strategy characterized by a force of inertia strong enough to slow the progress of their project down or, depending on circumstances, even bring it to a stop. After all, it could be re-activated if future events led him to think it would be to his advantage to do so.

I trust you will not be tempted to come down too hard on our young man for finally choosing this opportunistic, even egoistical course of inaction. After all, wasn't he like most, if not all of us at some time or other in so much as his hopes, doubts and fears were simply stronger than his more noble intentions?

TWENTY

On Monday morning Sylvia gave her talk before the assembled school. Both it and the playing of *Amazing Grace* which followed seemed to go down well. The single, unaccompanied female voice gave the song a hauntingly plaintive ring which contrasted with the hymns the school usually sang and which frequently seemed to echo a sort of sanctimonious Christian smugness. Michael was struck by her assured manner. It worried him that he himself might not quite find the self-possession to perform so well. Though he now had enough experience to put on a show of authoritative confidence in front of a class, he feared that addressing a public containing his more discerning adult peers might be the cause of an agitation he wouldn't be able to hide. His own address was scheduled to take place some time after the Christmas holidays and, apart from the fact that it would in some way be connected with France, he hadn't given much thought as to its precise subject.

At the end of Sylvia's talk Headmaster Fowler stepped over to the lectern and gratified her with a nodded thank you and a feeble smile. For the benefit of the school he even added a solemn, 'I hope you will all think very carefully about what Miss Schofield has just said.' Michael made a mental note to congratulate her as soon as the first opportunity arose. It came only a few minutes later when the teachers had descended from the stage and were walking back to the staffroom. She was chatting to a lady colleague, and as he walked past he whispered a confidential 'Well done!' in her ear. She'd thanked him with a smile, and then raised her eyes aloft in a self-deprecatory attitude which seemed to suggest she thought her effort too humble to merit such selective praise. He vaguely wondered whether it was a kind of false modesty speaking.

As he was sipping his break time coffee in the staff room Adrian came sauntering up. His usually beaming face betrayed just enough anxiety to give Michael the suspicion that all was not quite right. His fears were quickly confirmed. Apparently, Adrian had gone along to two local open-air markets the previous Saturday afternoon, and after hunting around had only managed to find a dozen blanks. Disaster had struck when he'd been printing them in the evening. He'd already informed Michael that his mother's irritation at her son's invasion of her cooking area had been rising in much the same proportion as the increasing number of indelible ink stains that were appearing on table and floor. But even though the calamity had occurred during the printing session it was not caused by ink: for he'd dropped and broken the iron he was using to smooth out the creases in the freshly-printed T-shirts and fix the design. It was now beyond repair. He feared it was the very last straw: his 'old woman' had not only pointed out in the strongest possible terms that he'd be required to replace it without delay but she'd been adamant in insisting that all future production must be transferred elsewhere. Since Adrian supposed that relocation to Michael's mum's kitchen was out of the question he could only conclude that finding suitable premises at a reasonable rent was now at the top of their list. A small workroom with a sink, hot and cold running water, a workbench and some kind of heating would do the trick. He was, however, well aware it might not be all that easy to find, and that the coming Christmas holidays would give them the opportunity to have a good look round. Michael's immediate reaction was a feeling of discomfort at the thought that this development might mean him having to resist being drawn into the first stage of a financial involvement which he'd now resolved to delay until that time when events might cause it to suit his purpose. In addition, his pal had used the word 'reasonable' to describe the amount of rent they would be ready to pay. It occurred to Michael that neither of them had the slightest idea of the monthly cost of this type of facility. Moreover, he was inclined to think that for Adrian a reasonable rent, rather than implying moderation when compared to others of a similar type, simply meant one they could meet the expense of. He couldn't help feeling some unease at the thought that the rent required could exceed their expectations to an unaffordable degree. What added even more to his discomfort was his growing presentiment that, given Adrian's live-for-the-moment nature, his finances were not in the healthiest of states. What's more, there were limits beyond which he himself was not willing to go: not only must their contributions be on an equal basis but they must in no way cause him to reduce the monthly amount he was putting away in reserve for his French adventure. But for the moment any discussion regarding how much each would be prepared to pay was inopportune. Meanwhile, he'd try to calculate how much he'd be able reasonably to afford. He wondered whether his pal had given any thought to doing the same.

Adrian then proceeded to raise another problem: in view of the difficulty he'd encountered in obtaining adequate supplies of blank T-shirts on the local markets, it was his opinion that they'd now have to give some serious thought to buying larger quantities on a wholesale basis. They could once more take advantage of the Christmas holidays to obtain all the necessary information. As he had already indicated, T-shirts were imported in bales, and they'd have to phone or even make an appointment with an importer to discuss prices, delivery times and minimum quantities. Michael could only agree. After all, what did he have to lose by simply making enquiries? Adrian then introduced a change of subject.

'By the way, my mate who did the silk screen print's invited me to a Christmas party at the Technical College next Saturday. It's the last weekend of the term. You can come with me if you like. He told me there'll be plenty of birds standing under the mistletoe waiting to be kissed. My mouth's watering at the thought!'

He had thought of asking Sylvia out for a drink and perhaps even a meal that same evening. He knew a nice little pub which served typical French food. He had to admit that since last Saturday evening he was beginning to see her in a more seductive light; and he'd felt a thrill of pleasure at the thought of spending an evening out with such an attractive and elegant blond. But, after all, where was the hurry? Couldn't he put that off until the Saturday after? Wouldn't this arrangement have the advantage of giving the Christmas holidays a festive start as well as providing him with the opportunity of spending two consecutive Saturday evenings away from home?

'That sounds interesting, now!' he replied.

'It's a bring-a-bottle do,' his friend added.

Though he'd made it appear he shared his pal's anticipatory delight, this was not really the case. His own expectations of the pleasure the evening might bring fell far short of those which excited his friend. Even when he was a student he'd never been an avid party-goer. Didn't girls come to parties to laugh and enjoy the present moment? Didn't this include the hope of meeting a similarly minded male? Wasn't he too serious, too reserved a sort of person to relax and join in the fun? How could you expect a girl to be interested in a man whose sobriety of conversation rose in proportion to the amount of alcohol he imbibed? And wasn't a schoolteacher the very antithesis of what they were looking for? He wondered whether Adrian told them this was his job. It was something he very much doubted. It might even be one of the factors which explained his success. But there again, even if he did, it probably didn't matter. He neither spoke nor looked like a schoolteacher. As he'd already noted, girls were quickly attracted by his friend's engaging looks, his chatty sociability, his glibness of tongue and ready wit. What's more, there was always that 'Afro-style' haircut. It was the 'icing on the bun,' Adrian would joke. He'd once been witness to Adrian meeting a girl at a party and retiring with her to bed. Even if he had the same opportunity it was something he himself couldn't do. It was, perhaps, a certain old-fashioned prudery mingled with remnants of a juvenile, romanticized notion of the fair sex which made him feel scorn for the kind of girl who lent herself to this sort of one night stand.

TWENTY-ONE

'What did you think to Sylvia's talk yesterday?' Jennifer asked as they were walking back to the staffroom together at the end of the morning lessons.

'Personally I thought it was excellent,' she continued. 'On Friday she told me she had horrible stage fright just thinking about it. But she was so wonderfully calm and collected. You'd have thought she was a seasoned public speaker. I only hope I cope as well.'

'Yes, that's exactly what I thought,' he simply replied.

Jennifer was the German teacher Sylvia had been chatting to when he'd offered her his whispered congratulations. It was her first term at Barfield.

'Sylvia told me you'd helped her a lot,' she said, lowering her voice.

'Well, all I can say is she's being unduly modest. I only helped her with the Toussaint Louverture bit. And that wasn't much.'

'Now I think *you're* being unduly modest. She told me you'd spent a whole Saturday morning at the reference library finding out more about him. She's very grateful to you for that.'

'Honestly, I'd already heard of Toussaint Louverture. I just wanted to get a few details straight. It didn't take me all that long.' He didn't mention that Sylvia had invited him home. He'd frequently seen the two young women engaged in friendly conversation and wondered if their intimacy had gone so far as to have allowed her to inform Jennifer of this.

While he was inclined to consider himself lucky to have such a cheerful and friendly colleague as Jennifer, he couldn't say he had any real wish to spend more time in her company. Apart from the occasional chat in the school corridors, contact with her came mainly from the fortnightly, lunchtime meetings which Mrs Boxley, the head of the school's modern language department, insisted on them attending, and during which they discussed teaching methods, pupil progress and any discipline problems which as young, inexperienced teachers they might be encountering. He sometimes wondered why Ian, who taught elementary French and German to first form classes, wasn't included. It might be because he'd been teaching at the school longer than Mrs Boxley herself, and felt it was he who had the most experience. Jennifer thought it was more because he was too pig-headed, blinkered and set in his ways to want to discuss any form of change. Michael couldn't help wondering in what way Ian had offended her. Perhaps the injury was simply caused by him systematically ignoring her. As far as the meetings were concerned neither he nor Jennifer felt they were in any way a chore. Mrs Boxley was a dynamic, modern, attractive woman with a warm, vivacious personality, and these occasions took more the form of a relaxed, yet stimulating get-together.

Michael was happy that Jennifer was married. Her husband's name was Geoff and they lived in a small town some 20 miles away. He taught geography in a private school on the other side of Bridgeford. After driving to Barfield together in the morning, he would deposit his wife at the teacher's entrance and then continue on his way; and at the end of the school day he would pick her up to drive back home. Usually he waited in the school car park for her to appear; but on one occasion she'd been delayed and he'd ventured into the staffroom to see what had become of her. Jennifer had introduced him. He was a bespectacled, unremarkable looking, reserved young man, and they'd only exchanged a few words.

The main satisfaction Michael drew from his colleague's marital state was due to him never having had relations of a strictly platonic kind with a similarly-aged member of the opposite sex. He welcomed the opportunity it gave him to have an association based simply on friendly, mutually respectful and professionally helpful terms. Admittedly this was made easier by the fact that he felt no physical attraction for her: she was short and plump with a matronly bust and thick legs. And he'd lately observed that her thighs rubbed together when she walked. It was true that in view of his antecedents Michael could have entertained doubts as to whether nothing more than a cordial, relationship between a normally constituted young man and woman could ever exist. He'd come to the conclusion that it could be doing some a considerable injustice to be convinced it could never be so. As far as he could see, this was the case with Mrs Boxley and Ian. It was the subject of some staffroom amusement that something was 'going on' between them. After all, she was a trimly attractive, energetic woman; and it couldn't be denied that Ian, in spite of his quirks, was an athletic, handsome-looking man. And hadn't they both been entrenched in marriage for the last ten or so years? What provided conclusive proof for many, if not the majority of staffroom observers, however, was that, after lunching in the school dining hall, Ian and Mrs Boxley were in the habit of retiring together into classrooms on the floor above. But what is more natural with those whose profession requires them to act in an exemplary sort of way that this type of suspicion, rather than being expressed openly, should be conveyed by just the hint of an ironic smile? Michael had had what he considered irrefutable proof of their innocence. On one occasion he'd walked unknowingly into the language laboratory to prepare a tape for a coming lesson and found them both there together. She was sitting at the teacher's console doing some marking. As he stepped in she looked up and gratified him with a benign smile. Ian was busy repairing a microphone in a pupil's booth at the back. Neither of them showed the slightest sign of embarrassment at his intrusion, and he could only conclude that they simply preferred each other's private company to the public scrutiny they would be exposing themselves to in the staffroom.

While Michael now considered Mrs Boxley and Ian's relationship to be nothing more than one of cordiality, his own recent experience was suggesting their case was a rare exception: for despite him viewing Jennifer's company as simply that of a friend and colleague, he was becoming increasingly aware this wasn't the case with her. For one thing she'd begun to confide in him details of the history of her relations with her husband. She'd known him since their first university year. Apparently, while she was in Germany during her student year abroad he'd repeatedly written to tell her how much he missed her. He'd even hinted at marriage after their graduation. She'd written back informing him that this was not her main preoccupation. His reaction had been to take the first opportunity to go out to see her. Michael had listened sympathetically but had made no comment. One lunch time last week he'd informed her he was going into town, and she'd asked if she could go along for the ride. He could only reply with a polite, 'Yes, by all means.' While they were driving there she'd turned her earnest brown eyes towards him and declared, 'I feel so nice and safe when I'm driving with *you*!' This impulsive rush of intimacy had embarrassed, even irritated him. Wasn't she now flirting with the limits which a friendly yet professional relationship imposed? Nevertheless, he thought it would give too rudely abrupt an impression if he changed the subject of their conversation entirely, and that lending it a mechanical orientation might be a more diplomatic way of cooling her down.

'Yes, my dad taught me to drive. When I was learning he always stressed it was important to consider your passengers' comfort. For example, they mustn't feel any jerkiness when you change gear.'

He hoped that this would be enough for her to take the hint. After all, the last thing he wanted was it to be thought that they'd embarked on some kind of amorous adventure together and that staffroom tittle-tattle should focus on them.

TWENTY-TWO

As Michael lifted himself out of his car he gave a shiver. A biting wind was blowing and it crossed his mind that if it dropped they could be in for a frosty night. Rather than come together they'd each decided to take their own car and meet in a pub near the Technical College. 'After all,' Adrian had declared, 'we've got to be prepared for the best. I mean, if this evening goes the way I hope, we could be led our separate ways.'

He spotted his friend through the open tap room door. It wasn't a surprise as Michael had noted his banger in the pub car park. A half empty schooner of beer stood before him. It was a bit too early yet for the party to really get into swing, so they could take their time over a drink or two.

'Hello Mike. What'll it be? A pint of best?'

'No, this one's on me. The same again?'

'I wouldn't say no!'

He'd frequently noticed that Adrian never gave a direct 'Yes, please' answer to this sort of invitation. It was always something circumlocutory like, 'I don't mind if I do,' 'Go on, then' or 'You've twisted my arm'.

When he brought the drinks back from the bar he noted that, in spite of the cold, Adrian was wearing just a Xarkus T-shirt under his ice-cream man's jacket. He must have noticed Michael looking.

'Yep, I've got half a dozen of 'em in the car. You never know, we might be able to flog one or two at their retail price.'

Though he'd used an inclusive 'we', the idea hadn't even occurred to Michael. He wondered if Adrian might be inwardly reproaching him for not having decided to wear one, too. After all, he was right when he said it could result in one or two sales. The least it could do would be to

117

create a subject of conversation. A girl would certainly find it more interesting than teaching. That's if he chose to tell her this was his job. But sporting just a T-shirt at a party wasn't quite his style – especially when winter was near. Didn't he feel more at ease and, above all, warmer in the tweed jacket, the grey trousers and the polo-necked sweater he'd decided to wear?

As they were chatting Michael mentioned that he'd had a quick word with their colleague, Roland, about their project. He found it promising and expressed enough interest to ask to be kept informed. He'd said that the first thing they should do was to buy an accounts book in which to record all details of expenses and receipts. Michael had felt disappointed that Roland didn't seem to want his involvement to extend beyond this type of elementary advice. Perhaps, from a professional point of view, his past redundancy had now made him averse to anything which smacked of risk. Wouldn't it have somewhere acted as a salve to his conscience if Roland had given signs of being willing to commit himself deeply enough to have been in a position to replace Michael as Adrian's business partner in the event of him spending the following year in France?

Their conversation then turned to the evening's prospects. He wasn't really surprised by Adrian's unabashed optimism as to his chances of picking up 'a nice bit of crumpet'. It was in keeping with his character. It contrasted with his own fatalistic resignation.

'Well, I think it's about time we got stuck in – as the bishop said to the actress,' Adrian announced in his usual inimitable style. It was going on for nine o'clock and the party should now have got under way. Though this was his friend's usual way of intimating that they should move into action the effects of the beer Michael had swallowed helped him produce an acquiescent laugh. He was even beginning to view the next few hours in a more cheery light.

Adrian's art student friend was standing by the common room entrance. He was something of a colossus and had obviously been entrusted with the task of vetting arrivals and repelling any potential gatecrashers detected among them. Michael was conscious of a vague feeling of disapproval as he noted his scraggy beard and long, dark, greasy-looking hair which had been drawn tightly backwards and plaited into a long pigtail. He acknowledged the arrival of Adrian with a hazy smile. His eyes had a glassy look about them.

'I've brought my mate along. Is that all right?' Adrian asked with a nod in Michael's general direction.

'Yeah, no problem, man. Just go on through. You can leave your bottles over there,' he replied, at the same time indicating the direction to follow with a slight nod of the head. He hadn't even looked at Michael. He had the uncomfortable impression he wouldn't have done so even if Adrian had gone to the trouble of making a direct introduction. As they walked in a sudden confrontation with the heat of the room made him first ask himself why he'd put on his thick polo-necked sweater and then, more generally, why he'd come at all. Wouldn't it have been a far better choice to have invited Sylvia out for a nice quiet meal in that cosy little pub he knew?

The blaring music, the flashing lights and the entwined, slowly swaying couples packing the floor indicated that the party had now got well under way. It somewhere reminded him of the Saturday night dances of his student days. But during his teacher training year when he went to a party or dance he'd been in the enviable position of being accompanied by Sue. In addition, he'd been free of all professional and social restraints. Was it the sobering effects of the short but chilly walk from the pub which now produced in him the feeling that he was re-entering a world which no longer corresponded to his aspirations, age or job? For not only was he in the demeaning position of having to make an unconvinced effort to pick up 'a nice bit of crumpet', but he was suddenly struck by the alarming thought that this desirable type of female could well be one of his sixth form pupils. He doubted that Adrian would be much disturbed by similar considerations. After all, he was four years younger, and hadn't yet turned his back on those free and easy student days.

The 'over there' pronounced by Adrian's art-student friend indicated the corner in which was installed the small common room bar. Bottles of varying sizes and contents filled the counter. As they placed their own contributions on it, the young man behind beamed at them from beneath a red, pointed hat. It had white fur round the bottom and a pompon of the same colour dangled from the top. A barrel of beer – a ragdoll Santa Claus with legs splayed out on it – reposed behind. Apparently, it had been decided – wisely Michael thought – that, though participants had been required to make a personal contribution to that Christmas merriment which alcohol would undoubtedly bring, they would be denied the opportunity of having unlimited access to it.

They decided to stay standing with their drinks at the bar. In front of them an area had been furnished with plastic tables and chairs occupied by couples drinking, chatting or simply gazing into each other's eyes. It vaguely reminded Michael of the terrace of a French café. Their position gave them a vantage point from which they could discreetly survey the dancers on the floor. An interlaced couple caught Michael's eye. The girl's arms encircled her partner's neck. She'd inclined herself backwards, her eyes were closed and her lips slightly parted; and her face bore an expression of rapturous delight. As he followed their slowly swaying progress his gaze fell on a hand caressing her between the legs. That people could give themselves up to such intimate preliminaries in so public a place filled him with a mixture of shock and disgust which was partially attenuated by the amusing thought that her bright green panties might have been the signal for her partner to go ahead. It ran through his mind that such overt sexual display was typically English and that the French were too discreetly refined to allow themselves such raw, unrestrained indulgence. Then he recalled that second school trip to France. They were in a Paris *métro* train which had just stopped at a station. There amidst the swirling crowds he'd observed a man and woman openly embracing on a platform bench. The man had a slightly embarrassed, almost appealing look on his face – as if he was asking anyone who might care to look, 'Well, what on earth do you expect me to do!' As Michael lowered his eyes he saw his partner was gently stroking him between the thighs. Adrian had seen the intertwined dancers, too. 'God, they've got off to an early start!' he joked. Unlike Michael, he'd given verbal expression to the observation. There was a note of expectancy in his voice.

On scanning the terrace Michael's eyes fell on two girls sitting with their backs to them a short distance away. One, he observed, had straight fair hair falling onto bared shoulders. The disc jockey had switched on the strobes, and when she turned her head to speak to her darker-haired companion the flashing purple light gave the movement a weird, cinematographic effect. Her companion must hardly have replied, however, as no reaction could be discerned. Adrian had spotted them, too.

'Hey, those two over there', he whispered, giving Michael a nudge. 'They don't look all that bad. What do you reckon? You know, this could be our lucky night. Come on! Let's get in there while the iron's hot!'

Michael's natural reserve made him recoil at the thought of such a bold approach, and he found himself struggling to contain a growing unease. He apprehended a possible rejection of what might be interpreted as too brash an intrusion; and even if their reaction was favourable he wasn't quite sure of what to say. In the glibness of his brewery days it wouldn't have presented much of a problem; but he was conscious of having become a much more sober person since then and that he might now be at a loss to find suitably light, playful words. Admittedly, in the past he'd approached both Vicky and Susan in circumstances not totally dissimilar; but they'd been part of the same university establishment, and somewhere it was as if they were united by the same family ties. Wasn't he now about to be confronted with strangers from the great unknown? It was only after presenting himself with the thought that if two unescorted girls had come to a dance it was certainly with the intention of meeting men that he found himself quietly saying, not without a slight tremor in his voice, 'O.K. Let's go.' In any case he'd leave it to Adrian to do all the talking.

'Hello girls. You were looking so miserable and lonesome we thought we'd come and buck you up.' Adrian's voice had a familiar, confident tone about it. An impudent grin creased his face. It was certainly not the first time he'd used this approach. The fair-haired girl took both of them in with a quick sweep of the eye, and without so much as a look at her friend replied, 'Oh, so you're knights in shining armour come to rescue two poor damsels in distress!' Her eyes twinkled with amusement as she tossed her hair lightly back.

'Yeah, we had to leave our white steeds and swords outside. Otherwise they wouldn't have let us in. Are the two poor damsels grateful enough to let their rescuers sit down?' She glanced at her companion who gave a vague nod of her head. Her hair, he noted, was a reddish brown. Adrian immediately pulled a chair from under the table and sat down.

'Would you like a drink?' Michael asked, addressing the girls.

'Go on then. What are you having Molly?'

'Oh, just a Coke for me,' her friend replied.

'Well, I'll have a glass of red wine.

'A beer for you, Adrian?'

'Yep, I don't mind if I do.'

He was glad to be able to withdraw from their company for a short moment. It would enable Adrian to break the ice while giving himself time to reflect on the most suitable attitude to adopt. He'd already detected signs of an empathetic understanding between Adrian and the fair haired girl: she seemed to have the fresh liveliness of manner which suited his friend's exuberant, happy-go-lucky style and to be quite capable of meeting his unflagging repartee. So, he'd leave them to get better acquainted through the *badinage* they were probably already indulging in. As for himself, he'd simply be pleasantly polite to her friend who, for the moment at least, had presented no more than a taciturn, vaguely somber front. As he set the drinks down on the table he noted that the words and smiles being exchanged between Adrian and the blond seemed to indicate that the *rapport* he had initially sensed was already assuming an audible and visible form. Even before he sat down Adrian made the introductions.

'Mike, this is Jean and this is Molly. Jean and Molly, this is my business partner, Mike.'

During his absence at the bar Adrian had removed his jacket to reveal his Xarkus T-shirt beneath. It must have attracted Jean's attention as it was the subject of animated conversation between the two. Michael felt some discomfort that Adrian had not only presented him as his business partner, but now seemed to be doing his best to give the impression they were well on their way to success. While the two were chatting Molly and he did nothing much more than listen. It was only after Adrian had asked them if they were students at the Tech and Jean had replied in the negative that they all agreed to have a guessing game about what they did. It didn't take long to learn they were trainee nurses in their final year. It had been made easier by the fact that both men knew there was a nurses' training college just up the road. No guesses were needed to know that Jean originated from Birmingham, while the soft lilt in Molly's voice was unmistakably Irish. But after a while that conversation which had been shared by all four began assuming the characteristics of two diverging styles: the same uninterrupted banter on the part of Adrian and Jean, and the more serious, intermittent words which our young man exchanged with Molly. In an attempt to introduce a subject which might encourage a more fluid flow of conversation Michael asked her whether she was from Ulster or the Republic. She was born and bred in a small town near Dublin, she replied. He assumed this meant she was a Catholic. When he was a student Michael had had some Irish pals – mostly from Belfast. He was on the point of mentioning this but thought better of it: they had all been Protestants and he'd been surprised by the animosity, even contempt, which they had openly displayed towards those 'southern Micks'.

Adrian quickly invited Jean to dance. She accepted readily. Apart from an occasional glimpse of them bobbing to the surface of that slowly circling pool of dancers that was the last they saw of them. After their departure he tried to get Molly to talk more about herself. She became slightly more loquacious in a matter-of-fact kind of way. She was looking forward to going back home for Christmas. She missed her home and family. After qualifying as a nurse she intended to get a job in a hospital in Dublin. She seemed to lose herself momentarily in a distant dreaminess. She had aspirations just like him, he reflected; but rather than being inspired by the adventure of a new life abroad, hers reposed on the security of re-finding her roots back home. He mentioned he was a French teacher, and that he hoped to spend the following year in France. In view of the impression Adrian had given that they were partners in the same business venture, he'd expected a reaction of surprise. It brought only what he took to be an indifferent nod. They got up to dance but their hearts weren't really in it and they quickly returned to their seats. Then she gave a barely-concealed yawn. This intimation that he might be boring her irritated him. He even contemplated asking her if this was the case. She seemed to read his thoughts and apologized. She was tired. She'd been on night duty all of that week and wouldn't have come if her friend hadn't asked her. Jean had nobody else to go with and she hadn't wanted to let her down. When he offered to run her back to the student nurses' residence where they lodged she accepted with gratitude. He asked her if her friend wouldn't mind. She replied that Jean was 'big enough to find her own way back home.'

The wind had dropped, and as they got into the car he noted that a white patchwork of frost was beginning to glisten on its black roof. When they arrived she said she was sorry not to be able to ask him in for coffee, but men weren't allowed in nurses' rooms after ten. Even if she had invited him he would probably have refused. They exchanged telephone numbers, wished each other a merry Christmas, and parted with vague promises of getting in touch after the holidays. As he drove home he found himself thinking that the evening, while not being a resounding success, had on the whole been better than he'd thought. It had at least allowed him to put into his store another girl whose company might be called upon to help him ease his way through the chilly gloom of an English autumn and winter into warmer, more cheering foreign climes.

TWENTY-THREE

Michael could only exchange a quick word with Adrian as they crossed in the corridor on Monday morning. He and his department colleagues were in the process of reorganizing their arts and crafts room, and this involved them working most of the lunchtime with only the briefest of morning and afternoon breaks. In reply to Michael's hasty question as to whether he had enjoyed the party dance Adrian had replied with a broad wink, a thumbs-up sign and a promise to supply him with more details later on. He'd also walked past Sylvia but she'd been in conversation with another teacher. She'd turned her head briefly towards him and gratified him with a faint smile. He couldn't help noticing a small sticking plaster above one eye. At the end of afternoon lessons he drove straight home, and after greeting Grandpa he settled down in his armchair to peruse the contents of the local evening newspaper while waiting for his parents to come back home. The headline news wasn't of much interest and he was on the point of turning to an inside page when the title of a short article tucked into one of the bottom corners caught his eye. It read as follows:

Schoolteachers in Black-Ice Crash

Schoolteachers John Burton and Sylvia Schofield were lucky to escape injury late last Saturday night when their car skidded on a ring road bend and crashed into a lamp post. They were driving home after spending the evening at the Empire Ballroom in the town centre. 'Even though I was driving slowly I just lost all control as I was taking the bend,' said Mr Burton. 'The road was just like an ice-rink.' Mr Burton's Ford Escort car suffered extensive damage. Both were kept in Bridgeford Infirmary overnight for observation. Miss Schofield is the daughter of Herbert Schofield who owned the popular Majestic Dance Hall in Bankfield for many years. Miss Schofield and Mr Burton teach at Barfield School.

A simple definition states that surprise is that reaction of incredulity we feel on being suddenly confronted with an occurrence of an unforeseen nature. It could also be added by way of corollary that this reluctance of belief may be of a pleasant or unpleasant nature, and that these varying degrees of agreeability or disagreeability depend very much on whether we are directly affected or not. Thus, the news of a sudden, devastating earthquake under distant climes will probably have a more neutral impact on us than that of even the slightest of accidents concerning a close friend or relative nearer to home. The effect this particular disagreeable news had on our young man can be situated at a point somewhere between the two. Though less distressing than if it had involved someone preciously dear close to home, it was considerably more disturbing than if it had concerned a mere stranger in some far-away land. As he turned the implications over in his mind the slightly benumbed shock with which he had at first been seized gave way to mounting anger – despite a vague consciousness that it was fired by a good dose of wounded pride – to which a sense of betrayal was lending a markedly bitter taste.

His anger was directed at both Sylvia and himself. For the article supplied written confirmation of what he had suspected all along: that her recent invitation had simply been a ploy to lure him to the comfort of her home from where she could examine his eligibility more leisurely and in closer detail. The fact that it had taken this to make him realize that what had certainly been a preoccupation skulking at the back of her mind had been immediately obvious to Ian, and possibly others, added to the shameful feeling that by consenting to go along with it he had been stupidly naïve. What's more, he'd been pained by the circumstances of the accident as described in the article. Somewhere they seemed to bring it home that this shared misfortune had joined Sylvia and John Burton together so inseparably that he had now been irrevocably ejected from her scheme of things. The more he thought about it the more the pieces of the puzzle now seemed to slot into place. Didn't the level of familiarity required for them to go dancing together suggest that her *liaison* with John had begun some time before that Saturday evening he'd spent with her? Wasn't it quite possible that she'd spent the previous Saturday entertaining him? Wouldn't this explain her father's apparent indifference to him? Hadn't this been part of a plan to weigh them both in her balance? And wasn't he the person she'd found lacking? Now he knew the real reason why, on walking past her earlier that day, she had a sticking plaster on her forehead, and had only consented to give him the weakest of smiles.

The impact of that blow to his male pride was somewhat softened, however, by the thought that what he now supposed to be her rejection of him was not entirely based on personal grounds. Couldn't it be partly attributed to the fervour with which – the effects of the wine helping – he'd expressed his hopes of spending the following year in France along with his intention of never coming back? And even more wrecked pride was salvaged by the thought that John Burton could not be considered to be a serious rival. For here Michael had no sense of being put in the shade. Though he had never exchanged more than a few words with the man, he was the last person he imagined Sylvia would have been attracted to. He'd always struck Michael as being rather effeminate in his movements and manner; and he didn't seem to be at all sportingly inclined – a disposition which Ian's recent verdict that he was 'a bit of a namby-pamby' only served to confirm. It all went to feed his suspicion that for her finding a husband was less important than the marital state itself.

You would be wrong imagining, however, that a critical appraisal of his own motivations and intentions was beyond our young man's means. Once his anger had begun to subside he began to ask himself questions of a calmer, more objective kind. Could he really blame her? Hadn't he perceived her as little more than a convenient port of call? Hadn't he more or less made it known to her that he consented to some degree of involvement as long as it didn't interfere with his French plans? In short, hadn't he been caught less in her trap than in that of his own egoism? Finally, since there had never been any real commitment between them, didn't she have just as much right as him to frequent the person of her choice? So, when after dinner his mother, on reading the same article, had looked up, and turning towards him eyes that were more curious than worried threw out a, 'Wasn't that the girl you went to see the other Saturday evening?' he was able to muster enough composure to reply with a casual-sounding and what he thought reassuring, 'Yes, that's right. It was just to help her with the French part of her assembly talk.' As his mother's gaze returned to the page he detected what had all the appearances of a knowing smile.

Michael was in the habit of keeping his Monday evenings free to watch a much-praised television documentary series it would require an occurrence of substantial importance for him to be persuaded to miss. It was on the subject of age-old folkloristic events – fairs, feasts and celebrations of varying kinds – taking place in the depths of provincial France. This particular evening's programme was about a unique carnival dating back to the Middle Ages, and taking place in the small town of Saint-Claude in the heart of the Jura Mountains – a region which he'd hardly heard of, let alone visited before. A preview had revealed young men and children wearing long white nightshirts and colourfully ribboned bonnets and brandishing large bellows which they directed under the skirts of recalcitrant, yet giggling women – apparently, it was explained, in an effort to blow away the devil lurking beneath. He had been intrigued and wanted to know more. But he soon became aware he was not giving it that degree of unbroken attention which would normally have been his.

It must not be thought that this lack of concentration on a subject so dear to our young man's heart was the result of a resurge in the anger which the news article had initially unleashed: for the normal digestive process was now reassuming its rights, and the discomfort caused by the dyspepsia it had occasioned was gradually beginning to subside. But despite his reflections on the extent of his own culpability and the resulting return to relative calm they had caused he was unable to suppress the feeling that he'd been the one who'd been wronged the more. So, what he was now contemplating – though he would have been reluctant to admit it to himself – was something approaching what could be called revenge. And isn't revenge a dish which is best eaten cold? As a result, his thoughts were now focusing themselves with some coolness on the future attitude he would adopt towards the young lady – both to her own face and that of others. While his sense of propriety wouldn't allow him to make too noticeable a point of ignoring her completely, he quickly decided that reducing all acknowledgement of her existence to its most basic expression would be an effective way of sending her what he hoped would be the painful message that he had seen through and would never forgive her manipulations. As far as others were concerned his strategy would be simple. He had already put it to his mother that his relationship with Sylvia was no more than a friendly, professional one. He wasn't entirely convinced he had succeeded but, after all, wasn't she the person who knew him the best? With his colleagues, however, he couldn't prevent himself from hoping that the air of scornful indifference he was determined to affect whenever her name came up in conversation might go some way towards casting doubts on the favourable reputation she enjoyed among most of the teachers. And if the worst came to the worst and people like Ian or Adrian made ironic remarks, couldn't he let it be known that it was he himself who had put a stop to it all?

As the televised film of the carnival in the distant Jura Mountains was entering into one of its more interesting phases he turned his mind to reviewing those situations which might entail some likelihood of them meeting. Paradoxically, the risk of direct contact with her in the staff room was relatively remote: though it was crowded with teachers just before morning assembly, prior to afternoon lessons, and especially during morning and afternoon break, some powerful conservative force (the psychology of which I will not attempt to explain) caused staff to sit in the same seats, or to stand chatting and drinking their coffee or tea with the same clique of colleagues in more or less the same spot. Fortunately, Sylvia was in the habit of frequenting a part distant and unfamiliar enough for him to venture into on only the most exceptional of occasions. As far as he could see, the only serious risk was that of a face-to-face confrontation which a simultaneous free period might bring. In cases like this he would need to be careful; but since she was certainly aware he had read the newspaper article and had made all the necessary deductions, he didn't entirely exclude the possibility that her own plans might now be directing themselves along similar lines. Of one thing he was sure: she would no longer be found seated alone reading *Time Magazine* in a corner of the staff room after normal school hours.

The next day he noted her presence on the other side of the staff room during the morning break. She was standing side by side with John in earnest conversation with three or four colleagues. Its subject could only be the accident they'd had. Though he had to admit that the proper thing for him to do would be to go along and make polite enquiries about the state of their health, and that not doing so would be taken as an admission of the offence she had caused, he couldn't bring himself to do it: somewhere it struck him that this sympathizing circle of people openly discussing the misfortune the pair had suffered together provided confirmatory public recognition that they now enjoyed the status of a bonded couple. It wasn't as if he was jealous – he was now convinced she was simply husband hunting and that John was her only remaining prospect; but he hadn't been able to swallow his pride enough to overcome the feeling that her definitive rejection precluded any chance of him being able to present her with direct proof of those positive qualities he was sure he possessed.

That lunchtime he ate in the refectory with Jennifer and other colleagues. During the meal conversation took a fluttering course following sundry, insubstantial subjects, lightly tossed into the air, before settling on a topic that attracted them all: that of the impending Christmas holidays. It was at this point Jennifer announced that for her the coming Friday would be a doubly enjoyable occasion: not only would they be celebrating the breaking up of school by the traditional staff Christmas lunch but her birthday fell on this same day. As she spoke an idea entered Michael's head. Why not offer her a present to mark the event? It needn't be anything fancy – a nice box of chocolates would do the trick. He'd wrap it up in Christmas paper with a 'Happy Birthday from Michael' label and wait for an appropriate moment before the lunch to slip it discreetly into her hands. He was sure it would be appreciated. After all she was a colleague he felt a friendly affection for. Wouldn't it consolidate the pleasant working relations which existed between them? The thought made him glow with pleasure.

TWENTY-FOUR

Adrian needed very little, if any prompting at all to share with Michael his general impressions of the student party dance they had attended, and to supply more personal details as to the events which followed his encounter with that effervescent young lady who seemed to have made it all worthwhile. They'd stayed right up to the end; then, like Michael, he'd run her back to the nurses' home. Without going into any explicit particulars he did, nonetheless, reveal they had lingered quite a while in the car before the increasingly invasive cold had got the better of their conjoined body heat, and had compelled them to kiss a shivery goodbye. Despite the ambient freshness they'd got on 'like a house on fire,' and when more propitious circumstances presented themselves, as he was confident they would, the events of the evening gave every promise of more 'intimate' things to come. And by 'intimate', he added with a broad grin, he meant a union of both body and mind. Jean had a room on the same floor as Molly and he'd even paid her a surprise visit yesterday evening. However, it was her turn to work on the night shift during this last week before Christmas and, as she had to be on duty at 9 o'clock, the time they could spend together had had to be curtailed. He'd also had a quick chat with Molly; she'd asked him to tell Michael she was looking forward to seeing him when she came back from Ireland after Christmas. This was not without causing our young man some surprise: he'd not thought much of her since their first meeting and he'd imagined it must be the same with her. Her real name was Mary, Jean had informed Adrian, but everybody called her Molly. This was not just because the name was a familiar version of Mary; her surname was, in fact, Malone. It had brought to mind the famous song and this had led him and Jean on to talk about cockles and mussels.

131

He'd told her he liked sea food – especially mussels – and she'd told him she loved them, too, 'especially the big, juicy ones'. This had caused them to roar with laughter. She was going back home to Birmingham for Christmas – but only for three or four days. It occurred to Michael that the length of her stay might well have been abridged (Molly had told him she would be away for a week) as a result of her meeting Adrian. Oh yes, and he'd given her a T-shirt, too.

Given the enthusiasm with which he spoke, Michael had the impression that one of the results of his friend's encounter was, for the moment at least, to have pushed all thoughts of their T-shirt project to the back of his mind. A 'Now, to get down to business I've got some interesting news', proved this was not the case. This interesting news was provided by a telephone conversation Adrian had had. On arriving home yesterday afternoon there was a note waiting for him from his mum. A man had phoned while she was having lunch. He wanted to speak to the person who'd sold the T-shirts at Bridgeford Market and had left a number for him to phone back. Though it was a matter of some importance he wouldn't say anything more. So, the first thing Adrian did when he got home was to ring him back. He was the sales manager of a small garment manufacturing company located in a neighbouring town. They'd recently decided to include printed T-shirts in their range of clothes and were looking to outsource the printing of a batch of a thousand. Could they handle this? It could lead to regular business. They would supply everything: the blank T-shirts, the silk screen and design, the inks. The delivery deadline would be two weeks. If he thought this was possible they could go on to discuss prices. In view of the urgency he'd be grateful if he could have an answer as soon as possible. Adrian had told him he'd have to discuss this with his partner and would get back as quickly as he could. What did Michael think?

It was obvious they were neither equipped nor disposed of enough time to satisfy such a large-scale demand. Moreover, wasn't it their ambition to produce and market rather than limiting themselves to being simple outsourcers? Even though it was neither feasible nor desirable that they meet the request, it provided an encouraging measure of both the interest they had already aroused, and the speed at which things could evolve. It took some reflection before they finally realized how this company had got hold of Adrian's telephone number. It could only have been through that sole market stallholder to have requested a receipt. His was the last stall they'd visited and as they'd only had three T-shirts left he'd asked for their telephone number in case he needed more. Since the shirts were printed in his mum's kitchen, Adrian had given him his parents' number. A representative from the company had certainly called at the stall, seen their T-shirts and passed the information on to his boss.

Afterwards, Adrian's mum had been curious enough to enquire as to what the call was all about. When he told her, she'd asked him quite pointedly if 'they'd now found somebody else's kitchen to mess up with all that ink.' He'd replied in the negative while adding that they were looking into it. It had served as another reminder of what he was beginning to fear: that his mother was firm in her refusal to allow any more printing to be done in her kitchen. So, hadn't it now become a matter of some urgency to find some suitable work premises to rent? And not only that. Shouldn't they now start doing some serious thinking about starting up as a business concern? Couldn't they take advantage of the approaching Christmas holidays to obtain information about the costs involved in buying wholesale supplies of blank T-shirts and producing new silk-screen designs? They could even make enquiries as to the existence of automated machinery. Though Adrian had simply talked about making enquiries Michael couldn't help feeling alarmed that, contrary to his previous estimations, Adrian should be thinking along such committed lines, and that in a future which now seemed to be approaching much faster than he would have liked they could be plunged into deeper, more hostile seas where the right decisions and a determined commitment in terms of time, effort and money would be needed to keep them afloat. Wasn't there a risk that events might soon begin to run against the wait-and-see strategy he'd decided upon? Weren't things in danger of getting out of his control? It wasn't that he wouldn't go along with what his friend had just said. It was certainly information they needed to have. For the moment, however, he was not prepared to go beyond. They decided to phone each other after the Christmas festivities to agree on a mutually convenient date to view possible premises together and gain some idea of an average rent. They might even find time to visit the wholesale buying centre Adrian had mentioned in an attempt to dispose of the dozen or so T-shirts they had remaining. It was one of the main suppliers of shops specializing in low-priced teenage casual wear in both Bridgeford and neighbouring towns. Didn't it represent a step-up from the humble market stall?

You must not imagine by this that Michael hadn't once more thought about speaking frankly to Adrian about the dilemma he was afraid he might soon find himself in and his resulting wish not to get too involved at this stage. But another reflection was now beginning to dawn. If Jean and Adrian's recently-begun relationship followed the course it appeared to be taking it might not prove necessary: for though they didn't seem to have yet fallen completely in love weren't they both showing unmistakable signs they were quite prepared to do so? And if they did, wouldn't Adrian inevitably be led to devote far less time to their venture? So, perhaps he might be able to count on Jean's involuntary co-operation to help him along with his plans.

TWENTY-FIVE

The end-of-term staff Christmas lunch took place as planned that Friday. The two large rectangular tables which normally occupied opposite sides of the staffroom had been pushed end to end in the middle, and some twenty chairs positioned around. It had then been laid out in festive splendour by two apron-clad ladies, temporarily liberated from those exertions confining them to the kitchen and refectory. Two weeks previously a type-written notice had been pinned on the staffroom board informing teachers of this traditional event, and inviting those wishing to attend to append their names to the space provided beneath. Though its writer had chosen to remain anonymous, it was generally agreed that, given her official administrative functions together with the fierce efficiency with which she carried them out, it would not be unreasonable to assume it was Miss Dobson. As I have previously had occasion to mention, Miss Dobson was the senior mistress of this co-educational school whom – apart from the fact that she had straggly, mousy-coloured hair, watery blue, bespectacled eyes, was of an indeterminate age and had rarely been seen to smile – I will leave you to picture for yourselves. It was Miss Dobson who had also been allocated the task (or perhaps she had allocated it to herself), which she was now carrying out, paper in hand, with her customary zeal, of informing new arrivals as they came in of the seat that had been assigned to them and which, by some esoteric process in which coincidence played little part, bore an extraordinary resemblance to the rank teachers occupied in the school order of things. Michael had recently been given cause to believe he was now enjoying Miss Dobson's favours. It was Miss Dobson herself who had supplied him with an indirect explanation as to why.

Now at Barfield School not only was there a problem of truancy among pupils but an inclination towards absenteeism on the part of some of the junior teachers. Since pupils couldn't be left alone in a classroom other teachers had to be found to fill in for their lessons. Appointing these substitute teachers was another of Miss Dobson's duties. Naturally, she could only choose among those who would normally have enjoyed a free period that day. So, every morning when it became obvious that a teacher or teachers would not be coming to work she would quickly prepare a substitution list, slip into the staffroom, and pin it on the notice board a few minutes before they all trooped out for assembly. Understandably, those who would normally have benefited from a free period that day viewed this moment with some apprehension. They could, however, gain some comfort from the fact that, whenever possible, the teachers called upon to substitute were chosen from among those who were the most frequently absent. During his first year at Barfield Michael had sometimes been obliged to give up these forty minutes of relative freedom – not because he was one of those teachers who were often absent but simply because there was no-one else. And even when a more senior teacher's free period coincided with one of his own Miss Dobson would systematically choose him. It was as if as a new teacher he had to prove himself over some pre-defined period before any concessions would be made. Not that he considered these replacement lessons to be really a chore. The problem was that as a specialized teacher of French, it was not within his professional competence to give lessons in geography or mathematics. He'd solved this by the simple expedient of buying a book of short ghost stories and reading them aloud to the class he was substituting for. He was a good reader and it kept them enthralled. He loved seeing their open-mouthed, wide-eyed faces hanging on to each of his theatrically-pronounced words. Michael himself had never once been absent – a fact which Miss Dobson had suggested could be put down to him living at home. He'd taken a little exception to her explanation: he liked to think that even if he had lived independently of his parents, as was the case with his offending colleagues, he would have had enough professional conscience not to do the same. Fortunately for him, Miss Dobson seemed to base her choice of replacement teachers on effects rather than those causes which she herself seemed somewhere to consider as mitigating circumstances. The result was that now in this first term of his second year he hadn't once been called upon to substitute.

So, Michael wasn't totally surprised when Miss Dobson who, after positioning herself on the right of Headmaster Fowler's presiding seat at the top of the table (Deputy Head Cooper was strategically located on his left), beckoned him to sit at her other side. It was somewhere a public confirmation of her professional esteem. Though he would have denied this to his colleagues, he couldn't help feeling rather honoured. The sobering reflection did, however, pass through his mind that, apart from a willingness to resist the temptation to stay in bed, professional competence at this school didn't stretch much beyond a teacher's ability to establish and maintain classroom order.

While they were waiting for Mr Fowler to take possession of his seat Michael discreetly surveyed the participants. It was not so much to see who was present as to ascertain those who were noticeable by their absence. John and Sylvia, Adrian along with Ian and Mrs Boxley were among the latter. He had heard rumours that Mrs Boxley had resigned and after the holidays would be taking up a more promising post in a school of higher repute. It occurred to him that a rival gathering might have been organized in a nearby pub to celebrate her leaving and they'd all gone there. After Headmaster Fowler had taken his seat and was saying grace Michael remembered this same lunch last year when he'd been instructed to tell the French *assistante* to disappear. He still felt some pain at his servile display of compliance; and he couldn't stop himself from wondering whether this unfortunate incident was some-where the cause of the school having no French *assistante* this year.

Jennifer was seated at the opposite end of the table. As he looked down in her direction her eyes met his and her face lit up in a radiant smile. Conveniently, her last lesson on Friday mornings took place in the classroom opposite his, and when the bell rang its end he'd waited until he was satisfied all her pupils had filed out. He'd then slipped in and presented her with his birthday wishes along with the gift. She'd been far more touched than he'd anticipated. She'd rewarded him with a spontaneous, 'Oh, that's so thoughtful of you! And it's so beautifully wrapped!' Her eyes had moistened and she'd thanked him profusely several times. He couldn't avoid reflecting that once would have been enough. After all, her expressions of gratitude were out of all proportion to the value and nature of the gift, and the less than delicate artistry with which the wrapping paper had been placed around. On the whole, it wasn't quite the reaction he would have liked: it gave him the uncomfortable impression she was seizing this opportunity to let him know it was the man she valued more than the offering. But his unease was somewhat appeased by the thought that, contrary to Sylvia's apparent calm and collected restraint, her emotional reaction could probably be explained by her belonging to the more impulsive type. After all, some women were governed by reason while others were ruled more by the heart. He was not without being aware that he had allowed himself a judgement of the more sweeping kind. But in the tortuous recesses of the female mind didn't it serve as a vague guiding light?

I will not dwell at any great length on this festive staffroom moment during which certain rites were respected and others were not, and where conversation never found a strong enough force of momentum to propel itself beyond the rigidly professional or the stiffly banal. Let me simply state that a good proportion of the participants – especially those seated at the less senior end – felt some relief when Headmaster Fowler, after wishing them all the season's greetings, announced the end of the luncheon by rising to depart – not before reminding them that, as was the school custom each year, the final afternoon lesson would be replaced by a special Christmas service in the assembly hall. I will again not embark upon a detailed description of this more elevating Christmas event. Suffice it to say that solemn prayers were said, stirring carols were sung, and pious words were pronounced on the need to embrace more closely those elusive Christian virtues of charity, forgiveness, peace and love.

After the ceremony most teachers took themselves straight off home. Others, temporarily deprived of a means of locomotion enabling them to do the same, remained behind for a final, pre-holiday chat. Before driving home Michael decided to take the direction of the staffroom in the hope of seeing Adrian to confirm their plans. As he was walking back Jennifer came hurrying up.

'I wish you a lovely Christmas,' she said. There was a noticeable earnestness in her voice. He found himself feeling uncomfortable that her words should be so pointedly directed at him.

'Thanks very much. The same for you,' he replied. 'I hope you won't have to wait long before Geoff comes.' It was spoken more as a way of orienting the conversation in a more neutral direction than as an expression of any real concern.

'Oh, he'll turn up eventually, I suppose.'

He was surprised by the apparent indifference which her words implied. They stationed themselves by the staffroom window.

'Will you be going away for Christmas?' he asked.

'Oh no. On Christmas Day Mum and Dad are coming. And on Boxing Day it'll be the turn of my parents-in-law.'

'So you'll be doing all the Christmas cooking?'

'Oh, you know, it doesn't bother me all that much. It keeps my mind off things,' she replied. He couldn't avoid thinking – not without some irritation – that somewhere her remark was intended to show him she was open to any advances he might care to make.

'Does Geoff cook?' he asked by way of imparting a less personal tone to their conversation as well as giving her a chance to present her husband in a more redemptory light.

'Oh he does in a basic sort of way but I usually relegate him to setting the table and doing the washing up.'

The window they were standing by looked out onto the school car park, and after ten minutes of desultory conversation he was relieved to see her spouse arrive. He parked his car in its usual place but made no effort to get out. Jennifer seemed to be doing her best not to see him.

'Oh, talk of the Devil, here's Jeff now,' he said in an effort to oblige her to admit his presence.

'Yes, well he can just wait. What about you? What will you be doing?'

'Nothing really exciting. I'll be spending it with the family at home. My sister and her husband will be coming for Christmas, and I think we're going to their house on Boxing Day. My sister's expecting a baby soon.' He immediately regretted having introduced this new line of conversation.

'Really? When is it due?'

'I don't know exactly. There's still a bit to go.'

He'd decided that by providing brief and vague answers to her questions with no further interrogatives on his part she might take the hint that it was time for her to leave; but, instead of abridging the conversation, she seemed to want to draw it out. He again looked out of the window, this time with growing unease. Her husband was getting out of his car. A moment later he was marching into the staffroom. Without even looking at Michael he strode up to his wife, his face clouded in anger.

'Didn't you see me? I've been waiting for you for the past ten minutes!'

She continued talking to Michael as if deaf to his words. He expected this to produce an even more furious reaction on the part of her husband but his voice took on a distraught, uncomprehending tone.

'Jenny, what's the matter with you? Why don't you answer me?'

'I must be going now. Happy Christmas to you both. Goodbye,' Michael hastily declared, without looking at either. As he was leaving the apologetic glance he'd been unable to avoid giving her was enough for him to see the stupefaction and then the hatred which blazed up in her eyes.

TWENTY-SIX

All things considered, the Christmas festivities went better than Michael had expected. On Christmas Day his anxieties had been focused on those barely-hidden tensions simmering between his father and Grandpa and which he feared might surface enough to disturb that semblance of family peace which Yuletide custom requires. This is not to say, however, that the day was not marked by an incident which might justify us saying that it didn't get off to the most desirable of starts. And it didn't come from the quarter he'd expected.

As planned, Michael's sister and her husband came for the day. Almost immediately after they had divested themselves of their coats and the usual season's greetings had been exchanged, that normally agreeable ritual of present giving began. Michael's brother-in-law presented his wife with a bottle of expensive French perfume, exquisitely boxed and wrapped, accompanied by a sumptuous Christmas card in which his spousal feelings were fondly expressed. Michael's father had, on the other hand, deemed it more practical to bestow on his spouse a few days before the more down-to-earth gift of plain cash. This had the triple advantage of relieving him of the effort required in deciding on a suitable present and then going out to buy it, while at the same time enabling his wife to 'get yourself something you *really* want.' But the idea had not entered his head of buying a small, token gift to give her in return for the secateurs and gardening gloves she now offered him. This might have been forgiven had he not committed the additional sin of confronting her with the fact that she would not even be the recipient of a card. It was certainly the comparison she made between the thoughtfulness her son-in-law had shown towards his wife and the absence of any corresponding consideration on her husband's part which made her burst out into harsh words of recrimination. Though Michael felt his mother's anger could be justified, he could only note that a lack of discernment had been shown in choosing this place and time to give such vehement expression to it. Didn't propriety require that this type of marital reproach be reserved for a private moment? Didn't it reveal a lack of solicitude for their guests while humiliating the person to whom it was addressed? The wrath it aroused in his father was expressed by the two bitterly expectorated words, 'You bitch!' Despite the violence of the reaction Michael had felt some sympathy for his dad.

Though during the course of lunch his father did manage to regain enough composure to be able to address civil enough words to their guests, his son and even his wife, and had embraced the Christmas spirit to the point of pronouncing one or two not too ironic words in the vague direction of Grandpa, the incident added more force to Michael's growing resolution that if his application was again refused and he decided to accompany his parents down South he'd have no hesitation in renting his own little flat. Another result of this confrontation was to cause our young man to ponder – not without a certain bitter amusement – on the ravages which more than 30 years of marital co-habitation can bring. The extent of the damage could be measured by a recent discovery he'd made.

It all started when he read a magazine article on the value of old English coins. It reminded him that Grandpa was in possession of a golden guinea dating back to the early eighteen hundreds and which had been passed on to him by his own grandfather. When Michael was a child it had been frequently extracted from the small glass case in which it was always kept and presented to him as a precious family heirloom. So, being curious to know if it figured among the coins in the article and, if so, how much it was worth, he asked the elderly gentleman where it could be found. Grandpa informed him that he'd given it to his daughter some while ago. It didn't take much reflection for Michael to realize where it would be.

Now Michael's parents kept all important household documents and articles of value – the house deeds, insurance contracts, bankbooks, jewellery and things like that – in a large tin box reposing at the bottom of their bedroom wardrobe. After rummaging through its contents he soon found what he was looking for. He'd also come across an unsealed brown foolscap size envelope which seemed to have served no purpose. He couldn't resist the temptation to look inside. It contained a score or more of Christmas and birthday cards along with sundry gift labels from another age. A yellowing white envelope caught his eye. Its stamp bore the head of George VI. There was a Christmas card inside. On opening it he read, couched in what he recognized as his father's flowing hand, the words 'To my dearest, darling wife'.

TWENTY-SEVEN

It had been arranged that immediately after the Christmas celebrations Adrian would phone Michael to agree on a day when they could go looking for suitable work premises together. Being without news, it was Michael who rang. His pal's mother informed him that her son was down with a bad bout of flu and that the doctor had confined him to the warmth of his bed for the next few days. Given Jean's working *milieu*, it crossed his mind that it was she who had probably vectored the bug. As he asked Adrian's mum to give her son his best wishes for a speedy recovery he found himself hoping she hadn't detected the note of cheer in his voice. Didn't this all fit in with the delaying strategy he'd decided on? Didn't this mean that the plans they had discussed would now have to be put off to some later date?

This welcome news, along with icy weather, freed Michael of both the obligation and desire to set much foot outside. And during those post Christmas days of a fast-disappearing year he indulged himself fully in his dominical habit of spending the mornings reading and dozing in bed. In the afternoons, after desultory lunchtime conversation with Grandpa (his parents were now back at the shop) on things long since past, he would retire to his room where he resumed his laborious study of Hervé Bazin's minutely descriptive prose; and a French radio station allowed him to replace this exercise by one which required him to transfer concentration from eye to ear. He was also becoming increasingly aware that he'd have to start giving some thought to his future assembly talk. Though it would, of course, have some connection with France, he hadn't yet decided on anything more specific. During the end-of-term staff Christmas lunch he'd taken advantage of his position next to Miss Dobson to ask her if she could possibly schedule it for the second week after the holidays. The exact day didn't matter. He'd justified his request by pretexting absence from home for most of the Christmas vacation. It was one of those untruths which his work at the brewery had accustomed him to classifying as harmless. After all it hurt nobody and furthered not much more than his own minor interests. But she'd been curious enough to ask him where he'd be going, and he'd been obliged to expand the falsehood more than he would have liked by pretending he'd been invited to spend a few days with an old student friend and his wife who had just bought a house in the Midlands. It reminded him of the dry cleaning fib which had hastened the end of his engagement with Vicky.

'I'll see what I can do,' she'd replied with a nod and the glimmerings of a rare smile.

You will probably have guessed that Michael didn't belong to that category of people who so much hate being alone with themselves that the first thing they do on coming back to an empty home is to turn on the television or radio simply for the reassuring feeling of human presence this imparts. If you asked him whether he preferred to spend more time in his own company than that of others he might even have been tempted to choose the former. He enjoyed these moments of solitude: they were a time for reflection, the posing of questions and the search for honest answers. And as the afternoon hours began to fade into darkness he would close his books, turn off the radio, settle back in his chair and allow his mind to run back over the more notable events of this moribund year before pondering on those which the next one might have in store. Some of these questions and especially their answers gave rise to considerable pain.

It is barely imaginable in a young man of such an inward-looking nature that the causes and effects of that unfortunate culmination to the last school term did not occupy much of his thoughts, and that the meditative conditions provided by these limbo days between Christmas and the approaching new year did not prompt in him the rueful reflection that it is often only when we are faced with the distressing consequences of our own heedless acts that we attempt a more scrupulous examination of their motives. It was his handling of relations with Jennifer on which his ruminations first alighted. Hadn't it fallen not far short of disaster? And wasn't it he who had been mostly at fault? For he soon came to admitting that his main intention in presenting his colleague with a birthday offering was less to give her pleasure than the desire to produce the opposite effect in Sylvia: since he was sure Jennifer would inform her friend of his gift, hadn't his real aim been to create painful doubt in Sylvia's mind by suggesting she might be the loser in preferring John Burton to such a thoughtful person as himself? Hadn't he played with Jennifer's feelings in order to do this? Hadn't he used her as little more than an instrument of revenge? It had been a reprehensible act which, beyond the distress it had caused her, he was ashamed to think he'd been capable of. What's more, though Jennifer certainly didn't suspect the real reasons, the effect of his gift had been to lead her to believe that he returned the affection she obviously had for him enough for her to consider his sudden departure from the staffroom as an unforgiveable betrayal. How else could he interpret the hatred he had seen in her eyes? Hadn't he now alienated her for good? Wasn't the decision he'd taken to wash his hands on a regrettable situation he himself had been largely responsible for creating somewhere too facile a way out? Wasn't it Jennifer and her husband who would now have to bear most of the consequences? And didn't the falseness of his behaviour towards Jennifer make him guilty of that same manipulative conduct he reproached so much in Sylvia? This is not to say that these feelings of guilt were not made slightly easier to bear by the thought that Jennifer wasn't totally without blame. Why had she made it so obvious she was attracted to him? Hadn't he given her discreet but unmistakable signs that he rejected anything more than a friendly relationship? Why had she married a man she had so little respect and affection for? But he was especially cheered by the stern promise he made to himself that if ever again he was tempted to play this sort of masquerade he would first consider its possible consequences.

In addition, our hero (if I may be permitted the use of such a grandiose word) had enough self-honesty to be aware of a gross incoherency within. For though he had confided in Sylvia his great hopes of spending the following year in France and had even given her to believe he would never come back, he now seemed to be regretting not being able to pursue a relationship whose burgeoning evolution might have choked all immediate desire to go there, or could even have flowered into a union he had repeatedly expressed an aversion for and which would certainly have obliged him to abandon his dream for ever. But in his secret conscience there was enough deepening realization for him to see that, rather than being more involved with Sylvia than he had thought, he had allowed himself to be ruled by an excess of pride; and while this common human failing may be considered not too bad a thing when it helps us to conceal our hurts from others, it can only be nefarious when it causes us to hurt them.

As he turned his meditations to the coming year is it surprising that such a reflective person as Michael should have become conscious of other doubts and inconsistencies gnawing at him from within, and which seemed to feed the growing apprehension that he had only the vaguest glimmerings of who he was and what he really wanted to do with his life? And what is more understandable that in view of their potentially life-changing importance it was their business venture and his French exchange on which his thoughts then focused. Despite the wait-and-see strategy he had decided upon, he was still troubled by the nagging fear that a time might come when he would be obliged to choose between the two. How could he know his own mind well enough to be sure of making the right choice? Wasn't he attracted by both? Didn't they both represent a form of adventure? Didn't they both bring their own type of reward? For while the rewards of the one consisted mainly in outward material gain those of the other enriched the person within. But the more he thought about it the more he was seized by the chilling thought that they might both be illusory aims. Couldn't they simply be a way of escaping from himself? Were his disappointing academic results, his failed first love, his negative job experience, the growing tedium of school, the poisoned home atmosphere and that disastrous management of relations with his two female colleagues not simply due to youthful heedlessness or unfortunate circumstance, but the doings of some repulsive reptile which lived within the person? Would this loathsome inner creature which had poisoned his past and was now infecting the present leave its slimy traces on his future? But there again, was he becoming so overwhelmed by his imperfections that he was losing sight of the qualities?

It was certainly the thought that any successful adventure begins by an exploration of the self which led him to ask whether the solution to this *crise de conscience* lay in seeking out those more positive attributes that surely resided within: that by some interactive chemistry of self-discovery, a deeper, more prolonged analysis of his feelings, reactions and motivations would serve as a sort of catalyzing agent accelerating that process whereby those distant, sporadic and increasingly somber glimpses of himself would be transformed into a more acute awareness of who he really was, and where his natural qualities and propensities lay. Wouldn't the self-realization which such an analysis brought provide him with the means of building a more solid foundation to the path of his future life?

One of the first things these deepening introspective examinations brought to the fore of his consciousness was that, paradoxically enough, the distress he felt at his own shameful conduct towards Jennifer and Sylvia could be viewed as a reason for perceiving himself in a more redemptory light. Wasn't the very admission of his guilt both an indication of his basic self-honesty and a sign that the standards within him were stricter than he might have imagined? Wasn't the mental pain he'd endured a measure of the self-condemnation which his misconduct had brought? And didn't this all go to suggest that a lesson had been learned and that in future he would act in a more responsible and principled a way?

It was his former work at the brewery which next occupied his thoughts. What were the reasons for him not liking the job? The answers he pondered took the form of a series of rhetorical questions. Hadn't he been part of a system which tended towards objectives too restrictive in nature in so much as these were focused exclusively on financial gain? Wasn't this quest for mere profit an inevitable source of conflict and all too liable to bring out the doubtful, even sordid aspects of human nature? Wouldn't he have found it far more fulfilling to have been able to pursue, in a spirit of amicable co-operation, that nobler, self-ameliorative road which leads beyond the acquisition of material gain to a growing awareness of where your better self lies? And as far as his own better self was concerned, the main result of his inward ponderings was a growing awareness that deep within lay a person who, unlike the down-to-earth realist he had previously imagined himself to be, was struggling to see things as they could be rather than as they really are. He had to confess, however, that he didn't belong to that category of what he considered to be dangerously naïve idealists for whom money is a vile, befouling sort of thing. For he would have been the first to admit that filthy lucre, as it is termed by some, brought not just an appreciable comfort to life but could be an important factor of freedom. It was simply that he could never envisage it as a goal in itself. He also felt some unease at the thought that it could serve as a means of domination over others. He didn't aspire to command; nor was he one of those inspirers of people to come together and work towards a common goal perceived as being far greater than anything that could be achieved alone. He was of an independent nature and wished neither to lead nor to be led. He simply wanted to be at the helm of his own destiny, free to set his sails in the direction of territories which would add to the inner riches of the self.

It must not, however, be thought that our young man's search for improvement was limited to his own person and that there didn't lie within a wish to produce a similar quest for discovery in others. For as he pondered the more it became clear why his experience with the off-licence manageress had caused his cup of disillusion to overflow to the point of confirming his decision to resign. Though he condemned her deceit and thieving, he'd still been frustrated by the fact that they were both cogs in a machine which, when she'd been found defective, had obliged him to discard and replace her by another, hopefully more efficient one. Wouldn't he have found true satisfaction in being able to guide her along that same road to discovery of that better person which certainly lay hidden somewhere within? He did, however, have enough realistic appreciation of himself and others to see that he might have fallen short of his goal. But it went to reinforce his conviction that he had been right in taking the decision to leave this first employment and embark on a more vocational course.

Another effect of Michael's newly discovered ideality was the realization that their T-shirt project – though it did set an entrepreneurial chord vibrating within – corresponded less to his real nature than he had previously thought. It was true that it could provide him with a new and exciting diversion from the tedium, the conflicts, and the uninspiring prospects that were making their presence more and more intrusively felt both at work and home. What's more, by enabling him to prove to himself that he was capable of meeting those challenges necessary to achieving a worthwhile business goal, it could be a source of enough personal satisfaction to allow him to regain some lost self-esteem. But even though he had to admit he was also not insensible to the material rewards and social recognition this type of success would bring, it still remained that all his efforts would be too narrowly subservient to the dictates of financial gain. So, all in all, weren't these ruminations now making it increasingly clear that the added personal dimension that living in a foreign country would certainly bring was in closer correspondence to his deeper nature?

It was certainly in an attempt to add more brush strokes to that portrait of the inner man which was now beginning so encouragingly to emerge that during those same late December days he began a closer exploration of those reasons for him having always felt such a strong attraction for France. His first remembered vibrations could be traced back to an early age when, one evening during his final primary school year, his parents' conversation had, for some reason or other, turned to France and his mum had told him he'd be learning French at his new school. His excitement, with which mingled a strong dose of curiosity, was caused by the thought that he would soon be able to view through the telescope of its language a land he already perceived, without really knowing why, as being intriguingly different to his own – despite the fact that the children's comics he read at the time frequently portrayed the Frenchman (especially in his Canadian form) as a treacherous, *béret*-topped, pencil-moustached fiend who'd take advantage of the slightest opportunity to stab the upright, blond-haired Englishman in the back.

Even so, he couldn't say it was love at first sight. For his French lessons were conducted by a stern, elderly schoolmaster who not only seemed to make a point of never speaking to them in French, but succeeded in mystifying (and boring) his pupils by attempting to drill into them (without the slightest explanation as to what it was all about) the phonetics of the language: the spoken language was broken down into its individual sounds to each of which was attributed an odd-looking symbol (so strange, in fact, that he remembered asking himself whether by some mysterious process learning French first involved mastering the letters of the ancient Greek alphabet). For the next two weeks or so lessons consisted in him suspending a phonetic chart on a hook above the blackboard and pointing to each symbol with a rather vicious-looking cane whose intimidating appearance was enough to persuade the class to chant in perfect unison the corresponding sounds. Individual boys were then randomly summoned to stand up and repeat the same. It was with a feeling of immense relief on the part of them all that suddenly, for no apparent reason, the body of phonetics was buried – never again to be exhumed – and a new life was infused into their lessons by the distribution of what was undoubtedly the standard textbook of the day. Curiously, it was its outdated nature which first set the young boy dreaming. For it was antiquated enough to be illustrated by black and white drawings of what he later came to learn was a bygone rural age: hens scratching on a huge farmyard manure heap; a smock-clad peasant guiding an ox-drawn plough; his sabot-shoed wife peeling potatoes by the farmhouse door; a donkey-mounted peasant girl taking her fruit and vegetables to market. And this close association between the French way of life and some picturesque, bucolic idyll opened up a perspective which allowed his young mind enough scope to transport him beyond existing horizons to a land perceived as being fascinatingly strange. And as he later came to realize, his dreams took their inspiration in this kind of limitless vista: for the reason he disliked chemistry at school was that, being restricted to the observation and subsequent write-up of known interactions, it left little room for him to express his own creative imagination. It was becoming increasingly clear, even at this tender age, that much of the appeal of France lay in a desire to take flight: that the attraction he felt for these long-past rural scenes was prompted by the release they gave from the grim, polluted industrial environment he felt imprisoned in at that time and from which he'd already resolved to do all in his power to escape.

But it was a school trip which set this budding affection well along the way to flowering into a lasting love. At school they were fortunate enough to have had a German teacher who, no doubt aware of the broadening effect travel can have on young minds, took it upon himself to organize trips abroad during the summer holidays of each year. One year it was to Germany, the next to Switzerland, and two whole weeks had been planned on the French Mediterranean coast for the end of Michael's first school year. As luck would have it (the egoism of childhood made him view things in a heartless sort of way), his dad's mother had departed this earth a few weeks earlier, and left his sister and himself the grand sum of £20 each in her will. Having confided in his mum that he'd really love to go on this trip, she gave him to understand that if he asked Dad 'nicely' – while at the same time suggesting his part of Grandma Morgan's legacy could be used to meet the cost – he might be given permission to go. This he did in a tentative kind of way. Perhaps she'd had a quiet word with her husband before but, contrary to his worst forebodings, paternal consent was immediately forthcoming. It was even accompanied by a spontaneous, 'That's a good idea. It'll broaden your horizons, my lad!' His dad's endorsement was doubly gratifying: not only did it cause him to perceive his begetter in a far more liberal light, but it filled him with an exhilaration he'd never known before. It was prompted by the realization that in only a few months' time he would be setting off on a fascinating voyage of discovery of a world that was unknown. From then on, each evening after going to bed and before saying his prayers, he'd pull out his Christmas diary; and, after crossing off that day, he would proceed to count those separating him from that longed-for departure date. And early one bright August morning his dad, accompanied of course by Mum, drove him to Bridgeford Station where he joined the 60 or so pupils and teachers who were to be his companions, guides and protectors during the following two weeks.

After chugging down to King's Cross (these were the days of the steam locomotive), they crossed London to Victoria Station where they took the train to Dover. Here they caught the ferry to Calais and then a train to Paris. Late that evening at the *Gare de Lyon* they embarked on that legendary night express, *le Mistral*, which was to carry them to their destination of Nice. Not even a mostly sleepless night spent trying to find a comfortable position on a French second class railway carriage bench, along with seven other restless little boys, could subdue the trembling excitement which seized him as dawn broke and he caught breathtaking glimpses of the indigo sea they were now running parallel to. This was nothing to the rapture he felt at the sights, sounds and smells that greeted them when the train pulled into the station. As he stepped down onto the platform he was seized by a strange feeling of walking on air: it was as if he was now entering a totally unimagined new world where a lighter gravitational pull caused ripe apples to float more gently to the ground.

You must not imagine, however, that the young Michael was allowed to remain long in the belief that what for him was a terrestrial paradise should necessarily be viewed by others in the same idyllic light: for he was quickly made aware that his own willingness to embrace those differences that are an intrinsic part of the lives of others was not shared by many of his schoolmates who frequently maintained an attitude of suspicion, distrust or even contempt when confronted with what he himself found so fascinating. Many of them criticized or even rejected the food they were given to eat, or constantly deplored the fact that they couldn't find in France what they enjoyed at home. He remembered being seized with a mingling of disappointment and incomprehension that the minds of some were closed to what he welcomed as being so excitingly new. It was as if they could only live comfortably within the safety of landmarks that were a constant, familiar sight, and that the uncharted world of adventure beyond, far from representing an irresistible attraction was a permanent, insidious threat. As he was later brought to reflect, this rejection could even take the form of a savage denial of the foreigner's right to be different. He recalled that incident his father would sometimes relate when, towards the end of the Second World War, he had been posted to Brussels on some police mission or other. He was walking along a deserted backstreet with another R.A.F. policeman when they spotted a man standing alone in a shop doorway. His father's colleague (he must have been a brute) for no reason other than that he was a foreigner and that he himself could act with impunity found nothing better to do than knock him to the ground with a single punch to the jaw. His foreignness had made him as much of an enemy as a German.

It was, nevertheless, during this same first trip that he had been made to see that in this paradise on earth snakes were lurking in the grass. Everything began when, on the day preceding their departure back home, his thoughts turned to buying something which might serve as a gift for his parents and a souvenir for himself. As far as spending money was concerned, each boy had the same fixed amount which was included in the total cost of the holiday. Its distribution was meticulously organized. Every morning at nine o'clock those boys in financial need were required to form a militarily-aligned queue leading up to a table on which rested a large cash box, an even larger ledger, and behind which sat their mathematics master, a Mr James Williamson, or 'Big Jim' as he was more commonly called. Though it was perfectly logical that a mathematician should have been entrusted with the accounting and issuing of pupils' spending money this choice of nickname was rather less so: for Michael had recently been looking at some old school class photos on which this teacher appeared, and he was struck by his relatively modest size. Perhaps it was his commanding class manner and the awe it inspired in his pupils which gave him such a disproportionate stature in their eyes. Now, for obvious reasons the maximum daily amount each boy was allowed to draw out was limited to 500 francs (these were the days of the *ancien franc*, and despite the two noughts this was not a particularly large sum). In order to be sure he had enough to cover the cost of his intended gift, Michael requested the maximum amount. Though Big Jim asked him why he wanted such a large sum he must have been satisfied with his answer: so, after carefully noting the transaction in his ledger, he extracted a crisp new 500 franc note (perhaps he had no smaller ones left) from his cash box, before handing it to Michael with an accompanying, 'And mind you don't lose it, my lad!' Then, with a couple of friends, off he trotted into town.

After surveying the contents of a number of souvenir shop windows his eyes alighted on a rather interesting-looking fish reposing in the corner of one. It seemed to have been carved out of a small horn. What attracted him most was its relatively modest price of less than 100 francs. So in he crept. My use of the word 'crept' is not inappropriate as this was the first opportunity he'd had to speak French with a native; and the fact that this native was an adult made the prospect even more daunting. Mustering all his courage, he muttered something resembling the word 'poisson', while at the same time pointing a finger in the direction of the fish. The shopkeeper took it out of the window, wrapped it in tissue paper and gave it to him. Michael handed him the 500 franc note and the man gave him back his change ... for 100 francs! At first the innocence of childhood made him think it was a genuine error and, as far as his single year of school French would allow, he did his best to point out the mistake. The shopkeeper would certainly not have been without knowing a little English but, much to Michael's stupefaction, it suited his purpose to reply with a, 'Ah non, mon petit, tu m'as donné un billet de cent francs! accompanied by an emphatic shake of the head. Then, turning his back, he began arranging some articles on the shelves behind the counter. It was as if the matter was now irrevocably closed and that the only thing left for this little English boy to do was vacate his shop. Though he was incapable of replying, the anger which welled up inside made him determined to stand his ground. There next happened something which had since led him to believe that certain innocents have guardian spirits hovering invisibly above, ready to summon earthly assistance in moments of dire need. Child Michael's assistants were képi-topped and clad in dark blue uniforms! For at that very instant two patrolling gendarmes strolled past the shop. Without hesitation he pointed to them before making a resolute step towards the door. It was with a show of extreme reluctance on the shopkeeper's part, but a feeling of immense relief on his own that he slowly reached inside his till and handed him his due.

Though his reflections on this sobering experience caused him to question his initial, naively-perceived impressions they didn't really undermine his attraction for France. I suppose it was something like a couple's first quarrel: it didn't destroy his affection but simply confronted him with the consideration that, when faced with closer acquaintanceship, some more down-to-earth revisions had to be made. He also comforted himself with the thought that the same thing could have happened in England. The experience also brought him to widen his field of vision and to ponder on the thought that the normal course of life can reserve other surprises of a similar, or even more painful nature. And so, rather than bringing much disillusion, he was able to integrate the experience into a positive, wider process of thought which allowed him to begin tempering his childish illusions by a clearer perception of how things really were. It was certainly a first step towards maturity. Perhaps it also marked the beginnings of a consciousness that there lay within him a certain propensity to that philosophical sense of enquiry which seeks those truths and principles underlying all knowledge and being. It was certainly this which during his later studies led him to ponder the fact that even though dreams and reality are an inextricable part of the human condition, their extreme forms must always be avoided. For dreams – that representation of things that are not, and can never be – can inspire in us hopes of a better world. But if they are so present as to blind us to reality, they can be a source of harm – even destruction. As he later came to discover, literature is not without examples of this. From Flaubert's portrayal of *Madame Bovary*, a woman who viewed the world as her romantic fantasies saw it to be, and who was annihilated by what it is, to Stevenson's classic of fantastic literature *The Strange Case of Dr Jekyll and Mr Hyde* in which the idealistic Dr Jekyll was destroyed by his dreams of cleaving Good and Evil apart so that each could be made to inhabit two separate bodies which could then go their own different ways. So, in his later, more metaphysically-oriented moments Michael gained some comfort from the thought that we are all this same inseparable amalgam of Good and Bad which, like Siamese twins, need each other in order to exist; and that the only thing we can do is to work on this impure clay with the aim of attaining some kind of working equilibrium between the two.

It was certainly this belief in the need to find a balanced middle course between dreams and reality that attracted our young man to the adage, 'If you can't get what you like, you must like what you can get'. This was what he was obliged to accept as far as his French lessons were concerned. For, he could never quite escape the feeling that it was impossible to address the object of his affection in any direct way. It was as if some sort of chaperone stood constantly between them. And his chaperone was male and took the three-times-weekly form of that same dry, stern French master who had introduced him to this living language at the age of eleven and whose approach was very much the same as if it had long been dead. Not only did lessons consist almost exclusively in translating from English into French (and occasionally *vice versa*), but the texts they were called upon to render were frequently drawn from the realms of 19th century literature. As a result, he began having serious doubts as to whether the ability to translate into French sentences such as, 'He strolled nonchalantly down the narrow, cobbled street sporting a scarlet riding coat and fleece-lined boots and jauntily waving a silver-knobbed walking stick' could possibly increase his ability to communicate on matters of present day concern. And not once did he remember pronouncing a word of French outside the context of the translations, or 'set' examination books they were plowing through. For even in the sixth form their 'A' level studies of those classical and modern authors, Racine, Molière, Lamartine, Stendhal, Saint-Exupéry, Camus – considered to have penned some of Marianne's finest literary offerings to the world – consisted in their grinding, page-by-page rendition into English. And this almost daily treachery, he had shamefully to confess, caused him to be unfaithful, too: for he ended up committing the ultimate betrayal by purchasing a paperback English translation of Balzac's *Le Père Goriot*.

Going on from school to university had always seemed a natural continuation. It was something his parents encouraged in him and something he'd always wanted to do. For them it was a first step towards a career in teaching. After all, what other job offered the advantages of total security, long holidays and decent pay? While he never openly opposed their recommendations it struck him as being too narrow a path to follow. His personal ambitions were wide enough to extend beyond any professional considerations. He'd been fascinated by the thought that his future encounters with superior minds could only result in the stretching of his own and, as far as any future job was concerned, he had simply imagined that a degree in his pocket would put the world at his feet. He couldn't understand (and was even inclined to pity) those among his pals who chose to leave school at the age of eighteen to start a career in banking or insurance in the town where they lived. Though the bank and insurance companies took charge of their training and career prospects were good (this was a period of full employment), what struck him was the confined, unadventurous nature of their choice: for some took this road simply because they wanted to start earning a living, others were reluctant to leave an environment they had known all their lives, while most seemed to be guided by a combination of the two.

He had no difficulty in choosing French Language and Literature as the subject of his degree course. Though he learned German as a second foreign language at school it was never a serious rival to French. Not only was German grammar extraordinarily complex but the guttural tones of the language could in no way compare with the soft musicality of French. But, above all, in his mind Germany never represented enough of a difference with England to prompt him to lean back in his chair and indulge in prolonged bouts of dreaming.

At that time university entrance was highly selective: not only was acceptance conditioned by the marks obtained in the official 'A' level examination which pupils sat at the end of their school career but the universities applied to (these could number as many as three or four) would summon candidates for an interview and, in many cases, even require them to take their own private exam. This was the case with Michael. He recalled his experience in all its detail. The interview was scheduled for eleven o'clock and, since the university was located in a town at a considerable distance from home, he was obliged to take the train the day before, and spend an anxious, mainly sleepless night in a nearby hotel. It was with dread in his heart that the next morning a shy, nervous 18 year old who'd rarely ventured any great distance from home alone presented himself at the French department office located on the second floor of the imposing red-brick faculty of arts building. He was immediately taken to a small room where an exam paper reposed on a desk. He had an hour to complete it in. It was divided into two parts: a *thème* (a translation from English into French), followed by a comprehension exercise which consisted in reading a text in French and then answering questions on it in English. But it wasn't so much the exam he feared as the interview which would follow. Exams were something he was used to and this one, though not particularly easy, was not beyond his abilities. It was a face-to-face confrontation with a university teacher which could be a highly intimidating affair. And when you feel intimidated you never give of your best. The events which followed brought home to him the extent to which fortuitous circumstance can play a decisive part in the fashioning of our lives: for he was lucky enough to have had an interviewer who by his understanding and modesty of manner immediately put him at ease. He later learned that he was of even more humble origins than himself. His parents were both factory workers in a Lancashire town. Apparently, he'd been such a brilliant student at school that he'd won a free scholarship to Cambridge where he'd graduated with a first-class honours degree in French and Spanish before going on to do research for his Ph.D. A few days later he received a letter offering him a place. He could scarcely believe it. That gate to a world he longed so much to discover was now swinging open. Though admission had certainly been partly based on his performance in the exam he couldn't avoid thinking that his interviewer had seen in him the working class youth he had once been. Perhaps he wanted to give him a chance to embark on the same voyage of discovery as his own.

He had to admit that at the beginning he'd felt homesick and over-awed in this rarefied world of elegant red-brick buildings set in a splendid parkland of cedars and elms where everybody spoke with superior accents and said 'Sorry?' instead of 'You what?' when they wanted you to repeat. But he'd soon made friends and the transition from school to university was made without any real problems. What's more, the freedom he was suddenly confronted with didn't go to his head. He was a sensible, serious-minded young man and, though he and his pals had good times together, he never lost sight of the fact that he was there to study and obtain a degree. In his end-of-school report one teacher had written, 'He's something of a plodder but he'll get there in the end'. Though he'd taken a little exception to the notion of unimaginative perseverance which the word 'plodder' implied, he had to admit he couldn't be described as brilliant. For his daily encounter with powerful intellects was not just a source of wonder but also brought out the limitations of his own. He was determined to make up for this lack by a sustained effort of application. So, he worked diligently throughout his first and second year and had been proud of the results obtained. He was not one of the best students but certainly not among the worst. He'd dreamed of coming back home at the end of that third year in France with an outstanding command of the language, and had been deeply disappointed when it was not achieved. But wasn't this due to those catastrophic accommodation arrangements, his regrettable choice of room mate together with his own deep shyness and in no way attributable to the country itself? For France had never ceased to live up to his expectations. It still remained this was the first time in his life he'd tasted the bitterness of failure. What's more, another reminder of his linguistic inadequacies had recently come to reinforce his determination. He'd written to the French Consulate in Bridgeford to enquire about alternative work possibilities in France, and had made a special point of penning his letter in French. He had the impression that the polite reply he'd received complimented him more on the effort he'd made than the result achieved. Thus, the French exchange was nothing less than that second chance he'd always vowed he would take the fullest advantage of to make up for that missed opportunity. His goal would be to master the language and immerse himself in the culture to such a point as to become indistinguishable from a native Frenchman. It was part of his perfectionist nature to set his sights as high as they could be and, even if, at bottom, he knew they would be difficult to reach, didn't the challenge lie in seeing how far he could go?

The more Michael guided himself through his boyhood, youth and early manhood the more he saw that, despite his timidity, his was an adventurous nature. Not that he considered the explorer within to be of the kind that is driven by the thrill which the discovery of wild, unknown climes may arouse. For our young man was indifferent to the physical challenges of steaming jungles, scorching deserts, icy wastes, pelagic expanses and vertiginous heights. His love of discovery was directed towards those vast, unmapped territories of the mind: what set him vibrating was the thought of embracing the traditions, manners, customs, codes and language of a land significantly different to his own. He was also not without becoming increasingly aware that beyond his longing to escape from the routine and conflict at work and home his dream of immersing himself in all things French was also a way of wiping his personal slate clean of all past failures and failings and starting a new debt-free life. And it was all reinforced by the growing realization that this was something he must not delay. For here lay a chance to re-mould his life as he wanted it to be. He was determined to seize it while he was young and free.

Though Michael was well aware that his hopes of living his dream were essentially an emanation of the heart, he was level-headed enough to take into account certain practical considerations. For one thing he'd weighed up his chances of success and found that the scales were well tipped in his favour. After all, when it came to successful expatriation the main obstacle was adapting to a country whose language you didn't speak. Wasn't this far from being the case with him? Even though his present level in French didn't measure up to his own high standards it was more than enough for him to get by. And didn't this introspective journey he'd just made back into his past prove he was enough of an adaptable, conscientious and open-minded person to be able to draw the maximum benefit from his stay? In addition, it wasn't as if he'd be going out there looking for work. Wouldn't he have the security of a guaranteed job paying a comfortable salary which was even supplemented by an allowance to compensate for the higher cost of living in France?

Though his deliberations were mainly focused on this prospect of a year of adventure Michael did have enough foresight to realize that he would be faced with a number of options when it came to an end. Since he would still be officially employed as a teacher at Barfield one of the choices he would be led to make would be either to rejoin his post there or apply for a job down South. But judging from the way he felt at the moment returning to England would be a last resort. What he'd really set his heart on was settling in more attractive climes. While this would probably mean him remaining in France he hadn't quite excluded the possibility of moving on to another country. It would all depend on how much he enjoyed his stay. For experience had taught our young man that there was a world of difference between a distant amorous attraction and everyday co-habitation. So he'd treat the year as a sort of trial marriage. After all, when he came to think of it he'd never experienced prolonged direct contact with the object of his desire. Whether it had been during his French lessons, the school trips or his student year in France somewhere his compatriots had always got in the way. So if things didn't work out (and he was realistic enough not to have quite excluded this eventuality), and he decided to move on to a far-away English-speaking country (South Africa, Australia and New Zealand sprang to mind) he was sure that his present teaching qualifications along with the linguistic improvement and added knowledge of French life and culture which his year's experience brought would not only be a source of personal enrichment but provide him with the guarantee of a stable job.

He was also aware that the real problems would come if he decided to stay in France. Since his native teaching diploma was not recognized by the French education system he would have to find a post teaching English in some private establishment with all the lack of job security this involved. And the thought had even crossed his mind that if the right circumstances presented themselves he might even be able to start his own language-teaching business. But weren't these choices he would have to make only when the time came? If the truth were known, however, there was one consideration he hadn't entertained: for certain recesses of his mind were still unexplored enough for him to realize that the *entrepreneur* might re-surface enough for him to say, 'If the worst came to the worst I might give in to the temptation of going back to England and resuscitating the business project – with or without Adrian.'

This, then, is a faithful *résumé* of our young man's thoughts, feelings and remembrances, his hopes, doubts and resolutions as they presented themselves during those closing days of December. All in all, it had been time well spent. For these moments of meditation had not only helped him to deepen his understanding of himself and his attraction for France but to trace out more clearly the path of his life.

Twenty-Eight

As he was driving to school on the first morning after the Christmas vacation Michael couldn't suppress a flutter of apprehension. It wasn't really due to the imminent prospect of renewing contact with his pupils. Though he couldn't say the thought inspired him with much more than moderate pleasure, it didn't fill him with the dread he imagined must be seizing some of his colleagues – in particular those who had been misguided, or inexperienced enough to treat them as equals. When he'd first started at Barfield he'd had one class of fifteen year olds with whom he'd been too familiar and not insistent enough on the respect of rules. He'd learned to his cost that this was a good way of giving immature youngsters too much control. But he'd gradually adopted a detached, imperturbable sort of pose – unlike the loud-mouthed, authoritarian role Deputy Head Cooper seemed to have chosen to play – which placed him in a position where he was not inaccessible to pupils but which allowed him to maintain enough of a distance between himself and those in his charge to create a controlled relationship based less on fear of punishment than that of the unknown. He'd previously had doubts on the desirability of such a strategy – especially since Sylvia had once confided in him that at the end of one of her lessons she'd asked her class which teacher they had next. They'd replied with an almost unanimous shudder that it was Mr Morgan. This had caused him to wonder whether the hushed attention he could now command was based on anything more pedagogically constructive than acute trepidation. Nevertheless, he'd been reassured by a parent teacher meeting at the end of last year's summer term when many of those parents interested enough to attend had informed him that their progeny were far from disliking French. It was even the favourite subject of some. And in class the naïve, often laughable ignorance which prevailed in many made it difficult for him not to reveal himself more than he thought appropriate. During the last lesson before the Christmas holidays he'd relaxed his normal teaching routine to the point of transforming it into a session where pupils could ask him any questions they wished on the subject of France and the French. Higgins, who seemed to be taking an unusual interest, had raised his hand and with a look of perplexity had proceeded to ask, 'Sir, is it true tomatoes are square in France?' Michael knew what had prompted his question. At that time in the early seventies the absurdist comedy series *Monty Python's Flying Circus* was all the rage, and one of the protagonists had surrealistically affirmed that French tomatoes distinguished themselves by their systematic presentation in this shape – the principle reason being that it made packing so much easier. The only explanation Michael could find which he thought might be within Higgin's grasp of things was that 'it was just a joke, meant to suggest that the French do things differently to us.' Higgins seemed disappointed by his answer; Michael had had the distinct impression his pupil would have preferred to have been told it was true.

As the school buildings came into sight his unease began to grow. It was mainly due to his uncertainty as to how he would behave towards Sylvia and Jennifer and, perhaps even more, as to how they would behave towards him. He was quite aware that his future attitude might not be without having some bearing on theirs, and that theirs would certainly have some influence on his. As to their behaviour he soon had his answer. He was just stepping out of the small staffroom kitchen in which stood the large urn used to prepare the coffee teachers would drink during the morning break when Sylvia and Jennifer strolled in. They were chatting together and as they walked past he gave them a glance. Sylvia presented him with a weak, almost apologetic smile. It seemed somewhere to contain her admission that they were now separated by a permanent barrier, and that she wished to apologize for what she now realized was the part she had played in creating it. Jennifer, on the other hand, tossed her head ostentatiously in the other direction in a gesture of unabashed scorn. There seemed to be a growing intimacy between the two young women. He rather suspected they'd met during the holidays and that he'd been discussed. Their two contrasting reactions went to confirm his previous assessment that the one was a woman not insensible to the call of reason while the other was an illustration of that famous French philosopher's observation that 'the heart has reasons which reason doesn't have'. Of one thing he was sure: he would now have to resign himself to the sobering fact that the woman of the heart had no forgiveness in her, and that her attitude towards him was now, and would always remain one of resolute antipathy, even hate. He couldn't avoid being seized by an inner shudder of fear.

His trepidation was somewhat allayed when Ian informed him that Mrs Boxley was no longer a member of the Barfield school staff and that the plump, matronly-looking lady he'd previously noticed on the teacher platform during morning assembly was the person appointed to replace her. He hoped she would spare him the embarrassment which a renewal of her predecessor's language department meetings would now inevitably cause. The same morning coffee break also provided him with an opportunity to exchange a few words with a rather wan-looking Adrian. Though he still felt 'a bit weak and wobbly', and had even considered staying at home for a day or two more, he had to admit that on the whole he was now 'on the mend'. Michael was quick to note that his friend made no mention of their business project. He found himself wondering whether he was being wishful in thinking that this could be taken as confirmation that his friend's growing amorous involvement was now causing things to start moving in the direction he desired.

That evening he was sipping his after-dinner coffee in the living room with his parents and Grandpa when the telephone rang in the hall. His mother got up to answer it.

'It's for you,' she announced when a few seconds later she came back. 'A girl wants to speak to you. She's got an Irish accent.' He couldn't quite decide whether the slight hint of disapproval he detected in her voice was caused by the fact that the voice was unmistakably Irish or was simply because it belonged to a girl.

I will not dwell in any detail on the conversation which ensued.

Suffice it to say that it consisted mainly of polite mutual enquiry as to the degree of enjoyment the Christmas and New Year celebrations had procured along with some rueful comments on the contrasting despondency which renewed contact with work had brought. I will, however, reveal that Molly (he now felt familiar enough to address her by this name) did ask him whether he was doing anything the following evening. She was now working the morning shift and would be free. When he replied he had nothing planned she suggested they meet for a drink together in a pub close to the nurses' home.

'Yes, that'd be nice,' he said, without being completely sure his words had been pronounced in a tone enthusiastic enough to make his acquiescence totally convincing.

'So where did you meet *her*?' his mother asked as he was walking back into the sitting room. This time there was no mistaking the disapproval in her voice. Michael was seized by a mixture of surprise and annoyance. Blunt questioning of this sort was something she hadn't accustomed him to. On the whole she respected his private life and her rare enquiries were tactful enough to leave him room to produce a non-committal answer if he so wished. What's more, her voice had come from inside the kitchen which was well within hearing distance of anyone speaking on the phone. Since he'd have to walk past its open door on his way back to the living room, he more than suspected she'd positioned herself there strategically while they were talking – not so much to eavesdrop on his conversation as to be able to prevent her ensuing questions and his answers from reaching her husband and Grandpa's ears. The emphasis she'd placed on the word 'her' left him in no doubt that her disapproval was not so much due to the voice being that of a girl as to some vague prejudice which stated that the vocal inflections of this particular female betrayed origins she was not entirely reassured about. He also objected to her beginning the question with 'so'. It seemed to confirm she was now intent on expanding that breach in his private affairs which her initial reaction of disapprobation had opened.

This was not to say he'd ever had any reason to consider his mum as having an excessively possessive nature. Not like the mother of one of the pals he'd had at school. Perhaps it was because her husband was considerably older than her and simply aspired to a quiet life that she had focused her affections on this only child. Her attentions also embraced Michael and other of her son's pals who were frequently invited for Saturday tea. But later when, as a student away from home in London, he became romantically involved, Michael was able to observe how insidiously she sowed her seeds of destruction. It was obvious she considered her son belonged exclusively to her for it was much the same scenario with the following two girlfriends. With the fourth he had been man enough to say, 'I'm going to marry this one!' It had meant an irreconcilable rupture between mother and son. His own mother had commented, 'How silly it is to be possessive to that point!' Though it was certainly true, Michael couldn't help reflecting that the credibility of his mother's indirectly proclaimed open-mindedness was undermined by her never having had to face a similar situation herself. But then perhaps he was being a little unfair. During their engagement he'd brought Vicky home for a weekend to meet his parents. His father had gratified him with a whispered, man-to-man, 'I can see why you've fallen for her!' while his mother had displayed a friendly politeness of such consistency that he'd never had cause to believe it was simply an appropriate veneer. There again, he was living away from home at the time and, even if she had disapproved, there was nothing much she could do about it. The person who had perhaps had most grounds for jealousy, though not of the same kind, was his father: for Vicky had been particularly taken by Grandpa; and during one of his momentary absences she'd turned towards his parents before declaring, the fire of enthusiasm in her eyes, what 'a lovely man' she thought he was. He had considered taking advantage of a private moment to explain the situation to her in the hope that she would appreciate the difficulties this *ménage à trois* presented his parents with. He'd decided against it. She was another of those women who allowed herself emotionally-based judgements on situations that she herself had never experienced. He was sure she wouldn't understand.

'Oh, I met her at that Christmas dance I went to a couple of weeks ago with Adrian,' he replied to his mother's question. 'She's in her final year as a trainee nurse.'

The fact that his answer seemed to go a visible way towards reassuring his mother suggested she had a more selective perception of the professional rank required by his female acquaintances than he had previously thought. Perhaps her reservations were also due to his age and situation now placing him in that perilous zone from which most marital unions emerge, and that she simply considered she had a right to let her opinion be known on someone who might eventually become a daughter-in-law.

On the whole he couldn't grumble about his parents. They had always wanted the best for their children and were well aware of the importance of a good education. At school the absence of any real brilliance in Michael had been to some degree compensated for by an assiduity of application which had always produced results encouraging enough for them to declare that they would support him as far as his abilities and the efforts he was prepared to make would allow him to go. His father had been born into a modest family at a time when most working-class parents could see no further than their children leaving school at the earliest legal age simply to become an additional breadwinner. This usually meant condemning them to a 'dead-end job' as a manual worker for the rest of their lives. Apparently, at that early period of his life it had been without the slightest reluctance on his part. On growing older he'd been made increasingly aware of his own limited professional horizons and educational deficiencies and, when in the company of others, the feeling of inferiority it sometimes brought. 'Work hard at school,' he would frequently say, 'so you'll never have to go to work wearing overalls!' Or sometimes he would add, 'And when you've had a good education you can talk to anybody.'

It was rather different with his mother. She'd been an outstanding pupil at school and would have loved to have gone on to become a schoolteacher. And since Grandpa drew a salary in keeping with his level of responsibility at the mine it would have been well within her parents' means for her to have done so. But somewhere she'd been the victim of her times, of her social background and her mother's blinkered inability to see beyond an established order which stated that a woman's allotted role did not extend beyond looking after the home, catering to the comforts of her husband and bringing up the children. Apparently, on leaving school at the age of 15 she'd been put to work as some sort of seamstress. It was rarely alluded to by his mother, and whenever this was the case it was mentioned in a vague, shameful kind of way. She'd been very unhappy and her parents had finally withdrawn her from this drudgery. She'd spent the remaining years – before, he suspected, being rescued by the first man she had known – at home learning those edifying household arts of cooking, cleaning and washing. Her brother, on the other hand, had been encouraged and financed to stay on at school and then go to teacher training college. It was felt as a burning injustice which she'd never accepted, and in later years she'd repeatedly reproached her mother for this. Michael couldn't quite rid himself of the thought that Grandpa was also not totally without blame. He was a gentle, generous and sociable man who hated conflict of any kind but lacked the strength of character necessary to resist sacrificing his daughter for the sake of peace and quiet at home.

Grandpa's own education had been more of a specialized, technical nature which was not broad enough to prevent the occasional, sometimes laughable appearance of the self-made man. One example of this stood out in Michael's mind. As a child they would often go out for summer Sunday afternoon runs in the car, and his grandparents would usually be invited to go with them. Their route frequently led them past the same fields of rhubarb. Whenever it did Grandpa would systematically inform them that, 'All that there rhubarb is exported to France to make Champagne.' Grandpa was used to talking to ignorant miners who would believe more or less anything that was pronounced in a tone of knowledgeable authority. Even though nobody knew exactly where he'd got this information from, there seemed to be no reason not to give it credit – until that day when the young Michael had learned better. The next time they'd driven past he'd pointed out in no uncertain terms that what Grandpa was saying was utter rubbish. The rhubarb fields were never mentioned again.

'You know, we want what you want for yourself,' his mother had once touchingly informed him. It was not mere words. His interest in

France had always been recognized and encouraged to the point of her frequently bringing to his notice a press article or television programme on the subject. Moreover, they seemed – his mother especially – to take it for granted that his French dream was something of vital importance for him. One thing he did hold against them, however, was the fact that their marriage had always been shaken by violent, recurring quarrels which, as children, had caused him and his sister some distress. The first time he'd become aware of this – he must have been nine or ten at the time – was when his sister informed him that the previous night their parents' dissension had degenerated to such a point that his mother had threatened to throw herself out of the bedroom window. He must have been fast asleep as he'd heard nothing. 'I hate men,' his sister had declared. It came as a great shock. He frequently wondered whether this alternating hot and cold emotional shower which he'd been regularly subjected to during his formative childhood years had been unbalancing enough to produce in him that vacillating sense of fragility he'd always been conscious of in his relations with similarly-aged members of the opposite sex.

TWENTY-NINE

They'd arranged to meet at 8 o'clock. He'd offered to pick her up at her nurses' home, but for reasons he hadn't asked her to explain she preferred to meet him in the pub. He arrived a quarter of an hour earlier but had only been sat ten minutes when she walked in. She gave him only the briefest hint of a smile. He couldn't help feeling disgruntled. Wouldn't he have been justified in expecting more warmth? After all, it was she who'd phoned him and not the other way round. And he wasn't at all sure that what he referred to as 'the other way round' would ever have come about. On the other hand, he was agreeably surprised to note that she was a little more attractive than he'd first thought. When he'd left her he'd had the impression she was nothing more than anonymously plain. And since then, during those rare moments when he'd thought about her, he was able to produce only the vaguest representation of her looks. It could have been due to the ambient semi-darkness of their encounter; but there again he was far from having an artist's eye for detail; and usually his thoughts were too concentrated on the impression he made on others rather than the impression they made on him to retain more than just a blurred picture of someone whose acquaintanceship he had just made. It was true that Vicky and Sue had been exceptions; but then, each had possessed looks which had been striking enough to leave an immediate, durable imprint. Perhaps it was a desire to add more details to this barely touched canvass which now caused him to note the scattering of freckles that dotted the top of her cheeks, a slightly up-curved nose and a gently pointed chin. And somewhere he detected a tired sadness in her blue eyes whose lightness seemed to be emphasized by the shadows beneath. But what struck him the most was her thick auburn hair tumbling down each side of her head. It reminded him – not without some inner amusement – of the ears of Rusty, the Golden Cocker Spaniel his grandparents had had when he was a child.

After inviting her to sit down on the bench seat beside him he asked her what she'd like to drink. She chose a dry Martini. As he brought it back from the bar and placed it on the table next to his own half-empty glass of beer, he saw that she'd taken off her coat and positioned it, carefully folded, between her and where he'd been sitting. He raised his glass with a, 'Here's to the new year. I wish you everything you'd wish yourself.'

'The same to you,' she replied. The charm exerted by the soft musicality of her Irish lilt was neutralized by the brevity of her answer. It seemed to come as a verbal echo of the fleeting smile she'd given him as she came in. He suddenly found himself wondering why he hadn't thought up some excuse not to come. The Irish he'd met with up to now had all, without exception, been a warm-hearted, chatty, open and frequently humorous lot. But then they'd been exclusively men. Perhaps, as a general rule, their women showed more reserve. Somewhere he couldn't quite rid himself of the thought that her attitude went beyond a natural reticence of speech: it was as if she had purposely erected a protective screen to defend some vulnerable part of herself against an anticipated attack. Was it because she was Irish with an accent which made her instantly identifiable as such? Did she think he might consider her origins as a source of scorn? Was she waiting for him to reassure her that this wasn't the case? If the reasons lay here he could feel some sympathy. After all, if his French adventure came about his own foreignness could cause him to be viewed as an object of suspicion by some. But there again, he could be searching too deeply. Perhaps this apparent lack of affability could be explained by her reserved nature, or was simply due to the down-heartedness caused by lingering memories of her recent Irish Christmas.

He decided to direct conversation back to the end of year festivities in the hope that it might touch a feeling nostalgic enough to induce in her a spontaneous willingness to talk. She became a little more open without allowing herself to proceed beyond the mundane. It had been nice to be back at home with her family. She'd appreciated being able to go to bed and get up at the times she wanted. He enquired whether she had any brothers and sisters, and she replied that, 'There are just two boys and two girls, including myself.' Her answer struck him as being strangely impersonal, and her use of 'just' appeared a little odd: it suggested a modest number, whereas for him a family of four children was already one of considerable size. They were perhaps dyed-in-the-wool Catholics. He also tried to find out in an indirect sort of way what her father did for a living and whether her mother worked. She remained what he took to be determinedly vague. In return, she asked him – simply, he thought, out of politeness – what he'd done at Christmas and on New Year's Eve. He replied in much the same vein. The holidays had been spent quietly. He'd done nothing special. He'd thought she might have enquired about their T-shirt project and especially about Adrian. Jean had certainly told her he'd spent most of the holidays down with the flu. But she proceeded no further; and their conversation began lagging to such an uncomfortable point that he found himself asking whether his time wouldn't have been better spent in the more prolix company of Hervé Bazin. But then, hadn't he asked himself the same question when he and Adrian had arrived at the student dance? It even crossed his mind that this could all be part of a ploy. Was she enveloping herself in a cloak of mystery as a way of arousing his interest? He'd had enough of female intrigue; if he so much as suspected she was playing this little game he'd have no compulsion in letting her drop.

'I suppose the next time you'll be going back home will be in summer?' he enquired in what he'd decided would be a final attempt on his part to engage her in conversation. He'd been gazing straight ahead as he spoke but in view of her silence he turned his head towards her with a glance severe enough to leave her in no doubt that his patience was wearing thin. Her pale blue eyes had become slightly moist. This hint of emotion caused his stiffening irritation to relax into a consolatory, 'Oh, it'll go a lot quicker than you think.'

'I'll be going back sooner than that. Probably in less than a month.'

Her words were uttered with such finality that it flashed through his mind she'd made some irrevocable decision to abandon her nursing studies and go back home; and he'd already decided to question her on her reasons with a view to discussing the wisdom of such a course. The thought that he might be able to dissuade her from taking such an ill-considered decision filled him with pleasure. Wasn't this an opportunity to engage in something beyond the superficial? If she would only confide in him he was sure he could give her some sensible, reassuring advice. After all, wasn't he older and certainly more experienced than her? What's more, as a student in his own final year of study he couldn't really say the thought of throwing everything up had never entered his head. But things would remain platonic. Yes, that was it. He'd act as a sort of wise, elder brother.

'It's my mum, you see.' It was an answer he hadn't at all anticipated, and the tone with which it was uttered made him realize it was more serious than he'd thought. He waited for her to continue. He knew she would. She choked a sob, the tears welled up in her eyes and two rivulets crept down her cheeks.

'She's very ill with cancer.'

It was again something he'd not considered, and for a moment he was at a loss what to say. He regretted not being able to find anything more consolatory than, 'But people recover from cancer these days, as you're well placed to know!'

'Not this type of cancer.' Her words were spoken with resigned absoluteness.

'Breast cancer?' he tentatively asked.

'No, it's a deal worse than that. Two months ago she went to the dentist's with what she thought was bad toothache. He found something he didn't like and sent her to hospital for tests. They found she had quite a rare cancer – cancer of the jaw. At the time we thought it could have been worse since it's something that can be treated surgically. It's a long and complicated operation which can leave the patient's face deformed. But it can be life-saving – provided the cancer's not too advanced.' She now seemed perfectly lucid and calm. Her tears had dried leaving two narrow, vaguely discernible traces down the sides of her face. It was certainly the nurse who had now taken over. He nodded but could find nothing to say to bring her any comfort. But then didn't the best therapy consist in letting her talk?

'Anyway she had an MRI scan just before the holidays and we had the results the day I got back home. It's spread into her lungs and chest. The surgeon said it was too late for an operation and I asked him how long Mum had got left to live. He said it depended. It could be three or four months or just a question of weeks.'

'But you never know. You must never lose hope.'

He'd wanted to say something which went enough beyond the commonplace to see her actually seize the straw he'd tendered that all was not lost. They were the only words he could find. He was uncomfortably conscious that they were empty-sounding and had been uttered in a sanctimonious, clergyman-like tone. He'd been on the point of saying, 'Miracles do happen, you know,' but found it had greater religious connotations, and even implied the opposite to what he wished to suggest: that, in reality, her mother was indeed lost.

'There's no hope at all. As a trainee nurse I've seen enough to be absolutely sure of that,' she continued. 'The only thing we can do now is to make her end as peaceful and as comfortable as we can.'

'Is your mum at home?'

'Well, she was when I left to come back here. I phoned my sister this afternoon and she told me that yesterday she couldn't even take a step and was in great pain with water on the lungs. They took her to hospital. But she's in a ward with others and there's too much bustle and clatter. So we're trying to get her into a special nursing home for the terminally ill on the outskirts of Dublin. At least she'll be able to die in peace.'

'Has your mum come to terms with her own death?' He now felt the nurse had imposed enough dispassion for her to accept with calmness the directness of his question.

'I don't think she's got used to the idea of dying. She's too young and has got too much to live for to do that. But she has accepted the fact that she's going to die. When she gets nearer the end they'll probably ask her to sign a paper saying she doesn't want resuscitating. It's usually what happens in this type of case. Anyway, it's only putting off the end, as she well knows. I'm sure she'll sign without hesitation.'

'I suppose you feel guilty because you're not there by her side?'

'Yes, that's the terrible part of it. But my sister and brothers are there. They all work but they manage to take it in relays; so at least one of them is always at her side. I do draw some consolation from that. And I've made my sister promise to let me know when the moment's near so I can be at Mum's side when she passes away.'

'And what about your dad? How's he taking it?'

'He's got a strange reaction. It's as if he doesn't want to know. He seems to be doing his best to convince himself that everything's fine. But I do believe in God and even though it's hard to accept I think somewhere there's a purpose behind all this.'

'Yes, I see.' His voice bore a dubious note. He himself was convinced that the only existence God had was inside the heads of men and that Molly was seeing things as she wanted them to be: for he couldn't help pondering on the paradoxical fact that, even though her God had acted in this agonizing way, she now considered Him to be a source of consolation.

He asked her if she'd like another drink but she declined. They left the pub and he drove her back to the nurses' home. He had debated whether to give her a chaste kiss on the lips or the briefest peck on the cheek on parting, but felt that neither corresponded to the gravity which the situation required. He ended by simply leaving her with a grave-sounding, 'I wish you all possible courage. I'll be in touch.' He was at a loss to explain why he hadn't even been able to pronounce the word 'Goodbye'.

'Well, if I'm not there, you'll know where I am,' she replied.

THIRTY

'Haven't you seen Ma Dobson's notice? She's scheduled your assembly show for next Tuesday.' Ian said as they were sipping their coffee together during the Friday morning break.

'Really?'

'Yes, and I just can't wait to hear what you've got in store for us! What's it going to be about? I hope it'll be entertaining at least!'

While it wasn't said in a sneering tone he could detect a trace of amused irony in his colleague's voice. Since Mrs Boxley had left Ian had been spending more time in the staffroom, and they'd had more opportunity to indulge in the kind of teasing banter he liked. For reasons he seemed reluctant to divulge Ian was one of those rare teachers to have refused Headmaster Fowler's invitation to address the school assembly. From what Michael could judge it didn't seem to be out of any great personal dislike as he showed a resigned acceptance of his headmaster's foibles. Perhaps he'd given up all hope of promotion. Or perhaps he just didn't care.

'Well, I'm not completely sure yet, but I was thinking of talking about some of those stereotypes the English have about the French! And perhaps the other way round.'

'Oh, right. So you'll be telling the kids it's not true French men are a randy lot, and that the reason French women are so good in bed is not because they've all slept with at least twenty black men with whopping great choppers. I mean, it's a well-known fact they never shave under their armpits and tend to pong. Apparently it brings out the animal in the male! What did Napoleon Bonaparte say to Josephine? "Don't wash, I'm on my way!"'

'Yes, that's what he wrote. And, as everybody knows, in France when men and women arrive at work in the morning they stick their tongue into each others' mouth,' he replied with a laugh. The coarse indelicacy of his reply didn't conform to the image of himself Michael felt comfortable with, but experience had taught him that the best way to counter Ian's brand of outrageous provocation was to reply in much the same tone.

Despite his apparent surprise he'd already seen the list. Just before trooping out to assembly that morning he'd observed Miss Dobson slip into the staffroom and pin it on the notice board. He'd been expecting her to do this and had quickly looked to see when his turn would be. His show of surprise was designed to make Ian think the talk was something he attached little importance to. He'd previously considered going into the history of Toussaint l'Ouverture's fight against slavery in more detail as an extension to the talk which Sylvia had given. In view of what had happened since he'd abandoned the idea. So, given the general ignorance of his pupils as far as the French were concerned, talking about the more common stereotypes might be enlightening enough to dispel, or at least cause them to doubt some prejudices. He'd already begun a mental outline of what he was going to say. He'd first explain in the simplest possible terms what a stereotype was, and then provide an example of one. Perhaps it would give the kids a better idea of how little they corresponded to reality if he gave them an instance of the standard image the French had of the typical Englishman: that he always went to work dressed in a dark, striped business suit with a bowler hat on his head and carrying a rolled umbrella with a copy of *The Times* under his arm; or that he had fair hair and blue eyes. And why not ask those kids in the assembly who didn't have blue eyes or blond hair to put up their hands? Wouldn't the fact that they'd be in the majority prove how stupid clichés were? He could then point out that, similarly, not all Frenchman had black hair, a moustache, dark brown eyes and wore a beret, a blue and white striped T shirt with a string of onions hanging round their neck. He could also encourage them to question some standard prejudices about food: that the French systematically ate frogs' legs and snails for breakfast. It was all a bit elementary, but Higgins's question about square tomatoes had made him realize how tenaciously naïve they were. Then he could move onto stereotypes vectoring prejudices of a more moral kind – that the French were a cowardly, frivolous or untrustworthy lot. He was aware that the field was limited since – as Ian had pointed out in his inimitable way – some of the clichés served up by both nations had a strong salacious flavour which made them unfit for pupil consumption. Even so, he was sure he could make an entertaining yet instructive talk out of it all. What he found daunting, however, was the prospect of addressing the school and, above all, being judged by his peers and Headmaster Fowler. Though in his last year at university he'd been called upon to give a short seminar talk on a literary theme, he didn't consider himself confident enough to speak to a far larger audience simply from a set of notes. But there again, as Sylvia had done, he could write it all down word for word and then just read it out.

During the week Mrs Hungerford, the teacher who had replaced Mrs Boxley, had introduced herself and they'd had a little chat. Her ripe, matronly figure was in marked contrast to her trim-looking predecessor, and he inwardly smiled at the thought of Ian now spending his lunchtimes alone in her company. He was relieved that she made no mention of the language department meetings. But there again she'd probably never even been informed of their existence. The only person who could possibly have talked to her about them was Headmaster Fowler. Ian would never have done this, and neither would Jennifer. It was not as if he hadn't found them both interesting and useful; but he was now doing his best to reduce the risk of a head-on collision with Jennifer to as close to zero as possible. The risk which alarmed him the most was that he should suddenly see her walking towards him in the school corridor. It was true that on Friday mornings they had lessons in opposite-facing classrooms and they could find themselves suddenly confronted with each other on coming out. But this eventuality was mainly avoidable, being simply a question of choosing the opportune moment to leave. His apprehensions were further eased by the reflection that Jennifer would herself now be devoting considerable thought as to how best avoid those situations bringing proof that he hadn't ceased to exist. As far as a direct encounters with Sylvia were concerned his fears were not felt to quite the same degree. If she deigned to acknowledge his presence by one of her faint smiles he'd resolved to reciprocate with a restrained nod. Apart from the corridors, however, the risk of direct confrontation with either was minimal. Next to the main staff room there existed a much smaller room which, for reasons no-one seemed to be able to give, was a generally accepted male preserve. Or could its presence simply be due to that old English tradition (the same that provided exclusive gentlemen's clubs, or men-only public house snugs) which states that activities of a male-oriented nature (among which the playing of dominos, darts, the discussion of politics and women, the savouring of a fine vintage port, or the quaffing of a pint of English ale occupy an important place) shall be indulged in without the potentially bothersome presence of the opposite sex? Up to then he'd only occasionally taken advantage of the protection it offered, but he now resolved to spend all his free periods and lunchtimes within the reassuring confines of its walls.

He was, however, becoming more and more aware that those de-termining circumstances which obviate the need for us to make important choices regarding the future orientation of our lives were now removing certain vacillations which had been causing him much preoccupation: for Barfield School was now presenting such an increasingly painful working environment that he'd now made the firm resolve to resign his post and accompany his parents down South were his application for the French exchange again refused. And other circumstances were making Michael even more aware of the preponder-ant part extraneous events can play: for he was now feeling increasingly sure that, in much the same way as two communicating vessels, the more Adrian's mind was being filled with fond thoughts of Jean the more it showed a proportional emptying of those which might lead to the development of their T-shirt project. Couldn't this be taken to mean that his planned strategy of inertia would now not be necessary? For though he'd been under the impression that their plans to visit the wholesale distribution centre, to contact an importer of blank T-shirts and to look for suitable printing premises during the holidays had simply been postponed by Adrian's bout of Christmas flu, only the vaguest of mentions had been made since. It was with the aim of obtaining a more precise idea of where his pal now stood that Michael judged it necessary to have some sort of chat. Not that he envisaged a totally frank talk. He simply viewed it as a way of obtaining confirmation of the present state of his friend's heart. So, when he next saw Adrian he'd suggest they had a drink together.

As things turned out, it was Adrian who provided the suggestion. During the afternoon break of this same Friday Michael was walking past the entrance to those narrow confines of male privacy which I have described above when a, 'Hey Mike, could I have a word?' brought it to his notice that his friend was seated within.

'I'll just get my tea. I'll be with you in a tick,' he replied.

'Yep, I just wanted to tell you,' Adrian began, 'that Jean phoned me yesterday. She told me to tell you that Molly's mum has had a relapse and, as far as she can make out, has got only days to live. So Molly's gone back to Ireland to be with her. It's terrible. I mean, her mum's only in her early fifties.'

It was what Molly had led him to expect – though it had happened sooner than he, and probably she had imagined.

'Oh, and by the way, are you doing anything tomorrow evening? Jean's on night duty and it's a principle with me never to spend Saturday evenings at home – especially when you've only got your old man and woman for company!'

'No, I've got nothing special on.' He was conscious of being treated as something of a stand-in, but found some consolation in the hope that it might be to his advantage not to be too pained by this prick to his self pride. After all, things seemed now to be moving in the direction he'd been wanting without him having to impart the slightest impulse. And wouldn't a chat and a drink or two make a welcome change? He could prepare his assembly talk on Saturday afternoon. If he didn't finish it then he'd have all day Sunday.

'What about the Market Tavern? Shall we say eight?'

Michael was only too happy to concur. He couldn't avoid congratulating himself with the premonitory thought that Adrian had suggested they meet for reasons which, while not being the same as his, might lead to a result which suited them both.

THIRTY-ONE

The Market Tavern was an old Bridgeford pub – old enough, it was claimed, to have been for a brief few months the chosen drinking haunt of the artistic, ill-famed brother – not much later to undergo a mental and physical decline of such disastrous amplitude that it would lead to his precocious death – of world-famous literary sisters whose lives, we are told by the more Romanesque of their biographers, were an inseparable part of the bleak isolation of the nearby windswept moorland village in which they lived. The pub was not unfamiliar to Michael. As they sat down with their pints of beer he was reminded of those happy times (now ten years ago) when he'd been in the sixth form at school, and he and his pals spent their Saturday evenings playing dominos or darts in this same little snug – not officially destined for men alone, but where women (apart from the more wilfully emancipated among their ranks) had no reason to enter. After an appreciative sip which left a thin creamy line above his upper lip it was Adrian who began.

'You know, I hate to have to say this but my old lady won't budge an inch. I mean, if we went along to the buying centre with only the six or so printed shirts we've got left to flog they'll laugh their sides sore. So, if we decide to go any further, finding some premises is our top priority.'

It was the 'So, if we decide to go any further' which retained Michael's attention. Before Adrian had met Jean he was sure it wouldn't have been said. It could only be inferred that he was now entertaining the thought that he might not want to go any further, and that the inclusive 'we' was a tentative probe designed to explore Michael's feelings on the subject. Here seemed to lie the confirmation he was seeking that Adrian was becoming aware that, for the moment at least, his priorities lay elsewhere. However, his pal certainly needed a gentle nudge that would ease him even further in this direction.

'Yep, and something tailored to measure might not be all that easy to find. And I haven't got a clue about how much it'll all cost. Probably more than we expected. I reckon we've got to give ourselves time to think,' he replied.

'Yeah, me too.'

Michael couldn't avoid reflecting that Adrian's brief words of agreement were perhaps his way of letting it be known that for him this apparent wisdom in not taking any immediate decision was, in fact, more than just a roundabout way of putting a temporary stop to their venture: it was an indication that he was now contemplating its definitive demise. They also signaled that the road was now clear for Michael to seek validation of Adrian's reasons by leading him on to that subject which was now closer to his heart.

'By the way, when did Molly go back home?'

'First thing yesterday morning. She took a taxi to the airport and caught a direct flight to Dublin'.

'Jean and Molly seem to be good friends.'

'Yes, well I suppose you can say that. Though Molly's not that easiest person to get to know. She's a bit on the quiet, reserved side. But Jean says there's a lot more to her than meets the eye. I mean, what do they say about deep waters? Do you hit it off together?' Michael ignored the question.

'Jean strikes me as being a very sociable sort of girl.'

'Yes she is. She's a fantastic girl. She loves a joke and a good laugh. We get along like a house on fire. An' I don't mind telling you we've talked about bedding down together once she qualifies as a nurse.' He raised his eyes dreamily towards the opposite wall before lowering his eyes in meditation of the contents of his glass.

'You know, Mike, if this doesn't work out I'll become the world's biggest smoothie.'

He was surprised at this revelation. Though he knew that Adrian and Jean's relationship had blossomed, he hadn't realized it was to the point of them deciding to live together. Michael's first thought was that, as far as future partners were concerned, nurses' ambitions tended more towards doctors or, in their wildest dreams, surgeons than modest arts and crafts teachers. But then perhaps he was being cynical. Above all, Adrian's avowal set him thinking that what just a minute ago he'd interpreted as a sign that his friend was now contemplating the demise of their project was, in fact, a tacit admission that for him it was already dead. Didn't this perfectly suit Michael's plans? Hadn't he been right in counting on Jean's involuntary co-operation? Not only were things working out as he had hoped but his conscience was now freed of any possible accusation of blame: for in his own mind and, perhaps more importantly, in that of Adrian abandoning their project could in no way be imputed solely to him. What's more, he didn't even need to mention the choice he had now made in favour of a new life in France. So, in the unlikely event of Adrian bringing the subject of the exchange up he'd simply reply lightly, as if it were still a matter of secondary importance which would in no way have been an obstacle to him pursuing their business venture. It was not quite the truth but, after all, what really mattered was that the T-shirt project had now been put to death. It did, nevertheless, strike Michael rather uncomfortably that in view of the fact that Adrian had found it necessary to give him an indication of where he now stood he might have done the same in return. He drew some comfort from the thought that even if he hadn't been totally honest with Adrian at least he was being honest with himself. For how can you ever be honest with others if you're not capable of being honest with yourself?

THIRTY-TWO

As was the dominical custom his mum brought him his breakfast to bed late the following morning. Her arrival had been preceded by a shouted 'Breakfast's coming up!' as she made her way gingerly up the stairs. He'd already been down for the Sunday newspaper and was sitting up in bed perusing its contents as she walked in through the doorway which he'd purposely left open.

'You don't get better service than this in a five star hotel,' he joked, folding it away. He always made this same remark and its effects were always much the same.

'Yes, well as long as you appreciate it.' She lowered the tray carefully onto his lap. 'I filled your cup a bit too full. It was a real balancing act bringing it up and some coffee has slurped onto the saucer. Pour it back into the cup, otherwise it'll drip onto your pyjama top.'

'You know, Mum, I really don't know what I'd do without you!' he replied. It was said in a teasing manner. A certain prudishness made him recoil from making declarations of this type appear as if they had come too nakedly from the heart. He preferred to clothe them in this light, jocular veil.

'I'll leave you to get on with it then. But when you've finished can you give me a call. I'd like to have a little word.'

He'd been curious enough to ask her what it was all about, but she wouldn't reveal more than that it was 'something to do with them moving down South.'

After finishing his breakfast he took his tray downstairs. His mother was in the kitchen peeling vegetables for lunch and he suggested they went back up to his room. He suspected that if Grandpa hadn't been there she would have waited until he'd got washed and dressed and they would have chatted in the sitting room. He sat down on the side of his bed while she remained standing. Her head gave an agitated twitch and her face, when the trace of a smile had passed over it, wore a tired, washed-out look; but what struck him most was the degree to which the dark-brownness of her hair was giving way to onslaughts of grey.

'As you know, last week we wrote telling your Aunt Marguerite and Uncle John we'd decided to sell up and move down to Rivermouth, and asking them if they could get the estate agents there to send us details of properties for sale. Well, yesterday evening while you were out your aunt phoned to tell us how delighted they were at the news and that they'd already been to see all the estate agents in Rivermouth. She also gave us some idea of house prices down there. The long and the short of it is that they're quite a bit higher than what we expected.'

'Well, that's understandable,' he replied. 'After all, it's a much sought-after area. And I suppose you're not the only ones who dream of retiring down there. It all boils down to a question of demand exceeding supply.

'Yes, well if we were really pushed we could pay a bit more than what we'd bargained for. But the thing is we don't want to put all our capital into the property. I mean, you can't live on bricks and mortar. Mind you, it's not that we won't have money coming in: we'll have your Grandpa's pension; and I don't think your dad'll have much trouble getting a little job down there. It's just that we'd like to have something behind us in case of emergencies. I mean, you never know what could crop up. Anyway, your Aunt Marguerite said that one of their neighbours had told them that with a bit of luck you can pick up something more reasonably priced at a property auction rather than going through an estate agent. Apparently, some owners are looking for a quick sale.'

'Yes, that sounds logical.'

'Well, the problem is we don't have the time to look into this in any great detail. Auntie Marguerite's neighbour said that if you're really lucky you could get quite a bargain. But you've got to know what you're doing. Anyway, we don't really know the pros and cons of it all. Your dad said he could handle it but I'm not sure he wouldn't get hold of the wrong end of the stick. Now you're the brains of the family. You'd be doing us a big favour if you could delve into things and get to know more about it. Oh, and by the way, we've decided to put the house and the shop up for sale right away. We're determined to go through with this, you know. If there's an auction at Easter we could close the shop for a couple of days and go down there.' Her head delivered itself of another jerk.

'Well, that shouldn't be difficult. I'm pretty sure the reference library in town will have something on the subject. The problem is they close at 6 o'clock on weekdays, so I'll only be able to go there next Saturday morning. I'll be refereeing a school football match until around 11 but I'll go straight there after. It doesn't close for lunch.'

'Oh don't worry about that. There's no immediate rush.'

This unexpected opportunity to assist his parents was a source of immense pleasure. Some of the pleasure came from the satisfaction of being able to accomplish what he considered to be his filial duty; but most of it was drawn from this confirmation that his parents were determined to pursue their dream, and that he had been invited to play a not unimportant part in helping it come true.

THIRTY-THREE

He'd prepared his assembly talk in note form on Saturday afternoon, and it hadn't taken him long to write it out in full the following day. He'd even read it out in front of his parents' full length bedroom mirror as a form of rehearsal. He was satisfied with the way it read. And the way he read it shouldn't be much of a problem: as a pupil he'd always been chosen to read out a Bible chapter at the school's Christmas carol service and had taken this as proof of his ability to read clearly and without hesitation. What worried him most about his coming performance was his own anxious disposition: for he couldn't help giving an inward shudder at the thought that in the stress of the moment when all eyes were on him he might find it impossible to control his nerves. He remembered that seminar during his final university year when he'd presented a short dissertation. It must have been the apprehension which had made him sleep badly the previous night and he couldn't stop his hands from quivering during the reading. This had been noticed and brought to his attention by one of his fellow students. He suspected it had been quietly noted by some of the others, too. At the brewery he'd been told that drinking a stiff whisky was an excellent and not uncommon way of combatting the tensions involved in exposing your performance to the judgement of others at an important presentation or meeting. It gave a boost to your confidence, or made you think it had this effect (which as far as the results are concerned often boils down to the same thing) by lowering the level of your inhibitions for a short while. Nevertheless, it had to be used with caution: alcohol taken in too large a quantity could affect your judgement and lead you to doing or saying things you might later regret. And when he came to think of it he wouldn't be surprised if Sylvia or some of the others hadn't resorted to this same remedy. So, he'd buy a couple of miniature bottles of whisky and, depending on how he felt when he rose on Tuesday morning, would drink one, or even both before setting off for school. It crossed his mind that what he was resorting to was a form of Dutch courage, but he preferred this kind of artifice as the only practical way to obviate the risk of exposing any jitters to the mockery of others. Among these others Ian, Cooper and, above all, Sylvia and Jennifer occupied a significant place. So, after the chat with his mum he drove to the shop where he was in the habit of buying his newspaper. It was one of those mini supermarkets which sold a bit of everything. They only had only two miniature bottles of cognac in stock. But what did it matter? It was alcohol and the effects would be the same.

He slept in fits and starts the night before and, since he'd got up feeling rather the worse for wear, had had no hesitation in putting his plan into operation by eating only the lightest of breakfasts and ingurgitating the contents of both bottles. As he was driving to school a feeling of exhilaration made him think he'd gone too far; but as he stepped out of his car it was replaced by a feeling of sober, lucid confidence which reassured him that things could only go well. He'd stumbled over one or two words at the beginning of his talk but had soon got into a fluid stride. In order to give a simple, practical illustration of how racial physical stereotypes don't measure up to how things really are he'd invited those among the assembled pupils who didn't have fair hair and blue eyes to put up their hands. Not only had these non-Aryans readily responded but, as he had anticipated, they had been in the majority. It had all gone to prove his point. On sitting down after his delivery the headmaster had thanked while at the same time gratifying him with what he took to be an appreciative smile. He was immensely relieved, even elated, that it was now all over.

The rest of the week passed without any notable occurrence, if it was not for that incident – the result of one of those unfortunate coincidences life's perversity sometimes keeps in store – which again brought home to Michael the fact that, in the eyes of his previously fond admirer, he was now in irretrievable disgrace. He was walking up the stairs to his classroom on the first floor when, halfway up, he was dismayed to see that Jennifer had chosen this same moment to begin stepping down. She immediately divested herself of the smile that had been lighting her face to focus her gaze in a mask-like stare on some undetermined object two feet above his head. It was a sobering reminder that, despite all the precautions he had resolved to take, he could not completely eliminate the risk of being faced with his past aberrations in the shape of their principal victim. It only strengthened his determination to sever all connections with Barfield School at the end of the year.

THIRTY-FOUR

As promised, after the Saturday morning football match Michael took himself off to the reference section of Bridgeford Central Library. The librarian helped him find a specialized property magazine and, on searching through some back numbers, he finally came across an article entitled *Why Not Buy Your Next House at a Property Auction?* He spent the following hour studying and then summarizing what he considered to be its relevant parts. When he arrived back home his mum was in the kitchen preparing lunch.

'Did you manage to find what we wanted?' she asked. Even though she'd tried her best to impart a matter-of-fact neutrality to both the wording and the tone of the question, her face betrayed enough hopeful expectancy for him to see that she could barely wait for the answer.

'Yes. I found a very good article on the subject. I think I've got what we were looking for. Shall we talk about it after lunch?'

'Right. I'll speed things up so we can be eating in twenty minutes or so. Just slip out and tell your father, will you? He's dying to know. He's been in and out of the kitchen half a dozen times this morning wanting to know if you were back.'

As they were leaving table at the end of the meal his mother told Grandpa to go up to his room. 'There's something private we want to talk about. I'll give you a shout when you can come back down,' she said, before adding what was certainly meant to be a consolatory, 'I'll bring your coffee up in a few minutes.' Grandpa left them with a gently pathetic, 'I'll leave you to it, then.' It pained Michael to see that the elderly gentleman had been hurt by this family exclusion, and he was on the point of suggesting that he be allowed to stay. In addition, he couldn't avoid a feeling of injustice: after all, wouldn't Grandpa's

BARFIELD SCHOOL

pension constitute a good part of his parents' future household income if things went as they planned? But he judged it better to say nothing. After all, wasn't his first duty towards them? Was it really his concern? And if things went as *he* planned wouldn't he be out of it all?

'Did you find everything?' his mum asked after taking a sip of her coffee. Though she tried hard not to show it Michael could detect a hint of anxiety in her voice. When she put her cup back onto the saucer she was holding a slight tinkle betrayed the trembling of her hands.

'Well, everything we need to know.' His reply was meant to be categorical enough to leave them in no doubt as to thoroughness of his research and his personal involvement in their plans.

'Come on then, let's have all the gen,' his father said. There was a trace of impatience in his voice.

'Well, according to the article, what Auntie Marguerite's neighbour said is true. The potential for getting a bargain at a property auction is much greater than if you go through an estate agent. Apparently it's possible to get an attractive property as much as 20% below market value. But it is a potential – so not systematically the case. You've probably got to be lucky to get that.'

'As much as all that?' his father exclaimed. His voice expressed not quite enough agreeable surprise for Michael to exclude a touch of dubiousness. He couldn't help noting the difference between his father's present restraint and the swaggering confidence with which he'd announced some twelve years ago their decision to buy the shop. While it had never been openly admitted, perhaps he now fully realized it was only fortunate circumstances which had come to their rescue, and that his plan of 'making some real money' had been blindly conceived and could have led, at best to bitter disappointment, at worst to financial disaster.

'Yes, but it's not all plain sailing, of course,' Michael continued. 'There are certain precautions you've got to take. First and foremost you must realize that a house often ends up at this sort of auction because the owner hasn't been able to keep up with his mortgage payments and the building society repossesses it. This sometimes means he didn't have the funds to spend on upkeep. As a result the property is in a poor state.

Obviously there's no point in getting what you think is a bargain only to find it's going to cost you thousands to bring it up to scratch.'

'So it's important to view it before,' his mother said.

'Right. After all it's only common sense to have a close look at the inside and outside of the property you intend to bid for. The first thing you'll have to do, then, is find out when and where there's an auction. And for every auction they print a catalogue listing all the properties on sale, so we'll have to get hold of one and study it carefully. They're usually available three or four weeks before the actual sale. Then, if you find something you're interested in you'll have to get in touch with the auctioneer to arrange a viewing. I must admit that not being on the spot could be a bit of a handicap.'

'Well, we can always ask Marguerite and John to keep us in the know. I can't see that being much of a problem,' his mother said. 'Did it say when these auctions are?'

'Usually on Saturdays – especially bank holiday weekends.'

'So there'll probably be one at Easter.' Her words were accompanied by a nervous twitch of her head. 'Well, I'm sure your aunt and uncle will be only too happy to keep us in the picture. You know, they couldn't be more thrilled at the idea of us settling down there.'

'And what about payment?' his father enquired.

'Well, if you make the winning bid you'll have to pay a 10% deposit immediately and come up with the balance within 28 days. This means you'll need to have made all your financial arrangements before. It's extremely important as, apparently, it's been known for people to have paid their 10% and lost it all because they couldn't come up with the balance in time. And if you don't pay the balance you'll lose the property. You could even be sued for the difference if it eventually sells for a lower price.'

'So we'd better make an appointment to talk things over with the building society,' his mother said. 'Mind you, if we sell the house and the business before there shouldn't be much of a problem.'

'I don't think the house'll take much selling,' his father said. 'It's the business which could be a problem. The main thing we've got going for us is the mill. Mind you, I don't know how long it'll last. I've heard talk that the textile business isn't doing too well. There's more and more cheap competition from India and China, and I've heard rumours it could even be closing. So we're getting out at the right time.'

'Well, if it came to a pinch we can always get a bridging loan from the building society,' his mother added.

'Sure. And as far as the winning bid is concerned it all depends, of course, on how far other bidders are prepared to go. You've got to be aware that Rivermouth is in a very popular holiday region and you're certainly not the only ones who dream of retiring down there. So, you may have to contend with other determined bidders. Oh, and by the way, there are two types of auction: in the first the sale is subject to approval by the seller. This means that even if you make the winning bid it could be cancelled if he thinks the price is too low. You need to make sure you're in what's called an absolute auction where the winning bidder automatically gets the property. The main thing is to decide on the maximum price you're willing to pay and stick to it. I mean, there's no point in getting carried away and then finding yourself lumbered with a property you'll be stretched to pay for.'

'Don't worry about that, my lad. I *was* born with a bit of common sense, you know,' his father retorted.

Michael couldn't help contrasting the circumspect moderation which he had detected in his father's voice throughout their conversation with his mother's open enthusiasm. Though this could partly be explained by the cautionary effect previous experience was now exerting on future expectations, he was tempted to think that a down-to-earth representation of the value of money had caused him to take a more dubious view of the possibility of obtaining such an extraordinary saving as 20%. His mother, on the other hand, seemed to lend it more credibility. Perhaps it was simply wishful thinking. Or perhaps she was somewhat disconnected from reality: perhaps her childhood and adolescence of relative financial ease made it difficult for her to perceive a saving of 20% as having any real significance beyond the arithmetical processes she had been required to master during her mathematics lessons at school. The thought even entered Michael's head that she didn't make any real association between 20% and its fractional peer of one fifth; or that, had she done so, the two might not have been considered to be the same. His father, on the other hand, being issued from a family where ends were significantly more difficult to meet, went considerably further in his reasoning: not only was 20% firmly linked with the fraction but on a house whose normal market value was £10.000 this represented a saving of £2.000. And above all he had a realistic comprehension of the work effort required to accumulate this sum.

If the truth were to be known, however, Michael had to confess that certain compartments of his father's mind had always been something of an enigma. It was generally agreed in the family that his dad was 'good at figures' and that, had he been allowed to pursue the appropriate studies, he would have been quite capable of qualifying as a chartered accountant. It was undeniable that he possessed a form of numerical intelligence which enabled him to grasp arithmetical combinations and logical systems with such natural ease that he only needed a short moment of reflection to find the answers to those calculations which his son would have needed pen and paper and considerably more time to reach. What's more, – and here there was certainly a strong connection – throughout Michael's childhood and youth they had played draughts together many times; and such was his father's overall vision of the game's logicality that he couldn't remember emerging the winner even once. Yet, strangely, on a verbal level, there were certain elementary structures which seemed to be beyond his father's comprehension. Last Christmas, for instance, the weather had been mild enough for Michael to quote the French saying, 'Christmas on the balcony, Easter at the fireside'. Much to his mother's exasperation and his own astonishment the meaning had to be carefully explained to him. What's more, Michael was perplexed by a certain duality in his father's character which his mother put down to him being born under the Gemini sign. 'There are two sides to your father,' she would often say. And it was true. For, on the one hand he had showed enough adventurous spirit to have taken the risk twelve years ago of sinking all their assets in a business, and he now seemed ready to embark upon that radical change of life which selling up and moving down South involved. Yet when it came to the small things in life he could be remarkably set in his ways: on those very rare occasions when he was presented with no alternative but to eat with his family or friends in a Chinese or Indian restaurant, a *sine qua non* condition was that it also offered an English menu. For he could never perceive the native food served in such establishments as meriting anything more flattering than the epithet 'foreign muck', and his choice always fell on a 'good old English mixed grill' or just plain 'fish 'n chips'. So closed was his mind to anything unfamiliar that Michael had placed him in the same category as those of his companions whose chief complaint during those wonderful schoolboy trips to France was that it was impossible to find the things they enjoyed at home. Yet, paradoxically, this same person had given his permission and even encouraged him to go.

Somewhere, without really being able to explain why, Michael had put this ambivalence down to his father's religious upbringing. From what his dad had told him, his own parents had been fervent members of a strict Evangelical movement whose austere creed demanded extreme plainness of worship (no statues, no musical accompaniment to hymns, no graven images, no official minister), along with a literal interpretation of the Old Testament, a rigorous sobriety of person, an implacable observance of the Lord's Day in particular, and systematic abstention from all forms of entertainment in general. As a result, normal distractions such as card-playing, dancing, going to the cinema, playing (or even watching) a sport, gambling of all kinds and, above all, imbibing alcohol (at a very early age children were obliged to sign a formal pledge never to touch one single drop of tipple for the rest of their days) were considered so many enticements proffered by Satan, indulgence in which was assimilated to the most unacceptable forms of Popery. And no photos existed of his father as a child for the simple reason that only God had the right to reproduce the human form. Even though his father had considerably distanced himself from the movement in his late youth certain habits and attitudes suggested that its effects on him had never been completely nullified. For these were still frequently brought to Michael's notice early on weekend or holiday mornings in the form of sonorous, painfully out-of-tune renditions of hymns such as *All Creatures of Our God and King, Praise My Soul the King of Heaven, Onward Christian Soldiers, All People that on Earth do Dwell*, to name but a few. However, his monotonously repetitious singing of the praises of Godly supra-love had never enabled him to surmount his aversion to men with long hair, ear rings, tattoos, and especially beards (discreetly-sized moustaches were grudgingly tolerated); and he would never cease to castigate this form of facial growth, displays of which, Michael had concluded, were probably perceived by the Puritan within as an outward sign of personal vanity in so much as they were rooted in an excessive concern for the effect they produced on others. The results of a rigidly-imposed childhood observance of the Sabbath as a no-work, no-play holy day, devoted exclusively to the worship of the Almighty, also resurfaced whenever his father caught sight of a line of washing hanging out on a Sunday morning. On such occasions his fury could only be compared to that of a bull close to whose nose a bright red rag was being waved.

One thing Michael did understand was the perverse satisfaction his father took in 'cooking the books'. 'They're not going to take the cherry off our cake,' he would frequently declare. And so, though he had his own official accountant whom he would supply with all the figures and receipts necessary for the preparation and presentation of the shop's yearly profit and loss account and balance sheet, the amounts submitted to the Inland Revenue authorities were but a modest reflection of the business's true financial state: for his dad had his own private procedure which consisted in declaring considerably less than the actual takings (these, nonetheless, being recorded in his own private book) by means of that subterfuge termed 'milking the till' which consisted in him pocketing the difference in cash between those amounts actually received and those officially stated. While his father had not excluded the eventuality of a fiscal control he was confident he could justify his apparently modest profit margins by pleading the fierce competition he was confronted with on the part of the now ubiquitous supermarkets.

I will, nevertheless, not allow it to be thought that Michael's father's stubborn determination to reduce to a minimum his contribution to the nation's finances could be taken as a reflection of his lack of probity in monetary dealings as a whole. Enough evidence existed for it to be perfectly well argued that the opposite was, in fact, the case: for, apart from those liberties he allowed himself with regard to the taxman, his attitude to money was characterized by a mixture of scrupulous straightness and deeply-rooted common sense. The principle he followed was of elementary simplicity: if you didn't have the cash to buy something you did without. In consequence, purchasing on credit was contemptuously referred to as 'the never-never'; and his proud boast to his children was that 'this house and everything in it is paid for.' Though they hadn't had the means to buy the house they lived in before coming to the shop without resorting to a mortgage, he hadn't been able to rest until the loan had been paid off – and this well before the due date. What's more, while his job as a commercial traveller didn't offer a large salary, he always managed to find something to put away. And as a child he'd always insisted on Michael doing odd jobs in the house and garden – setting the table, drying the dishes, cutting the lawn in summer, weeding the flower beds – in return for his weekly spending money. Later, when Michael helped him paint the house, glaze his new greenhouse or mix cement for a garden wall he always insisted on paying him extra for his toil. So his dogged determination to deprive the country of its legal due was fed by the unshakeable conviction that strict compliance with its fiscal requirements would have deprived them of those just rewards which their considerable efforts deserved. Michael could never avoid thinking, however, that with his father there were always limits – especially when it came to matters of money. During his final sixth form year when he'd been called to interviews at universities in distant parts of the country he'd had no alternative but to travel there by train. After two or three journeys, and much to his mother's disgust, his father had begun to complain about the accumulative cost of the fares. It brought home to Michael the sobering fact that in his begetter's mind financial considerations could even predominate over the educational future of his son.

'Well, do you think there's anything else we need to know for the moment?' Michael asked as a way of suggesting they might now consider ending their chat.

'No, I don't think so,' his mum replied. His father contented himself with an acquiescent nod.

'And thanks very much for all the trouble you've gone to,' she added. 'We're very grateful, you know. I'll just go and tell Grandpa he can come down now.'

THIRTY-FIVE

On Monday morning shortly before that moment when Headmaster Fowler was in the habit of strolling into the staffroom and inviting his teachers to follow him out to take their allotted seats on the assembly hall platform, Adrian walked in, looked around him and on spotting Michael came striding resolutely over. A somber frown had replaced the expression of light joviality his face usually wore when he addressed his pal. It flashed through Michael's mind that he'd been ruminating on the conversation they'd had in the Market Tavern and now wanted to inform him directly of his wish to abandon their T-shirt project. Or had something happened between him and Jean? But then, wouldn't he have waited for a more discreet opportunity to communicate this sort of news?

'Mike, I don't really know how to tell you this,' he began, looking to both sides of him to make sure no-one was within hearing distance. His voice had a hushed, uneasy ring of urgency about it, as if the message he was about to deliver was too ponderous for him to keep to himself for long.

'Jean rang me last night with some very bad news. Molly's mum passed away yesterday morning.'

'Really? I'm very sorry to hear that. But Molly and me had a drink together last week and she told me it was more or less expected – though it's happened sooner than she thought.'

'Yeah, the thing is, Mike, that's … that's only part of it. I don't know how well you knew each other but … I'm sorry to have to tell you this but, you see … well … Molly … she's dead, too. She killed herself just after.' He gazed uneasily down at his feet. It was as if he somewhere felt he was in the wrong for having to announce such a tragic event.

For a moment Michael remained in a state of dazed disbelief.

'I just can't believe it.'

It was all he could manage. He was not just conscious of the laconic triteness of his words but he couldn't quite rid himself of the guilty thought that they betrayed less a sense of sorrow than one of simple incredulity that the girl he'd been talking to only a few days ago no longer breathed. The feeling of guilt was heightened by the thought that when they were in the pub together he hadn't detected any real sign of what he now realized must have been a deeply fragile mental state. If he had, he would have been far more supportive. Perhaps this would have made her think twice before taking her own life. But could he really be blamed for not having seen what was going on in her mind? After all, he hadn't known her all that well. Even her best friend had admitted she was a difficult girl to get to know. In addition, he'd been accustomed to a certain lightness on the part of his friend, and he was now obliged to admit that Adrian might be capable of more true feeling than he had given him credit for, and that, as most of us do as some time or other, he himself had fallen into the trap of judging others severely while remaining airily tolerant with regard to himself. But there again, wasn't his apparent sadness more a vicarious manifestation of the sorrow Jean was certainly feeling? Since both he and Adrian seemed to be uncomfortable with the feelings the tragedy aroused Michael decided to give their conversation a more factual orientation.

'When did it happen?'

'Yesterday afternoon. Apparently she told everybody she was going for a drive, took her brother's car, drove out to a local beauty spot overlooking Dublin Bay and jumped from the cliff top.'

'Good God. I hope she didn't suffer.'

'No, I don't think she did. Jean told me she died from multiple fractures and injuries, so I think it would have been more or less straight away.'

'You know this is the last thing I'd have thought she'd do.'

'Yes, well it's the same with Jean. It's a case of still waters running deep. Jean told me that, as with most suicides, it was a combination of depressing circumstances. They managed to get her mum into a special nursing home for the terminally ill where she could die in peace. An' according to Jean, Molly would have had to sign a sort of disclaimer stating that she agreed to no medical resuscitation. Her mum wasn't in a state to do it herself. Jean says it's what usually happens in hopeless cases like this. It probably made her feel as if she was signing her mum's death warrant. An' I don't know whether she told you this, but she broke with her boyfriend at Christmas. They'd been going out together for years an' he wanted to get married as soon as she qualified. She told him she wasn't ready yet and he gave her an ultimatum. They had a row and she broke it off. An' then there was the worry of her final exams. It was all too much for her to cope with. It pushed her over the brink. I suppose she just couldn't see any future. Jean's very upset, of course. She's going to the funeral.'

Michael nodded his head slowly in sympathetic understanding. This was only the second time he'd been confronted with the death of a person who'd been a part of his life. His first encounter had been at the age of sixteen when his maternal grandmother had suddenly passed away. The news had been announced on the telephone and his mother had burst into tears. He'd never seen her show this type of lachrymose reaction before and it had caused him some disagreeable surprise. Though he'd been fond of his grandmother and over the days preceding the funeral had made an effort to assume the required sad looks, he himself had been aware of nothing much more than a feeling of discomfort that she was now no more. A good part of his unease was prompted by the blanket of lugubriousness which the event threw over the house along with a vague feeling of resentment that for the next few days her demise would be the cause of unavoidable perturbation to the habitual course of his life. In short, he couldn't wait for things to get back to normal. And just before the internment his grandmother had been laid out in her coffin at home on the dining room table so that everybody could pay their last respects. She looked cold and waxen and he'd given an inner shudder when Grandpa had kissed her colourless lips. It was true her death had come as something of a shock; but once its initial effects had been got over everybody's grief was muted. She had suffered from chest angina and perhaps in the sub-conscious depths of the family mind the likelihood of her sudden death had never been considered as totally impossible. As far as Molly was concerned it was different: she had been approaching the prime of her life and the unexpected, self-inflicted nature of her demise brought home to him the brutal fact that life and death are held apart by only the flimsiest of temporal strands. At the decease of his grandmother it was the egoism of early youth which had caused him to feel so little sorrow. With Molly it was also perhaps because he was now old enough for experience to have taught him to see things in a more detached, relative light: that what appears to be an insurmountable tragedy at a certain age can be the subject of indifference, even self-directed mirth only a few years later. But, while youth is generally too occupied with its own future to dwell in any great depth on the loss of it by others, he still remained aware that, though they'd only begun to become acquainted, she'd opened up her heart enough for him to be haunted by her memory. It still remained, however, that he was unable to comprehend how someone with most of her life before her could be pushed to such an irremediable extremity as to seek her own death. Perhaps it was because reality had momentarily stripped her of all her dreams. It only went to strengthen his resolve to pursue his own of starting a new life in France.

THIRTY-SIX

Not even the most devastating of tragedies can prevent life from sooner or later re-treading the familiar path of normality; and so it was that during the course of the following week a post was planted in Michael's parents' front garden bearing a sign informing neighbours and all those who chanced to pass by that the house reposing behind was now for sale. According to Grandpa (his daughter had finally informed him of their plans to move down South and being now a keen observer of events we can lend total credibility to his report), a young man had appeared one morning, camera in hand, and had taken several different-ly-angled photos of the house. It might, therefore, be confidently assumed that its sale was now being brought to the attention of a wider, more targeted public by means of a notice in an estate agent's window carrying an image and description of the property together with the price at which its owners would consent to it changing hands. It might equally be supposed that a similar specification had been placed in the 'Proper-ties for Sale' section of that same evening newspaper which only a few weeks previously had for our young man been the vector of such disagreeable news.

During the following weekends a steady trickle of visitors had been interested enough (though it is not to be excluded that mere curiosity drove some) to wish to examine the house in more direct detail. It was his mother who had taken it upon herself to guide them round. She was a sociable woman and on the whole carried out her task well. But Michael was sometimes the amused witness to her naïve and sometimes tactless attempts at ending these viewings on a cordial note. Two examples stood out in his memory. One Saturday afternoon an elderly couple presented themselves. Even though the lady spoke with what was unmistakably a northern English accent his mum declared as they were leaving, 'There's no guessing where you come from!' She then found turned pointedly towards her husband who had a broad Scottish accent, and with what appeared to be genuine curiosity had asked, 'And where are *you* from?'

But the most awkward incident happened when a well-spoken, smartly-dressed, middle-aged man came accompanied by an attractive, mini-skirted, blond-haired girl whom Michael judged to be in her early twenties. As usual his mother showed them round, and when they came back down into the lounge after viewing the upstairs Michael was seated in an armchair reading the newspaper. As she was showing them out and with her usual intention of culminating the visit on a friendly note she found nothing better to ask the man, with a nod in the direction of the young lady, 'Oh, is this your daughter?' Michael had difficulty in suppressing a burst of laughter.

As his father had anticipated, much less interest was aroused by the sale of the shop. At one stage he had seriously thought about liquidating the business; but his accountant had pointed out that even though supermarkets were forcing corner grocery shops out of existence, the attractive margin obtained on the sale of sandwiches and cakes up at the mill justified them placing it on the market as a viable concern. He even recommended the services of a specialized broker in order to determine a fair price and then proceed to market the shop with a view to achieving a quick sale. Albert Morgan was, of course, astute enough not to mention the rumours he'd been hearing that the textile trade was facing increasingly fierce Asian competition to such a point that there was even talk of closing the mill down. But, if the worst came to the worst and it couldn't be sold as an on-going business it might sell more quickly, though at a lower price, if it was simply offered as residential property. The living premises were vast – in fact it was two houses which at some time in the past had been joined into one. In addition, he'd be satisfied if they could only get back what they'd paid some twelve years before. After all, if you took both properties into account they wouldn't be losers: the house they now lived in had shown a considerable increase in value over the last eight years. So, all in all, he was confident that by the time Easter rolled round the sale of one, or even both, would put enough cash behind them to envisage bidding for something worthwhile in a property auction down South.

THIRTY-SEVEN

One Saturday evening just a couple of weeks before Easter Michael had retired early to his bedroom with the aim of expending what remained of that day's energy in yet another concentrated attempt to develop his understanding of spoken French. He had just pressed his right ear close to the radio in the hope of being able to follow the French eight o'clock news when the left one brought it to his attention that the telephone had started ringing in the hall downstairs. His mother's loud exclamation, 'Oh, Marguerite. How nice it is to hear from you!' left him in no doubt as to whom the call was from and what it was about. As soon as she'd put the receiver down he switched off the radio and went downstairs. The television had been turned off and his parents were in excited conversation. Grandpa sat looking on with a steady smile. 'Oh Michael,' his mother announced, 'your Auntie Marguerite has just phoned with what could be some very good news.' He was quickly informed of all the details.

An auction was scheduled in Rivermouth for Good Friday, and Auntie Marguerite and Uncle John had managed to obtain a listing of the residential properties which would be up for sale. She'd posted it off that very morning but had previously taken the liberty of having a look through. She'd folded down a corner of a page on which appeared a photo and description of a small, brick-built bungalow they thought might be of interest. They'd been informed that the owner, an elderly widower who lived alone had died recently and that the bungalow was up for auction. Apparently, his children wanted a quick sale. The gentleman had had a small building company and the property had actually been built under his supervision some twenty years ago specifically for his retirement. Auntie Marguerite and Uncle John thought this could be taken as pretty good proof that it wasn't 'jerry-built'. That morning they'd even been and had a look at it. As they didn't have a key they could only view it from the outside. Their first impressions were that it was nice and private. They'd walked round the garden: there was a good piece at the front and a long stretch behind – ample enough room for Albert to have a reasonably-sized greenhouse. And it was all bordered by a high mixed hawthorn and privet hedge. The garden was certainly overgrown and neglected but they reckoned it wouldn't take long to knock it into shape. The only problem was that the bungalow might be a bit too small: they'd peeped through the windows and, even though there was a good-sized lounge and kitchen along with a small dining room and what seemed to be a spacious toilet and bathroom, there was only one bedroom. Judging from the fuel tank outside it had oil-central heating. Oh yes, there was also a detached garage. All in all, they thought it would be well worth their while to come down and bid for it. If they decided to do this they'd be only too happy to put them up for the length of their stay.

'It sounds just like what we're looking for,' his mother had excitedly declared. 'It's true it's only got one bedroom, but if we manage to get it at a reasonable price we might have enough left over to have one or even two dormers built. In the meantime we can always use the dining room as a bedroom for Grandpa. And if we close the shop at lunchtime on the Thursday we could be down there by early evening.'

Michael could scarcely escape the envious feeling that his parents might soon be one big step nearer than him to their dreams coming true.

THIRTY-EIGHT

During the weeks that followed their conversation in the Market Tavern snug Adrian made not the slightest mention of their T-shirt project. By this Michael could only conclude with much satisfaction that in his pal's mind their venture was now more than just dead; it had been long since buried. Some time after that promising news from Auntie Marguerite which had caused his parents such anticipatory joy and himself those stirrings of envy, Michael, as was his occasional habit, came home for lunch. As he walked into the sitting room Grandpa pointed to a letter which he'd stood up against the mantelpiece clock.

'It's for you. There's a French stamp on it.'

His words were pronounced with a strong note of drama. It was as if he was perfectly aware of the significance it might have, and wanted to show his grandson that he shared his anxiety as to the message it contained. Grandpa's reaction was not without causing some surprise as Michael had mentioned to him in only a vague, matter-of-fact way his plans to spend a year in France. Perhaps he'd overheard his parents discussing the importance it had for him. Though he was willing to admit that Grandpa's strong interest might spring from a hopeful anticipation of the gratification which favourable news would bring, he couldn't help feeling some irritation at the thought that it could also be motivated by a wish to impinge upon some of that private territory he considered to belong exclusively to him.

The origins of the letter caused Michael some puzzlement: it couldn't be of an official nature as the address was hand-written; and there was nobody he knew personally who lived in France – unless it was his former tutor, Mr Naylor, who might be there at the moment and was simply writing to say hello, or to enquire whether his application had been accepted. After all he had been kind enough to give Michael a good reference. This was what he read:

Hello Michael,

Your name and address have been supplied to me by our French Ministry of Education. Permit me to introduce myself. My name is Jean-Paul Combe and I've been designated as your future exchange partner. I'm writing to give you some information about myself, my family, the region in which you'll be living, and the lycée where you'll be replacing me for a year. I hope you'll find it useful.

At this juncture may I be permitted to offer my apologies at having to resort to a stereotyped description of those deeply-felt reactions which require that, on receiving the news we have been so eagerly awaiting and which can herald such a radical change in our lives, our heart begins to beat wildly and our hands to assume a trembling existence of their own? These were, nevertheless, the immediate effects these words had on Michael. His emotion was, however, tinged with incomprehension. Why hadn't he received official notification from the *Bureau for Educational Exchanges* before? The only plausible explanation was that his exchange partner had been informed a few days before and had taken it upon himself to write to Michael immediately. So, it could simply be due to a lack of co-ordination between the French and English sides. In that case a letter informing him that he'd been accepted was probably in the post. Still, wasn't the result the same? Couldn't this be taken as a sure sign that his French dream was now coming true? Grandpa had, no doubt, detected some of his emotion as he gave Michael a look of hopeful expectation. It was as if he was waiting for his grandson's enthusiastic confirmation of the good news the letter contained. But Michael simply said, 'Yes, it's what I was hoping for,' before retiring to his room: for rather than manifest his triumph to others by throwing up his arms and squealing with joy, he found more pleasure in first savouring it alone with himself. The rest of the letter read as follows:

I'll begin with myself. I'm 33 years old, a bachelor and live with my parents in a small village called Montbel. I've got a married elder sister and a brother two years younger than me. My sister is a nurse at a hospital in Lyon. She's married to a surgeon and they've got two boys. My brother (his name is Julien), has just finished his English studies at Besançon University and is doing his military service in Dijon at the moment. He's training to be an English teacher like me and when his military obligations terminate next year he'll start the practical part of his CAPES. As you probably know, this means 'Certificat d'aptitude au professorat de l'enseignement du second degré'. It's a competitive exam you must pass to become a state-recognized teacher here in France. Teaching is, in fact, in the family. My mother was the village primary school teacher for all her career. She's now retired. My father was the village baker and confectioner, but since he closed his baker's shop five years ago he's been working as a representative selling animal feeds to the small farmers in the region. His company's headquarters are in Besançon.

Except for one year as a co-operation teacher in the Ivory Coast I've spent the whole of my career (8 years) teaching English at the lycée of Vernois. I have (and you will have) 18 hours of lessons per week. The school is situated approximately 20km from Montbel. It takes less than 20 minutes by car. Vernois is a small (and not very interesting) town of around 12 000 inhabitants located about 45 minutes from Vesoul, the capital of the Haute-Saône département, and a one hour and a half drive from Besançon, the capital of the neighbouring département of the Doubs. Perhaps you already know the region a little.

The Haute-Saône is a very rural département with lots of forests and étangs. These are small, man-made lakes ('meres' in English) with plenty of fish in them – especially pike, carp, trout and perch. My father has got one, so if you're an angler bring your fishing tackle with you! The region is perfect for someone who likes being at one with nature. It has, however, the reputation for being backward and is sometimes disparagingly referred to (especially by Parisians) as the Haute-Patate. Please find enclosed a picture postcard of one of the surrounding forests. It's a bit banal but it will give you some idea of what to expect. I hope you're not a night owl as there's not much to do in the evenings – unless you're prepared to drive quite a way. The climate is a semi-Continental one of extremes with hot summers (+30°C) and very cold winters (-20°C). If you're a skier there's plenty of snow in the nearby Vosges Mountains.

The lycée has a total of around 800 pupils from both Vernois and the surrounding villages. You'll be glad to know they're calm, undemonstrative, country children who pose very few discipline problems. The teaching staff is very friendly and we all get on very well. We have a very good headmaster. His name is Monsieur Grelot and he's a hunchback.

I'm very much looking forward to hearing from you and to knowing more about yourself, the region and the school I'll be spending my year in. It might be a good idea if you arrived a week before the start of the school term here as this will give you time to acclimatize and find some accommodation. I'll be spending two weeks of the summer holidays in the U.S.A. with a teacher friend, but will be back well before the school term begins. We'll be renting a car and seeing as much as possible. My friend is very interested in the cause of the American Red Indians. We may even be spending a few days living with a tribe on their reservation! You can stay in Montbel with me and my parents while you're looking for somewhere to live. You should have no problem finding lodgings in Vernois, but in any case I'll be there to help you. Could you find some accommodation for me? It doesn't have to be permanent – just something that will give me time to look around. I plan to go to England two or three days before the beginning of the term.

I think I've covered the most important points. If there's anything else you'd like to know please don't hesitate to write. I'm really looking forward to hearing from you soon.

Friendlily yours,
Jean-Paul

On the application form which Michael had completed candidates had been requested to name, in order of preference, the three regions they would like to spend their year in – with the proviso that their choices could not always be met. Fond memories of his school trips had prompted him to indicate the *Côte d'Azur* as his first choice, followed by Burgundy and the South West. He'd never heard of the *département* of the Haute-Saône, let alone the town of Vernois, and had to look the region up on his map. It was true that quite a distance separated it from the

Mediterranean Coast. But did this have any real importance? What mattered, above all, was that in just a few months he would be leaving Barfield and England, and heading for a new life in the heart of France. And judging from the warm tone of the letter his future exchange partner seemed a friendly, helpful sort of person. What's more, he could only note with envy that it was written in precise, faultless English. It was with a desire not to reveal by comparison his own deficiencies in French that he penned his reply in his mother tongue. This is what he wrote:

Dear Jean-Paul,

Many thanks for your letter. I was really excited to read it. In fact I'm still waiting for official notification that my application has been accepted. I think this is probably due to a lack of co-ordination between your Ministry of Education and the Bureau which organizes educational exchanges on this side of the Channel. I'm sure I'll be hearing from them soon. It might even be on its way. Please accept my congratulations on your excellent English. To be honest, my French pales in comparison, and that's why I'm writing back to you in English. However, the main reason I applied for this exchange was to improve my everyday spoken French as well as broaden my professional and personal horizons. So, once I set foot in France I've resolved to banish English entirely (that is outside lessons, of course!).

Like you I'm a bachelor and live with my parents. I'm 28 years old and have been teaching at Barfield School for two years now. Right after leaving university I spent two years working for a brewery as an area supervisor responsible for the profitability of a number of pubs and off-licences (shops selling alcoholic drink to be consumed 'off' the premises) in and around Birmingham. But I didn't like the job and decided to go into teaching. Barfield is a relatively new (it opened only eight years ago) mixed comprehensive school of around 700 pupils aged between 11 and 18. The headmaster, Mr Fowler, is a bit of a stickler for discipline and is not particularly liked by some of the teachers. Apparently, he was captain of a ship (some people say it was a submarine) in the Royal Navy before — so that explains a lot of things! However, I've heard he'll be retiring at the end of the next school year. The teachers here are a mixed bunch. Most of them are reasonably young, so you should be able to make friends without any problem. I'll speak to one of my pals about you. His name is Adrian. If you have any problems I'm sure you can rely on him to help you as much as he can.

I'm afraid neither the weather we get here nor the city of Bridgeford are particularly attractive. We seem to get more than our fair share of rain and don't see as much of the sun as we'd like – even in summer. Temperatures, however, are usually quite mild with not too much cold or snow in winter. It certainly never gets down to -20° as it does with you! I'm beginning to doubt whether I'll survive to see next spring! Bridgeford has a population of around 300,000 and was for many years famous for its heavy woollen industry with plenty of 'dark, satanic mills', as the poet, William Blake, put it in his famous hymn 'Jerusalem'. There are, however, signs that the textile business is beginning to decline (there's more and more competition from India and China), and some of those grimy mills are now being cleaned up. As you probably know, the Brontë sisters were born and lived in a small village only a short distance away from here, and there's some very pleasant countryside to the north. Talking of sisters I've got just one (no brothers). She's two years older than me, married and lives quite near. Her husband works in a bank. At Christmas they informed us she was expecting a baby in July. My parents are a part of that 'nation de boutiquiers' Napoléon described the English as being. They've had a grocer's shop for the last 12 years but are hoping to sell up this year and retire to the southern coast of England.

By the way, regarding your accommodation I'll have a word with one of our teachers, Mr Bennet, who I'm sure would be willing to accommodate you. He's head of the English department at Barfield so he'll be in a good position to correct your English – that's if it needs it, which, judging from your letter, I very much doubt. He's quite a friendly creature, though perhaps a bit on the 'prim and proper' side. I've not met his wife, but apparently she's a teacher, too. Anyway if they don't suit you can always find a place of your own to rent.

I've just read this letter through and find it a bit rambling. If I've missed anything out please don't hesitate to let me know. I'll be writing to you later to tell you when I'll be coming – as you suggest it will probably be at least a week before the school term starts. Many thanks for your offer to *put me up while I look for suitable accommodation. It's extremely kind of you and I really appreciate this. Enjoy your holiday in the States.*

Very best wishes,
Michael

P.S. I've enclosed a couple of picture postcards showing some country scenes just a few miles to the north of Bridgeford.

He'd judged it preferable not to dwell too much on the pupils they had at Barfield School. They were certainly not calm, country children – some of them at least – and he couldn't escape the uncomfortable feeling that Headmaster Fowler's fears of future discipline problems might be prophetic in their purport. After all, the last thing he wanted was to give Jean-Paul reasons which might cause him to have second thoughts.

It might be imagined that these considerations were once again not quite in line with those previous promises he had made to himself of being more honest towards others. Michael was certainly not unaware of this; but like many young people of his age he was still in the making and, depending on circumstance, his merits and failings were capable of expanding or contracting. And what is more normal that, as the days progressed, the bubbling exhilaration he'd felt on receiving this good news should be slightly deflated by the prickling apprehension which the certainty of soon embarking upon an unprecedented adventure caused. He comforted himself with the reflection that his fear was caused by a deepening awareness that the insubstantiality of his dreams was now being replaced by material structures and persons. So, wasn't it an inseparable part of the jittery excitement we feel when, on the eve of departure into a mainly uncharted land, we are led to a closer, more realistic examination of the dangers involved?

THIRTY-NINE

Michael's assumption that official notification of his acceptance was already on the way proved to be correct: the following evening a letter from the *Bureau for Educational Exchanges* was waiting for him in that same place on the mantle-piece. It indicated the name and address of both the *lycée* and his exchange partner, while requesting him to confirm his acceptance of their offer and, in order to avoid causing any undue disappointment, to do this before getting in touch with the latter. Presumably, this was something Jean-Paul had not been asked to do, or had chosen to disregard. Once they had received his agreement they would be writing with details on the procedure involved in obtaining a visa and *carte de séjour*, the residence card that would be required for his year-long stay. This he hastened to do. The following day he took the first opportunity to inform Adrian that he'd been accepted for the French exchange. His pal seemed genuinely pleased. He made no mention of their T-shirt venture.

Now that our young man's dream was well on its way towards being transformed into reality what about his parents? What progress were they making towards the realization of their own? They had promptly received the promised catalogue of residential properties to be auctioned that Good Friday, and could only agree with Aunt Marguerite that the bungalow she had drawn their attention to represented enough of an enticing prospect to justify them closing the shop at midday the day before, and setting off for Rivermouth as speedily as driving back home, changing clothes and loading their suitcase would allow. And the potentially worrying relation of cause and effect between the rumours Michael's father had heard about the slackness of the wool trade and the management's decision to close the mill for the long Easter weekend at the end of that same Thursday morning was overridden by the more comforting thought that the immediate consequence for him was that the shop's early closure would be scarcely detrimental to the week's takings.

They had also received what could be conceived as encouraging news regarding the sale of their home. The estate agent had telephoned to inform them that they had received an offer. But since the sum in question was below the advertised price and was also dependent on the prospective buyer selling their present home they advised his father not to accept immediately. He was, however, quite confident that someone prepared to pay the full asking price with no upper chain involvement would eventually come along. His father had agreed that it would be more judicious to wait. Previously, Michael's parents had come to an arrangement with their building society: they already had enough available funds to cover a 10% deposit, provided the price of the bungalow fell within the limits they'd fixed, and had been assured that in the event of a successful bid without previously having sold their shop and home there would be no problem in them being granted a bridging loan to cover the balance that would normally be payable four weeks later.

The Thursday came and his parents set off as planned in the early afternoon. His father had reckoned there shouldn't be too much traffic on the roads this particular day and that they'd be able to make it down to Rivermouth in not much more than six hours. If things ran smoothly they might even be able to stop for a cup of tea on the way. They had gratefully accepted Aunt Marguerite and Uncle John's invitation to accommodate them; so, if they managed to make a winning bid they would certainly be taking them out for a meal on Good Friday evening to celebrate and to thank them for their hospitality. And if things didn't turn out as well as they hoped this would in no way discourage them. They'd spend Saturday and Sunday viewing other properties and would be setting off home on Easter Monday. In view of the heavy traffic they were sure to meet they could only be expected back late in the evening.

The result was that Michael, apart from a Saturday afternoon cricket match (the season had just started), was faced with the prospect of spending the long Easter weekend alone with Grandpa and his memories of things long since past. It wasn't that he had little esteem for his mother's father. His qualities far outweighed his defects: he was a kindly, generous man who hated conflict of any kind, and Michael was sure that inwardly he was suffering from those tense domestic circumstances he was now so inextricably caught up in. Poor Grandpa! At his age wasn't his only way of escaping from harsh reality that of losing himself in nostalgic memory of those hope-filled days of childhood and youth when life stretched so endlessly before him? Michael's respect was mingled with enough understanding for him to resolve to lend a sympathetic ear to what could be an object of indifference to many, even mockery to some. So, while he knew in advance that he would probably have heard it all several times before, he would encourage Grandpa to express himself on what he held so dear with a freedom which the presence of his daughter and son-in-law denied. Moreover, it wasn't all without interest: somewhere Michael didn't dislike hearing Grandpa talk about those 'good old days' when he had been too much of an eager participator in his own life to want to share much in that of others. What's more, during his lifetime hadn't he been a living testimony to changes sweeping enough for the world to have never known before, and which extended from the beginnings of the horseless carriage to Man's first landing on the moon? And didn't the fact that it had all been experienced by Grandpa make his narrations more graphically real than if they had been set down on the mute white pages of a book?

After lunch on Good Friday they settled down in the sitting room to enjoy their cup of coffee. Over the meal they'd discussed his parents' chances of making a successful bid for the property. As was his habit when volunteering his opinion on the outcome of events significant enough to have a major impact on the family's orientations in life Grandpa had advanced a generalized, 'Don't worry. It'll be all right.' Though it could in no way be said he was a man of deep religious belief he always seemed optimistic in his conviction that in matters of domestic importance occult forces were at work on their behalf. After finishing his coffee he proceeded to fill and light his pipe. Michael had always compared the resulting billows of smoke to a steam locomotive getting under way. It brought back memories of that time as a boy – he must have been aged 11 or 12 at the time – when having a puff on his Grandpa's pipe had been the object of compulsive desire. One day when his parents and Grandma were out he'd asked Grandpa if he could have a go. The first time he'd been met with a refusal. But even at that age he knew Grandpa well enough to know that it only needed a little more insistence for him to have his way. It was with a resigned 'Here you are then,' that Grandpa finally handed it over. Two minutes later the previously fixed verticality of the room, the walls and their contents assumed a disconcerting, floating movement in the direction of the horizontal. He'd only just made it to the toilet where he was horribly sick. Naturally, the incident was brought to the notice of his parents and Grandma when they arrived back home. Grandpa told them he'd let him 'have a go to teach him a lesson'. Michael had always suspected the true reason was that Grandpa's love of pleasing others was so much a part of his character that he had considerable difficulty in saying 'no' – especially when that 'no' would go against the wishes of a child.

'What did you use to do at Easter when you were a lad, Grandpa?' Michael began by asking. He used the word 'lad' knowingly. The right word in the right circumstances always has its power. He had thought of saying 'boy' but decided against it: not only was it a word Grandpa would never have employed but Michael couldn't help thinking it didn't have enough of a homely ring about it to open up the same fond memories of the past. Grandpa took his pipe from his mouth and laid it carefully down on the chair arm. It was as if he wanted to remove all doubt in the mind of this unexpected listener that he might prefer the pleasures of solitary reminiscence behind its curls of smoke.

'Ho. When I was a lad it wasn't like today, you know,' he began. His eyes took on a gleam that Michael had not observed since those days when his parents listened with deference to all he had to say.

'Well, to start with there was none of your chocolate Easter eggs. No, there was none of that. Before breakfast on Easter Sunday our mum and dad'd hide thirteen hard-boiled eggs in the garden when it was nice. An' when it poured they hid 'em round the house. You see, everybody kept hens in them days.'

'Why thirteen?' Michael knew in advance that there was no superstitious intent. His question was meant to give Grandpa the pleasure of being able to repeat what he'd been told many times before.

'Well that was because there was thirteen of us – twelve brothers and sisters. An' believe it or not, the thirteenth was adopted! We all went out seeking 'em, an' if you found the most you got an orange. You see, oranges were a real luxury in them days. We all got one for Christmas. Mind you, the eggs weren't wasted. We had 'em after as a treat for breakfast. As a rule, all we got was a couple of slices of bread with margarine and jam, an' sometimes a bowl of porridge in winter if we were lucky. Then we all went to church.'

'So you were a poor family?'

'Yes, we were. But I can't say we really went without. An' we were content with what we had. Life was hard but you accepted it. People want everything these days.

'Your mum must have had her work cut out looking after all you lot.'

'Well, in them days it was the eldest girl who looked after the youngest. When he was on his deathbed my dad called out for Mary, his big sister, and not his mother. Old Horace, he was a right character, he was. He'd even put it in his will that as they were taking him to the cemetery they all had to stop at *The White Horse*, and have a drink on him. He was sorry but he couldn't be with 'em on the way back!'

Grandpa paused for a second to take off his spectacles and carefully place them on the chair arm by the side of his still smouldering pipe. It was as if the act of removing them from his short-sighted eyes increased the clarity of his vision of past time.

'Of course, there were no cars when you were a little lad,' Michael said. He knew for a fact that this was not quite true: that during Grandpa's boyhood at the end of the 19th century they did already exist. But wasn't the object of the exercise to encourage him to talk?

'Oh no, just horses and carts. An' they used to put straw on the road in front of houses when there'd been a death in the family. You see, it was to deaden the noise. An' I remember the first motorcars as plain as this day. In them days we called 'em horseless carriages. They scared the horses out of their lives; an' people thought they were dangerous. I remember a law coming out saying that in town a man carrying a red flag had to walk 50 yards in front of 'em.'

'And when did you first meet Grandma?'

'Well, we both lived in the same village and our families used to visit. It all started there. Your Grandma's dad was a real stickler, he was. I remember one Easter – we'd just got engaged and we were walking arm in arm in the park – when he came walking up to us. An' you know what he said? "What's up we thee lass? Is tha lame?" It takes some believing but it's the truth. Aye, things have changed a bit since then. We were ignorant in them days. Not like now.' His voice assumed a lower, more confidential tone as if indiscreet ears might be listening to what he was about to say. 'You know, when I was first married I didn't even know what a woman's period was!'

'How old were you?'

'Twenty-six.'

'And where did you go for your honeymoon?'

'Nowhere. I was on nights at the time. So just before we got married I went to see my undermanager to ask him if he could let me have a week's summer holiday in advance. An' you know what he said?'

'No.' Michael replied with a note of simulated expectancy.

'He said, "I'm sorry, lad, I can't do that. But I'll tell you what I can do: I can put you on days for a couple of weeks!" An' that was our honeymoon.' His words were followed by a dry chuckle. 'Mind you, we did manage to have a week on the Isle of Man that summer.'

The conversation continued in the same desultory way. Grandpa's father-in-law had spent the last two years of his life living with them. 'It was never a problem,' he remarked with a resignation discreet enough to stop short of a sigh. The thought crossed Michael's mind that such a restrained reference to his own painful situation was revelatory of Grandpa's deeply rooted family spirit. Apparently, Grandma had sat up through long nights watching over her father as he lay dying. It was all beginning to get her down. So, when their doctor saw the state she was in he'd given her a mysterious white pill. 'Give it to him this evening before you bed him down,' he'd said. 'That's all you'll need.' And it was true. Their sadness was mingled with relief when the dawning day revealed that the old man had passed peacefully away. All in all, Grandpa thought he'd had a good life. In many ways he'd been lucky. Though work down the pit (Grandpa always used this word and never 'mine') was terribly hard, coal was such a vital commodity that miners had been granted dispensation from military service. Otherwise, he might have joined those scores of thousands of entrenched soldiers who'd died on the battlefields of the Somme. Grandpa had even revealed that he himself was aware of his propensity to want to be liked – especially by children. After the end of the Second World War Michael's father had been de-mobbed, and the family had left Rivermouth to come back up North. While they were looking for a home they'd lived with Grandma and Grandpa for a few weeks. When they arrived after the long train journey from the South both grandparents were waiting for them at the garden gate. His mother was carrying the baby Michael who was wailing at the top of his voice. It was the first time his grandparents had seen the little chap and his mum had invited her father to take him in his arms. Grandpa had categorically refused.

'If I take him when he's crying like that he'll never take to me!' he'd declared.

Though it had been the energy of enthusiasm which had driven Grandpa on, the weight of his years gradually began to tell; and when he'd finally nodded off to sleep Michael resumed his reading of a book he'd borrowed on the architecture of French cathedrals. It wasn't that he was passionately interested in the subject. He simply felt he couldn't allow himself to remain in ignorance of what was such an important part of the French cultural heritage. An hour later the telephone rang. It was his mother.

'We've just come back from the auction, so I thought I'd ring you straightaway,' she began. Her voice was pitched high with excitement.

'Well, you'll never believe this. We can scarcely believe it ourselves. We've done it. We've managed to get the bungalow. An' it's all due to your father. I'd never have thought him capable of it. You know, I'm really proud of him. An' we got it at a reasonable price, too. He sounded so determined in his bidding. He just put the others off!'

'That's fantastic news. So the bungalow's what you were looking for?'

'Well yes, I don't think we could have found anything much better. We got hold of the keys this morning and managed to have a look around before the auction. On the whole it's in a reasonable state. The bedroom and lounge are quite big but they could both do with redecorating. But your dad'll see to all that. An' the dining room's a bit on the small side. For the moment it'll do as a bedroom either for you or Grandpa. We'll just have to eat in the kitchen. You might have to sleep on the floor in your sleeping bag before you set off for France – though Auntie Marguerite did say Grandpa could stay with them for the two weeks or so before you go. An' once we get ourselves sorted out we'll probably have a couple of dormers built in. So Grandpa'll have his own bedroom and you'll have yours for when you come home. It's just the garden which is a bit overgrown, but your dad says he'll soon knock it into shape. There are tall hedges all round, so it's lovely and private. Anyway, I've got to go now. I just thought I'd give you a quick ring to tell you the good news! We're going out to have a celebration drink or two shortly. I'll tell you more when we get back home. All we've got to do now is sell the house and shop. By the way, you can tell Grandpa. See you some time on Monday, then. I can't say exactly when, but it could be late. There'll be some heavy Easter traffic on the roads. Bye.'

FINALE

Would I be flirting with the limits of your credibility when I say that the same lucky star which had brought the mill's personnel manager to Michael's father's rescue some twelve years before, and which had guided him so unerringly during his recent auction bidding should have continued twinkling benignly above when it came to selling the family home and shop? And even if the more sceptical among you may have difficulty in believing what I have just stated, perhaps they will find greater plausibility in the fact that it didn't shine in enough of a glowing light to steer them clear of the bridging loan needed to pay off the balance on their newly-acquired bungalow at the due date. It did, however, soon re-emerge from behind that thickening cloud of gloom which the usurious interest rates this type of credit was causing to form: for two weeks later, as the estate agent had inferred, a suitable buyer came along. As for the shop I must confess it took a little longer. I would even go so far as to say that the nearer the planned removal date approached the more Michael's parents were inclined to despair. But once again his father's lucky star re-appeared overhead. Or was it simply because they had been persuaded to reduce – and this significantly – their original asking price? So, at the beginning of August they were ready to move. The family heirlooms, crockery, China and glass were carefully wrapped in newspaper, delicately placed in packing cases and these, along with the furniture, carpets and other voluminous household items were deposited within the spacious confines of a furniture van. It had been decided that Michael and Grandpa should drive down to Rivermouth on the day before the official removal and spend the night at Auntie Marguerite and Uncle John's. Michael's parents and furniture would follow the next day. You will hardly be surprised to learn that as

Michael got into his car he didn't for one moment feel even the slightest hint of regret that he was now departing – probably for ever – from that life he'd been leading over the past two years. But wasn't the call of France now echoing too loudly in his ears for his thoughts to be focused on anything other than that great adventure which now stretched so gloriously ahead?

ABOUT THE AUTHOR

Born and educated in the U.K., Barry A. Whittingham has lived a long expatriate life in mainly peaceful co-habitation with the French. You can connect with Barry, the fiction author of *Barfield School*, Book 1 in the *CALL OF FRANCE* trilogy, on Twitter at: @Barryawhitt

Or pay him a visit at:
www.calloffrance.com

OTHER BOOKS BY
BARRY A. WHITTINGHAM

Barry is also the non-fiction author of *FTT's FRENGLISH THOUGHTS*, a homorously comparative review of two countries geographically separated by just a narrow stretch of shallow brine but mentally a vast ocean apart.

Connect with him on Twitter at:
@Frengthoughts

Or visit him at:
www.frenglishthoughts.com

You can email Barry at:
Contact@frenglishthoughts.com